THE COVEN'S DAUGHTER

THE COVEN'S DAUGHTER

Lucy Jago

Disney • Hyperion Books
NEW YORK

Printed in the United States of America
First published in the U.K. by Bloomsbury Publishing Plc. in 2010
First U.S. edition, 2011
10 9 8 7 6 5 4 3 1

V567-9638-5-11046

This book is set in 11-point Requiem Display HTF.

ISBN 978-1-4231-3843-3

Reinforced binding

Visit www.disneyhyperionbooks.com

To Paul, for everything, and Susie,
passed into spirit but always with me

MAY DAY

Saturday 1st May 1596

News of the dead boy spread through the church as fast as a pig runs from the butcher's sack. His body was black and blistered, they whispered, like the Devil himself had danced upon it. His tongue stuck from his mouth as if someone had tried to pull it out.

Overhead the bell tolled. The villagers of Montacute had gladly heeded its merry call that morning to celebrate the start of May. Now they heard it as a death knell. Huddled in small, frightened groups they shivered as if the dark and cold of past months had returned.

CHAPTER 1

Ugh, droppings between my toes." Cess kicked off her clogs anyway, because they were rubbing. She had walked to work through a misty dawn, but now the early morning sun was breaking through the clouds, and it had stopped raining. She swept the poultry yard in time to the matins bells, unaware they were ringing out a warning that death and pestilence had come to the village.

"They wriggle, but they're not worms." She laughed as the hens pecked her toes. Some of the birds had been in her care since she was taken on at Montacute House three years before, and her heart lifted when they rushed to greet her. She was lucky to have this job, and she knew it.

"It is my birthday today," she announced, used to one-sided conversations. It was also a feast day, and Cess could leave the yards once they were swept. The whole village would meet to celebrate the start of the summer, to drink, flirt, and forget their worries, but she knew that she would be left to one side like a branch without blossoms.

Cess bent to her work again, enjoying the patches of warmth on her back. She noticed how strong her forearms had become after so much sweeping. The skin on them was still pale, for the winter had been hard and the spring wet, but by the end of summer she would be burned brown and freckled, for she liked to work with sleeves rolled up and her head bare. The straw hats other girls wore to keep their skins fair itched her. She stopped to scratch her scalp just thinking about it. She knew she ought to wash her hair now that the weather was warmer. She had the ashes and a little beer to make it shine, but no pig-fat soap. Cess considered her hair to be her best feature, hazelnut brown and thick, though it was usually braided and pinned under a linen coif, as her work was dirty.

"This is my frayed cap," she said ruefully to the hens. "Have you eaten my good one?" She had searched everywhere for it. "Now I am thirteen I am supposed to look like a lady," she continued. Her mother's mirror had been exchanged for food so long ago that she had forgotten her reflection. She knew her eyes were large, because she was sometimes called "owl eyes," though more often "cesspit." Or "bastard." Her real name was Cecily, but only her friend Edith called her that, or her mother when cross. She did not mind "Cess"—it was familiar.

Boys should come courting now, or even crown me Queen of the May, she thought, laughing, although it sounded hollow even to her. She knew that for other girls the day was marked with a new skirt, a cap, or even a kirtle. Her cousin Amelia had turned thirteen two springs earlier, and paraded about in an outfit smelling of fine, crisp wool and soft shoe leather. She could still remember the sweet scent of Amelia's new clothes even against the acid reek of the poultry yard.

As Cecily had lain awake that morning, in that silent time before dawn, she had made a wish with a longing that took her by surprise. *Let this day be different.*

If only her wishes were as powerful as her dreams. For as long as she could remember she had dreamed of where to find a lost hen or whether a woman with child carried a girl or boy. Her premonitions were always right, but she had quickly learned to keep quiet about them, for when she told people, they looked at her suspiciously.

Cecily threw down her brush and took up a wooden pail. She always found pleasure in the delicate task of collecting eggs. She opened the door of the largest coop and ducked to enter. Inside, the musty darkness was pierced by shafts of light that came through gaps in the plank walls. Cecily sneezed a few times as the dust filled her nose, then bent so that her deft fingers could root out the warm, chalky eggs from the straw of the lower nesting boxes. She had barely filled a quarter of her pail when she yelped and jumped back as if she had been stung. The hen on the nest stared at her glassily and shuffled her feathers at the intrusion.

"What is this strange thing you have laid today?" Cecily whispered as she gingerly pushed her hand again under the bird's warm weight. She retrieved a box the size of her palm, covered in pale blue velvet and held shut with a tiny hook.

"God's wounds," she swore under her breath, fingering the box nervously. She could feel something shifting within as she turned it. She longed to know what it was, but opening strange boxes was dangerous. She might unleash an evil spirit or bind herself to the faerie world and be forced to do their bidding. Perhaps it was put here to take so that she could be accused of stealing. There were many who felt no goodwill toward her.

"This cannot be meant for me," she mumbled as she bent to put it back. But then why had it been left there?

"I should forget about it," she said sensibly as she moved the box into one of the beams of sunlight that penetrated the gloom, and picked at the golden catch with a grubby finger. Slowly the lid opened, and she could see black silk within. As if a hatchling nestled beneath, Cecily gently lifted away the silk and revealed a jewel of such costliness and sparkle that she had to squint as the light reflected off it. Stones of red, fiery blue, ice, and deep green edged a heavy oval pendant of rich gold. In the center was a portrait of a woman dressed in furs, silks, and jewels. There was a crest to the right of her head, and although it was very tiny, Cecily thought she could make out a black bird, like a crow or raven, standing on a white stag. The woman had a pale, almost blue-white oval face, out of which stared hazel eyes. Although the portrait was small, Cecily felt those eyes boring into her as if the woman was offended that a peasant girl should be holding her. She knew she would do well to snap the box shut and shove it back under the hen, but she was mesmerized.

"I'm just looking; there's no harm in that."

The woman's hair was swept under a curved French hood, but Cecily imagined it to be honey-brown, like her eyebrows. Her hands could just be seen, one gloved in calfskin, the other bare with long, ringed fingers, white as ice.

"Who are you? Why are you here?" Cecily whispered to the portrait.

She knew a girl like her could never own something so precious, but there was no law against trying it on. No one could see her and she would put it back afterward. Carefully, she passed the heavy gold chain over her head. She had never worn anything this valuable, and the weight of it upon her neck was delicious. She shivered as she imagined the pendant transforming her inch by inch from grimy, illegitimate poultry girl into a noblewoman.

Very slowly she began to sway then twirl inside the cramped coop as if it were a great hall filled with sweet music. Silks and Dutch lace caressed her body, and pearls and precious stones sparkled against her skin and in her hair. The stench of chicken droppings was replaced with the scents of fine food, spiced wine, and the perfumed clothes and hair of the highborn men and women dancing with her. All around were faces smiling and nodding. She was beautiful and admired and knew how it felt to be wanted.

A harsh whistle and the clucking of alarmed hens in the yard outside pulled her up short.

"Oi! Cesspit! I've come for ten birds!" shouted the kitchen boy as he neared the yards. Cecily shoved the pendant down into her bodice and dashed outside to shoo her favorite birds into the farthest coop to keep them from the pot.

"Oi, where are you, girl?"

"Coming!"

"I want ten . . . What's with you?" he said as he let himself in. Cess did not reply, but her cheeks were flushed and her eyes glittered. The boy stared at her a moment, then shrugged and began a strange, jagged dance around the coop as he tried to catch the wary creatures.

"Reckon you'll actually have to do some work, eh, when the Queen arrives," he sneered unpleasantly.

"The Queen?" repeated Cess in amazement. She usually ignored the kitchen boy, for he strutted around her like a pompous ass. His trips to the coops were the only time in his day when he was superior to somebody, and he reveled in it.

"Do you hear nothing?" he said. "She's expected here in a few weeks. They'll be needing more food than was on the Ark. You'll have yer work cut out then." Cess watched him scrabbling after the terrified birds and forcing them into the baskets he carried with him.

"Don't suppose you'll be helping," he grumbled.

"Not in here!" she yelled at him furiously as he went to wring a bird's neck.

He looked at her with contempt, and smiled as the sound of cracking bones filled the air. Cess turned away. She could not bear to watch her beautiful hens die at the hands of this brute.

She left the boy to his murderous task and took refuge behind the largest coop. She thought of the pendant deep inside her bodice and wondered what she should do with it.

"If I put it back and someone finds it, I'll be accused of stealing it," she reasoned. "If I give it to the steward, he won't believe I found it under a hen and will call me a thief just the same. I will be hanged from the gibbet either way." She took out the pendant, questions turning endlessly in her head about how it came to be there and who the woman was. Only when the hunger in her belly outgrew the excitement she felt as she gazed at the portrait did Cess take a deep breath and drop it back down her bodice. It felt cold against her ribs, reminding her that she had just made a decision that could cost her life.

Her cloak bundled under one arm, with the empty velvet box inside, Cess picked up the pail to take the eggs to the kitchens. Even though she was one of the lowliest servants on the estate, she felt proud to belong to Montacute House. Halfway across the vegetable gardens she stopped and gazed at the beautiful building as the morning light fell across it. She had watched it grow from its foundations since she was a little girl. It stood proudly amongst the gentle rolling hills and woods of the county, a great monarch of a house ruling over a kingdom of hamlets, small towns, and villages, including Montacute itself. Visitors came from afar to marvel at the sight of the soaring facade, its walls of golden Somersetshire stone, pierced with so many windows that they looked to be made of lace. Hundreds of saints, marvelous creatures, and armored knights kept guard in delicate niches in the walls, and a forest of chimneys told the world how comfortable, modern, and wealthy was the owner.

She walked across the south drive, used by servants, tradesmen, and visitors of the poorer sort, past the stables and into the kitchen yard. As she handed over the eggs, an apprentice cook thrust a cup of small beer and a chunk of rye bread and beef dripping at her in return—breakfast. The kitchens were in uproar with servants flapping from dairy to storeroom, brewhouse to larder, fire to pastry table, in a fluster of preparation for the evening's banquet to celebrate the fact that Montacute House was finally finished. It had been ten years in the building, and Sir Edward Mortain, Earl of Montacute, now had one of the most beautiful houses in the country.

Smells of roasting and the thick, greasy smoke of spitting meat made Cess's stomach roll in longing. People came and went, stepping round her as they might a puddle. Small groups of men-at-arms hung idly about waiting for the stable boys to prepare their horses. Some of the men were in Sir Edward's livery, but others wore the silver and black of his son, Viscount Drax Mortain, who had been a guest at the house for the past few weeks. Cess had not seen him. Unlike his father, he had shown no interest in the poultry yards.

Eyes down, Cess walked quickly across the kitchen yard. She tried to be invisible when the men-at-arms were about. Their manners with unmarried servants were lewd and rough. She hurried past the stables to the south drive and walked quickly toward the village. She was halfway down the drive when a strong prickling sensation ran up her spine and made the roots of her hair tingle unpleasantly. She stood still, unsure whether to look or to run. She knew the sensation. Someone was watching her.

Her breath quick and shallow, she turned very slowly. The path was deserted. The servants in the gardens and orchards were busy with their chores. Her eyes were drawn to the southern facade of the house, where there was a great oriel window. As she squinted against the sun she felt her heart jump in her chest. Someone was looking out the window, straight at her. At such a distance Cess could not tell for sure who it was, but she could see the glint of gold chains. It was one of the noble guests, the steward or her master himself. Cess's heart thumped uncomfortably with the guilty knowledge of what she carried in her bodice. Although she had not thought of it before, something of such great value must have come from the House. She raised her hand to shield her eyes, hoping for a clearer impression, but the figure backed away into the darkness of the room behind.

CHAPTER 2

Cess walked homeward blindly, absorbed by the figure in the pendant and the face she had seen at the window. It seemed too great a coincidence that she should be observed on the very day she had found something that did not belong to her.

She sped up as she entered the village and passed the large group of well-made houses with barns, stables, and a brew house that were home to her Perryn cousins, aunts, and uncles. Cess had no desire to see them, but out of habit she glanced quickly at the comfortable house in which she had been born. She instantly regretted it. Her cousins Beth and Amelia were standing outside, watching her. Cess was astonished to see Beth blush, and even Amelia, usually so smug, was looking surprisingly furtive.

They're up to no good, Cess thought. Then she noticed two maypoles leaning beside their front door, one for each cousin. As tradition allowed, during the night, the village boys had adorned the maypoles of girls of marriageable age in the way they saw fit. Beth had awoken to find her pole draped with stinking potato peelings, moldy cabbage stalks, weeds, and all manner of rubbish. Amelia's, identified by the long blond ringlet she had carefully tied to it, was crowded with bouquets of wildflowers and May blossoms.

Cess thought it was hard on Beth to have a much prettier sister, but when she looked back she saw that Beth's blushes had been replaced by a look of determination. She and Amelia turned away from Cess and swapped Beth's pole with a neighbor's, which was festooned with gorse. To be thought of as prickly was hardly flattering, but better than being rubbish. Cess was shocked that Beth and Amelia could be so dishonest. The neighbor, who was also a cousin, would be mortified.

"Gorse, cousin? Be glad it is not elder," quipped Cess before she could stop herself. With its strong smell and easily drilled wood, that plant festooned the poles of girls who had been easy with the boys, as Cess knew Beth had, for all her superior airs. Beth's lips pressed together spitefully, but it was her younger sister who replied.

"Are you laughing, cousin?" Amelia said in acid tones. "You must have roses and ribbons on your pole."

Cess turned to walk on, sickened that her cousins would switch maypoles, but cross with herself for interfering.

"Oh no, of course not, silly me," Amelia called after her. "You don't have a pole at all, do you? No one would ever dream of marrying a bastard like you!"

Cess's face burned.

"I would happily roll you in the gorse prickles you have just pinched! One day, Amelia . . ." she muttered angrily as she walked on, dreaming up revenge that she knew she would never be able to inflict. Amelia and Beth were the daughters of her uncle, Richard. He had inherited the Perryn estate after her grandparents had died in the plague of '94, three years earlier. He was ambitious and ruthless, and his farms were doing well enough for him to call himself a gentleman. His daughters could taunt Cess as much as they liked without fear of retribution. She was as insignificant as the donkey that walked endless circles to turn the mill wheel.

Amelia's taunts hurt more for the fact that she and Cess had been friends as children, until Amelia became aware of what the word "bastard" meant and of her own, more elevated, position. Her parents had encouraged the distance between them.

Cess kicked hard at a stone in the lane, almost losing a clog. Amelia's rejection of their friendship had made Cecily herself acutely aware of what it meant not to know her father. Although she had begged her mother to tell her who he was, Anne Perryn had refused to give her daughter the slightest clue. She seemed both convinced and relieved that he would never turn up at their door, and told Cess to forget about him and be grateful for the roof over her head and the little food she had in her belly. But Cess could not let go of the mystery of her father and prayed that one day he would come to claim her. She had dreams about him: He was a nobleman, unaware he had sired a child until some extraordinary event alerted him; he was a spice trader in the Orient who had finally made his fortune and come to collect her. He was never just a farmhand. Cess knew they were probably her imaginings for they felt different to the dreams that came true.

As she walked through the Borough, past the guildhall, the lock-up, and the shops, she noticed people huddled in small groups, deep in discussion. Many had just come from matins and were on their way home to break the fast, their faces unusually somber. Cess wondered what eternal hell the parson had threatened to make them look so serious.

Outside the tavern a few men were brawling. The fight looked as if it had started the night before and had revived now the men were waking. Some were groaning, clutching their heads and bellies. Others wrestled through pools of vomit and piss, arguing over who would reign once Queen Elizabeth was dead.

"King James! A man at last to end these times of misery!" shouted one, who was immediately set upon.

Cess doubled back to Wash Lane to avoid being entangled in the mess of punching fists, bleeding lips, and foul language. As she squeezed past the gossips at the narrow entrance to the lane, she overheard their whispered conversation.

"Who found it?"

"Maggie. She's only six. A terrible thing. She poked it with a stick!" Cess heard the other women tutting. She could not imagine what they were talking about and only half listened as she crouched to remove a twig that had caught in her clog.

"He was only a boy, not more than twelve. Someone thought they recognized him, from Yeovil. Still had a farthing in his pocket."

Cess's attention was caught. She wondered how long she could fiddle with her clog before arousing suspicion that she was eavesdropping.

"No one would steal a farthing off a putrid body. Had he a reason to be in Montacute?"

"No one knows. He had no horse, and it's a long way to walk."

"He was under the thorn trees by the river. Eyes open and staring as if the Devil himself took his last breath."

Many unpleasant things happened in the village: men beat their wives, women their children, babies died of hunger, and farmers were crushed by their own cattle. But to find a dead body far from home was a different thing altogether.

"How did he die?"

"Not by human hand." There was a pause as the women absorbed the dreadful thrill of that thought.

"The Devil?" one said quietly.

"Who knows? The boy's teeth and bones were broken. He was bruised like ten bulls ran over him, and his skin was raw with boils."

"The Good Lord preserve us!"

"If it was illness that took his life, then others of his kin or village will die, so word has been sent."

"Perhaps it was his family who sent him away when they saw he was ill." Again the women tutted, although Cess knew several in the village who had boarded up dying members of their own families in empty barns, even tiny children, to protect themselves from the plague.

"Is it witches?"

The reply was drowned out by the shouts of several brawling men who were now fighting their way down Middle Street to the top of the lane. The women were forced to move on, and Cess risked a brief glance to see if they had noticed her. They were clutching their Bibles and frowning with worry, too engrossed in their imaginings to care about her.

Sometimes it is useful being a nobody, she thought as she walked quickly away, trying to shake off the hideous image she had formed of the dead boy.

CHAPTER 3

Ignatius Bartholomew, the village parson, muttered crossly under his breath as he heard a rap at his front door. On May Day morning anyone devout should have known not to disturb his preparations. Today of all days he needed peace in which to write a sermon that would deter his flock from the abominable heathenism he saw all about him.

"These villagers with their maypoles, dancing, and fornicating in the woods . . ." he muttered angrily as he rose from his table. Although he had lectured them on the matter for the past ten years, Ignatius was aware that he had had little noticeable effect on the villagers' behavior.

"Sir Nathaniel Davies, steward to His Lordship, sir," announced his manservant.

"Ah, that's different. . . ." mumbled the parson, smoothing a few sparse strands of dark hair onto his balding scalp.

He bowed as Sir Nathaniel strode in. "At your service, sir," said

Ignatius in his reedy voice. The parson was a tall man and thin. He did not approve of display, thinking it "womanly" and frivolous, and believed that the nobility of a man's soul and the sharpness of his mind was all the adornment needed. He also loathed spending money, such that his clothes were shabby and ill-fitting, and he kept a poor table. The only guests he invited were local magistrates whose decisions he wished to influence, or men of the cloth with whom he talked about Good versus Evil. No women crossed his threshold other than to collect his laundry. He had once thought to have a wife, but was turned down by the object of his decision, and had thereafter abandoned any such notion.

"You have heard, I presume, of the boy found dead this morning?" asked Sir Nathaniel, without preamble. Ignatius, never a great admirer of the steward's blunt manner, could not hide his astonishment.

"You have not?" said Sir Nathaniel disapprovingly. Ignatius was aware of the steward's disdain for him. Inexplicably, Sir Nathaniel seemed to place great store by his wife's opinions, and she had left the parson in no doubt what she felt about his belief in the inferiority of women and the evilness of papists. It had occurred to him that the steward and his bossy goodwife might be secret Catholics themselves, but so far he had held his tongue.

"I do not involve myself in the villagers' lives," Ignatius said loftily, "but prepare them to meet their Maker at their end."

"Indeed," said Sir Nathaniel, his jaw clenching in irritation. "The boy lies in your crypt. The church warden opened up, I believe."

"Probably. He knows I don't like to be disturbed before a sermon. He is quite capable of making the necessary arrangements for the body to be returned to the proper parish once it has been claimed—"

The steward cut Ignatius short. "Finding a young boy dead is a shocking event, even on such a busy day as this," said Sir Nathaniel sternly. "He was recognized as hailing from Yeovil, and we have already heard that he went missing three days ago. The magistrates were treating it as a case of truancy, although the parents swore there was no reason for their son to run away. Finding his body has thrown doubt on a number of other cases of missing boys, of which there seems to have been rather a spate recently."

Ignatius's eyes narrowed in irritation. He liked to think he had an ear to the ground amongst the magistrates of the county. The fact that Sir Nathaniel was so much better informed than he was showed that the hospitality he afforded at the parsonage was not being rewarded.

"Please keep your eyes and ears open and report to me anything that might shed light on the death of this boy or the other disappearances," Sir Nathaniel said, more an order than a request. "The Queen has honored us greatly by agreeing to visit, and it is of vital importance that nothing occurs which might disrupt matters."

"The Queen?" whispered Ignatius as if Jesus himself were expected. Sir Nathaniel nodded. "Have you considered Catholics?" the parson blurted out, daringly, given his suspicions about Sir Nathaniel's religious leanings.

"What?" said Sir Nathaniel testily.

"The boy. Could he be dead at the hand of Catholics?"

"To what possible purpose?"

"To put off the Queen's visit?"

Nathaniel paused; the parson's notion was not impossible. "We do not yet know if the boy was killed or died of natural causes," he said. "His appearance was that of someone dead of the sweating sickness."

Ignatius's eyes opened wide in horror.

"It seems not to be spreading in the usual manner; no other cases have been reported," said Sir Nathaniel, much to the parson's relief.

"Has witchcraft been considered?" said Ignatius intently. It was a subject about which he was passionate.

"No, parson, nothing has been considered. We are simply looking for information."

"I shall be glad to serve in any way I can," Ignatius assured hurriedly, bowing low as Sir Nathaniel left.

Back at his table, the parson took a small sip of wine to calm his thoughts before returning to his sermon. One dead boy. Hardly a plague. He hoped it stayed that way. Last time plague struck the village he had been away at his brother's farm at Porlock Bay on the north coast, close by Devonshire. He had returned once the last of the bodies had been buried. He remembered the eerie quiet in the village. One in three dead. It had been a necessary release of anger and fear to hunt the witch responsible, easy to rouse his flock into following him, although disappointing that she had evaded capture. The fear of God had been struck into the villagers' hearts, and that year at least there had been no maypoles or reveling. Perhaps, thought Ignatius, the dead boy provided the perfect excuse for a new hunt. He, of course, would lead it. This time the witch might be caught, and anyway, the exercise would provide valuable lessons on sin that the villagers needed to hear. How easily the Devil seduces his victims. The parson bent over his table and began to write furiously.

It was nearly midday by the time Cess found her best friend, William Barlow, and slumped down on the ground next to him. He put aside the slate he had been drawing on and began fishing about inside his leather jerkin.

"What bit you?" said William, noticing Cess's frown.

"I heard about the dead boy they found this morning."

William nodded but did not reply as he searched his inside pocket. Cess felt her worry diminish in the presence of her quiet, thoughtful friend. He was not someone to gossip or spread gruesome stories; he rarely spoke unless he had something useful to say, and Cess liked that about him. Indeed, having only one friend in the village now that Edith no longer lived there, she was glad it was William. People assumed they were friends because both were outcasts. She was a bastard and William had a clubfoot, the "Devil's mark," but Cess knew that was not the truth. She had saved his life once, when the other children refused to pull him from the fish ponds because of his deformity. His near drowning was "God's will" in their eyes. That day had created a bond between Cess and William that they believed would last for as long as they lived.

"Ah!" said William, at last finding what he had been looking for. "This is for you." He rushed the words out and blushed as he thrust a small packet toward Cess.

"You knew it was my birthday?" she said in surprise, turning pink with pleasure. Cess untied the dull brown wrapping of the parcel, and gasped. In her hand was a length of velvet ribbon, richly colored in reds and yellows, and trimmed with gold thread. Other than the pendant, it was the loveliest object she had ever held. Unlike the pendant, she knew this was really for her.

"It's beautiful," she mumbled, tears brimming in her eyes. She hugged her friend so tightly she heard his joints crack.

"It's for your hair," William grinned, pulling off her cap and reaching to undo the braid.

"I daren't," said Cess, stopping him. "People will see."

"That's the point! It will look lovely on you." But Cess shook her head, pulling her cap back into place.

"People will talk," she said. He opened his mouth to disagree, then shut it, knowing Cess was right. But she was so happy with the ribbon, her face shone as she tucked it away with the same care she had the priceless pendant. A thrill went through her to think of the treasures concealed in her tatty bodice.

"I should have bought you a mirror instead of a ribbon," William said, staring into Cess's face.

"Why?" she asked. "There's not much point having a mirror with no ribbon to admire."

"You have less need of ribbons than most, Cess," said William, looking away to hide what Cess suspected was another blush.

She blustered on. "All that writing on your slate has weakened your eyes, just as your mother said it would," said Cess. William fell silent, and Cess felt cross with herself for laughing at his compliment. It was not as if she received so many that she could be careless with them. During the silence between them they heard distant music. The sounds of fifes and recorders, the sackbut, cornets, and shawms, drums, and flutes, and cattle bells, were growing louder.

"They are bringing in the maypole!" cried Cess, eyes alight with pleasure, the awkwardness with William instantly forgotten. She helped her friend to his feet, and together they hurried to the edge of the Borough. The music grew louder as along Bishopston and Middle Street swayed a herd of cows and oxen, their horns decorated with May blossoms and ribbons. The largest two oxen were yoked to a great pole, painted with stripes and covered with spring flowers and boughs. Ribbons, strings, and handkerchiefs were tied to one end. Among the cattle were villagers, who had found ingenious ways to cover themselves and their best clothes with the May blossoms that signified fertility and love. Flowers sprigged their hats and caps, buttonholes and bodices, and were twisted into crowns and necklaces and even tied on to their shoes and clogs.

Cess and William, along with every villager well enough to leave their home, joined the crowd in the Borough. They stood to one side as the men heaved the pole erect in the center of the small green to such a cacophony of cheers it was as if it were carried aloft on the voices of the village. The girls came forward to dance, holding the ribbons that were pinned to the top of the pole. William pushed Cess forward, but she dug in her heels and stayed near the back of the crowd. The dancers wound the ribbons around the pole while others tucked more blossoms under the ribbons so that the pole looked to be bursting with fresh growth. Cess noticed Beth among them but could not see Amelia.

The music and clapping grew to a crescendo. Then the crowd fell silent with expectation. The taverner stood on an upturned log at the base of the pole, clutching in one huge hand a large pewter tankard from which he took a sip before bellowing out a poem.

May all our beasts birth babes,
And our fields grow tall with corn,
May our hives run forth with honey,
And our men all blow the horn!

At the last line the crowd shouted and whistled, and the men pulled their wives, sweethearts, or the nearest woman toward them and planted kisses upon them. To Cess's amazement, William grabbed her in a clumsy embrace and kissed her cheek. She was speechless that he dared show her such affection before a crowd, but no one seemed to notice them. The taverner cheered to see the lust he had unleashed, chucked the contents of his tankard at the base of the pole to symbolize the coming together of man and woman, and signaled to the musicians to start up a tune. He jumped off the log to grab his wife, and moments later the whole village was carousing around the maypole, lifting skirts, whooping with pleasure, and drinking deeply.

At the end of the first dance a loud fluting hushed the crowd, and a veiled girl was led into the Borough. At a signal from the drum the young men raced each other to capture the crown of blossoms at the top of the maypole. A strapping cooper beat the others and swaggered over to the girl. He lifted her veil and planted the crown on her head with a great smacking kiss. Cess was not surprised to see that the May Queen this year was Amelia, who was even more pleased with herself than usual. Cess had to admit that her cousin looked lovely, her golden curls crowned with a frothing circlet of blossom. She wore a green overdress that showed off her smooth, creamy complexion and bright blue eyes. Although Amelia smiled sweetly at her May Day beau, it was clear to Cess, even at a distance, that her cousin did not consider the barrel maker a fitting companion and that she would shake him off as soon as possible.

As the May Queen looked on from her throne, and Cess and William found a vantage point on a pile of beer barrels, the villagers played games on the green, competing against each other in the long jump, skittles, high jump, and throw-the-stone. As the afternoon grew long, couples wandered into the woods, and the children ate greedily from small baskets of sugared treats that they had exchanged for pieces of fruit at cottage doors that morning. But despite the drunkenness and boisterous high spirits, Cess noticed a current of fear running through the festivities like a ground fire spreading along bracken roots, more frightening for being hidden. Among the carousers, Cess passed several huddled groups whispering about the boy who lay dead only a few measures away in the cold church crypt.

"What do you know of the dead boy?" said Cess to William, taking up the conversation that had been interrupted earlier. Visitors and travelers wanting William's blacksmith father to reshoe their horses were expected to share their news while they waited.

"A Yeovil man came through this morning. If it's the same boy as the one missing from there, he disappeared three nights ago," said William. "And there are others."

"Others?"

"They say two others have gone from Yeovil and . . ." Cess stopped William with a poke in the ribs. The parson was passing on his way to the church. He had a way of striding forward and poking his small head to left and right, searching for souls to save but looking no one in the face. Cess noticed that he seemed unusually interested in his flock, cheerful even. But she had no desire to talk to him, so she and William shrank back among the barrels, and he passed without seeing them.

"And at least one other from Martock, and there may have been more," William went on.

"They've not just run away?"

"This is the first body that's been found. No one knows what has happened to the rest, but there've been no sightings of them, which is unusual. This one seems to have had the sweat."

Cess was silent for a while. The sweating sickness was a terrible way to die. Sufferers shook so hard that they broke their bones and teeth. It felled everyone in its path, not just the old or babes, but the young and strong too. William seemed quite excited by the news. Cess knew he did not revel in death but that illness fascinated him. He had heard that in the great cities like London and Edinburgh it was possible to study the human body and its ailments. To become a physician was what he wanted above all else, though he knew it would take more money than he was ever likely to have. Cess wondered if he sought a cure for his foot, but had never asked.

"Some are saying that witches are responsible," continued William doubtfully.

"Witches?" said Cess, nervously. She was not only frightened of what witches could do, she was terrified of how easily someone could be called a witch, even if they were not. Her friend Edith Mildmay had been one of the most sought out women in Montacute for her healing skills, yet, in the grief and terror that accompanied the plague, the villagers had fixed their fury on her, accusing her of being a witch and bringing the plague upon them. The parson had brayed especially loudly for her blood. "Thou shalt not suffer a witch to live!" he had screamed from the pulpit, quoting the Bible. But how could anyone believe that one woman, who had lived nearly fifty summers among them in peace, could have caused such devastation? Cess had lost what little faith she had during the witch hunt that had ensued.

Edith had escaped alive, just, but the episode had shown Cess how normal people could turn overnight into a screaming, murderous mob and hunt down someone they had respected, even relied upon, the day before. Cess had withdrawn from village life, stopped trying to make friends, and accepted that to most of the villagers she would never be anything other than a bastard anyway. With the boy lying dead so close by, Cess wondered who might be blamed this time if the disease came to the village.

"Do you believe witches could be behind all this?" asked William.

"I've never met a witch, so how could I know?" said Cess pointedly, even though she knew William meant well and had not agreed with the hounding of Edith. The church bells rang out for evening prayers.

William did not take offense but smiled at her. "The parson says witches dance with the Devil and allow him to suckle from their breasts," he said, as if this was something he might rather enjoy seeing.

"He also says the Devil is hot from the flames of hell, so the witches suckling him would be burnt to cinders, wouldn't they?" said Cess, always pleased to pick holes in anything the parson said. "I know nothing about witches and I don't want to. There's your mother." Goodwife Barlow, pretending not to see Cess, was signaling sharply for her son to join her.

"Will you come with me to see the fireworks at the great house tomorrow night?" William asked as he began clambering awkwardly down the barrel stack.

"The what?" asked Cess.

"I heard the grooms speak of them," he said over his shoulder as he limped toward the scowling woman. Cess saw the thin line of her lips tighten further as his mother watched her hobbling son.

"Pull down your jerkin. Your shirt is hanging all about. Go on with you." Goodwife Barlow pushed William down Middle Street toward the church and then marched ahead, too fast for him to keep up. Cess's own mother hurried past minutes later, head bowed and eyes downcast.

With a deep sigh, Cess lowered herself down the barrels and walked to the church to join the other villagers, most the worse for drink but too poor to pay the fine if they stayed away. There was an air of expectancy, and as the church bell tolled five o'clock, another sound could be heard. The thud of many hooves through the village, and a single drum. The crowd hushed as the nobles of Montacute House arrived to attend the May Day service.

CHAPTER 4

Forest grew thickly to the west of Montacute village. Rising from the trees was the steep hill of Saint Michael's Hill, a place no villager would venture to. In a small clearing, two women worked hard and quickly, alert for the sound of footsteps approaching. Their hooded cloaks hid them completely so only their hands could be seen, gripping long brooms. Back and forth across a patch of bare earth the women swept until the last twig and leaf was banished. Not a word passed between them, yet they seemed to anticipate every move the other made. They placed their brooms against the wall of a small wooden shack. The taller woman brought a flask of water, and the shorter poured in salt to purify it. From a pouch at her waist she pulled a small black dagger and dipped it in the flask, quietly whispering:

Cast out from thee,
O spirit of the water,
All impurities and uncleanliness

Of the World of Phantasm.
In the names of the Goddess and the God.

In the air she drew a circle that mirrored the shape of the cleared space. She sprinkled the rest to the north, west, south, and east points of the circle. The taller woman poured salt in an unbroken line between the cleared space and the world beyond. The circle was now sacred; no spirit would dare cross into it. Only then did the women push back their hoods. The shorter of the two was younger but had a powerful presence. Her hair was fair and her skin had a translucent quality, like sun shining through water. The older woman was angular, gray, and careworn, a wise creature who had witnessed both the honorable and the ignoble in the world. She walked around the younger woman, drawing straight lines in the earth until she had created the shape of a five-pointed star.

"There is little time. Do you have something belonging to the girl?" said the fair-haired woman.

"I have her best cap."

"Has it been worn?"

"Much," said the older woman, fondly smoothing out the yellowed and thinning square of cloth in which one or two long brown hairs were still trapped. She hoped her friend had not missed it.

"Then let us begin."

The liveried drummer parted the gawping villagers like a dog through sheep, allowing the men-at-arms to follow. They forced back the crowd for the mounted nobles and their retinue, led by the Earl of Montacute, Sir Edward Mortain, owner of Montacute House and its vast estates.

Sir Edward occasionally inspected his fine birds in the poultry yard, but today Cess thought he seemed much grander, dressed in red and green brocade and wearing an ornate gold chain of office, more the great aristocrat of Queen Elizabeth's court than the portly man interested in hens. He wore a short, square-cut gray beard and mustache, and his richly embroidered clothes and gold chains made a magnificent sight. Peacock feathers fluttered jauntily in his hat, and he smiled at the crowd, greeting several by name.

Sir Edward's family had owned land around Montacute for generations, but he was the first to be sent to court. The Queen had shown him great favor. He had risen fast and been given several titles including, lately, an earldom. His life had been visited by tragedy as well as success though. His wife and six of his children had died during a smallpox outbreak before Cess had been born. Only one son had survived. Sir Edward had been so overcome with grief that he had fled to London, abandoning Montacute for nearly ten years. When he finally decided to return, to pull down his father's gloomy home in which there had been so much death and build in its place a house of great beauty, everyone had been overjoyed that the village would get its heart back.

Cess's eyes were drawn to the rider behind Sir Edward. It was hard to guess his age, for he had no hair at all. His eyes without lashes or brows looked naked, and his cheeks were as smooth as a baby's. He did not attempt to disguise his baldness with a cap or hat, seeming to enjoy the startling effect it produced. Tall and powerfully built, he was less colorfully dressed, but Cess judged his attire at least as costly. His black velvet doublet was worked in silver thread, fine lace edged his ruff and cuffs, and his cape sparkled silver as brightly as summer starlight. He rode a huge black horse with a white star on its face, and on his left arm perched a great bird, white from head to tail, hooded in pearl-encrusted leather. It looked to Cess like a hawk, but she had never seen a bird so large, larger even than the great owls in the barns. The rider gazed ahead as he passed, ignoring the crowd.

"He would look more at his cattle," Cess thought. His indifference provoked her. Sir Edward at least showed an interest in the villagers who served him.

"Who is that?" she whispered to the old woman squashed in front of her.

"His Lordship's son," she said, "Drax. Viscount Drax Mortain. He's not been here for many a summer."

"What happened to his hair?" Cess asked.

"It fell out after all his family died except his father. You'd see his little sisters, the sweetlings, in the village, beautiful they were. And his brothers were strapping lads, God rest their young souls. Suddenly six of them dead and their mother," said the crone, twisting round, about to say more, but when she realized who had asked her, she pursed her lips and turned away.

The crowd surged forward as the nobles dismounted from their horses, followed by their guests. Most ignored the villagers, a few smiled, but one bug-eyed man in a page's uniform glared as if to ward them away from his fine livery. Indeed his straight, thigh-length coat was made of very fine linen, dyed deep green, and his hanging sleeves were embroidered with a coat of arms, though she could not see whose it was. Standing close to His Lordship was Sir Nathaniel Davies, Steward of Montacute House, wearing black, as always, with a starched white ruff that made his head look detached from his body.

Cess was pushed to one side. She kept her hand to her bodice, not wanting its treasures dislodged. She knew it was fanciful, but she could have sworn that the necklace was heating up like a fire poker. If it got any hotter she would not be able to bear it against her skin. She looked about until she saw a clump of dock leaves by the graveyard wall. She picked one and, as unobtrusively as possible, tucked it down her bodice between her skin and the pendant, sighing with relief.

"May Day cider, my lords!" cried the taverner. Cess saw that Amelia had pushed her way to the taverner's side and was looking up under her lashes at the nobles. Even with her crown atilt from dancing, she looked beautiful, and Cess noticed Drax Mortain watching her. Amelia also noticed, and tried to look demure.

"God's blood," swore Cess. "Surely even Amelia could not think a nobleman would be interested in her?" Amelia's parents, Uncle Richard and his goodwife, Alice, pushed their way next to their daughter and bowed to the nobles in the manner of gentlefolk and not the lower sort. Sir Edward had little choice but to acknowledge them and their pretty daughter. The Perryns looked as smug as cats in the buttery, and Cess felt sickened by the pantomime of their gentility. Amelia and her family had been ruthless in their treatment of her and her mother, and had shown them less signs of humanity and gentleness than a herd of wild boar.

Sir Edward downed a cupful of cider as tradition demanded, followed swiftly by Sir Nathaniel. The crowd stirred as Drax Mortain calmly refused the cup held out for him.

"I do not take drink," he said in a tone that invited no persuasion.

In the awkward silence that followed, Sir Edward's face was a mask of good cheer such as any courtier at the Queen's side learned to adopt, but as he turned to walk into the church, Cess noticed that his smile faded abruptly.

Cess slipped last into the church and remained near the back. Although she disliked the parson, she liked his church. The place reminded her of her grandparents, whom she had always accompanied there. Her grandfather had told her that the church had once been full of precious things, but that when he was young, men had come from London and taken all the statues, the candlesticks, and incense burners, even the stained-glass windows. Edward, Henry the VIII's son, who was a Protestant, was King then. He had commanded his people to pray and read the Bible in English instead of Latin so that everyone could understand the word of God. But he had died at fifteen, and his half sister, Queen Mary, a staunch

Catholic, put everything back into Latin. Then Elizabeth came to the throne and everything changed again. Her grandfather had smiled wryly as he described all the chopping and changing that went on. The church was now plain, with clear glass windows that allowed the light to stream in, the only furniture being the altar table, the choir stalls and a few benches either side of the aisle below the pulpit, facing each other. The pulpit was richly carved with detailed scenes that gave Cess something to look at while the parson droned on.

From where she stood, Cess could see that the benches were filled with the Mortains and their visitors. The few remaining places were taken by her Uncle Perryn and his family, who paid an annual subscription to sit in church. The rest of the congregation stood, although a few leaned against the pillars, and one old fellow snored on his feet. The crowd was noisier than usual, fueled by drink and excitement. Small children ran about while older ones whispered among themselves, earning the occasional slap from their parents. They quieted for the parson's sermon, although now and then someone shouted out a comment. Ignatius Bartholomew suffered these interjections as long as they came from men. For women, he held that it was not seemly to have an opinion.

"This day you drink and dance around a pole," noted the parson with obvious disdain. Cess could see that Sir Edward was frowning, whether with concentration or disapproval she could not tell. "For many years I have asked of you, should you not pray instead? Ask forgiveness for your sins?" Ignatius stared at his parishoners, a few of whom shifted uncomfortably. Cess jiggled her leg in irritation and repeatedly tucked away a strand of hair under her frayed cap until her mother, who had moved to her side, stayed her hand.

"Sin was brought into the world by Eve, who ate the apple of knowledge in Eden, and you women"—he ran his eyes over the motley crowd—"must lead the way in repentance." Cess groaned. Why did the parson never address the sins of the menfolk? Goodman

Porrit had got three different women pregnant. And Browning beat his wife so hard she died.

"Even now I look about, and what do I see? In full view of the angels there are women with no symbol of subjection upon their heads, bareheaded, or worse, with the May crowns of pagans!" Cess noticed Amelia look uncomfortable and put her hand up to remove her crown. Drax Mortain, sitting on the benches opposite, was drawn by the movement and watched her closely, a fact not lost on Amelia. Cess knew her cousin would be loathe to take it off, for the crown enhanced her looks and proved that she was the prettiest girl in the village. However, with a coy glance at Drax, she slipped the circlet of May blossoms into her lap.

"She really is tipping her cap at him," breathed Cess, dismayed for her cousin despite their mutual dislike of each other. Amelia would be like a lamb to the slaughter with a man like that, and Cess thought that her parents should care more than to use their daughter in their quest to become more important.

"Today we are reminded to think hard upon sin and salvation, for death has come amongst us. A boy lies cold beneath this very church," said the parson dramatically. The congregation fell silent. Cess wondered if this latest calamity would also be blamed on the sinfulness of women. "My flock, be vigilant. As your minister, I insist that any information you might have that could shed light on this death be brought to me at the parsonage immediately, no matter the hour." Cess strained to hear what else he had to say, but her ears began ringing strangely. Shaking her head had no effect, and the sound was soon dwarfed by a strange sensation in her legs, like intense pins and needles. The feeling traveled up her body; her head began to spin and her vision to blur. When she went to lean against a pillar, she could not move. She tried to cry out, but her lips were frozen and her voice mute.

She felt herself floating upward and looked down at her body, still rooted to the spot. The parson's lips were moving, but the sounds around her were becoming distant as she felt herself rising up and out of the church altogether. Her stomach lurched as she flew higher and faster, like a bird blown about on a stormy day.

Am I dying? wondered Cecily.

In the forest clearing, two women stood perfectly still, more so than the trees and bushes around them that moved in the breeze. Their faces were transformed in their stillness by an inner radiance and calm. Cess recognized one. It was her friend Edith.

"Your spirit comes to us," said the younger woman, who had fair hair. Cess thought she might have seen her before. Perhaps she was from a nearby village. She gave Cess a brief smile. "We call you here to offer our protection, for we felt the presence of evil and have foreseen danger. We can wait no longer, for you will encounter it soon."

"Edith?" Cess turned to her friend, confused about what the fair-haired woman had just said and unsure whether she was dreaming or awake. Edith's expression was of such seriousness and care that Cess felt fear squeeze at her heart.

"I guided you from your mother's womb, Cecily, and have looked over you these past thirteen years. I know you trust me. Alathea and I have seen that you have a power that could challenge the evil. We gladly offer you our loyalty, though it may lead to our deaths. Will you receive our protection?" asked Edith, her eyes boring into Cess's as if to communicate to her the importance of the request. Although Cess had no idea what was happening, she sensed in her gut that she must agree. After a slight hesitation, she nodded.

"We must start," said the younger woman, looking at the sun dipping behind the trees in the west. "Kneel before me." Cess obeyed, although it worried her not to feel the prickle of grass at her knees or the breeze on her cheeks. She looked up at the stranger whose light hair and shining face glowed like ripe corn. As the woman placed her hand on Cess's head, she could feel no pressure, but a deep sense of peace flooded her body. The words chanted by the two women streamed over and through her.

> *That which you seek is within you,*
> *The strength of the God and the wisdom of the Goddess.*
> *Do not look without you*
> *But know 'tis all within.*
> *For behold I have been with you from the beginning*
> *And I am that which is attained at the end of desire.*
> *You are your best Protectress,*
> *Learn to trust yourself.*
> *In you is the strength of a thousand hearts,*
> *Have courage to fight for your life.*

Currents of power and hope such as she had never felt before coursed through Cess's mind and body. Eyes shut, she savored the new feelings of strength they created.

But before she could open her eyes to smile at the women, a terrible pain made her gasp and double over. It was so great she feared she would split apart, like a chestnut in flames. Her companions had turned to ash and the clearing was burned black and naked. She screamed and flailed around to hit out at the evil spirits flying at her out of the shadows.

"The evil is too close!" shouted the younger woman. "Surround her!"

Both women fell to their knees and circled the girl with their arms, fear in their faces. They bellowed the protective spell: "Goddess, save thy child! Goddess, save thy child!"

Gradually the pain subsided. After several minutes, Cess dared to open her eyes. The suffocating dark had vanished and the clearing was as before, bathed in the golden light of early evening. The women were kneeling beside her, eyes wide with shock.

"That was the presence of the evil that is amongst us," said Alathea. "It comes from one who feels no love for any person. His heart is dead, and that makes him more dangerous than any other foe, for there is no way to reach him," she whispered, shaken by what she had just witnessed.

"I cannot ever face that," said Cess, trembling. "Whatever power you think I have, you are mistaken," she gasped. The forms of the women in the clearing were fading.

"If you do not triumph over this evil, it will kill you, and many others with you," said Edith, as if from a great distance. "You are young for such a task, but we will arm you as best we can. Poor child, have courage." The last thing Cess could make out were the tears in her friend's eyes.

"Child? Cess? Cecily!" her mother was shaking her arm, hissing her name into her ear in the hope that the rest of the congregation would not notice her daughter's stupor. Cess opened her eyes and staggered, unable to feel her limbs. Her mother helped her stay upright until the peculiar feeling of being poured back into her body was over. She was shivering, and her heart thumped in her chest as if she had sprinted away from something frightening. She could remember nothing from the middle of the sermon to the end of the service.

Gradually her body steadied, but her mind was whirling like hops in the brew pot, at one moment elated, then angry, a moment later tumbling into sadness and fear, then joy again. She could make no sense of what had happened. It was as if she had been pulled into someone else's dream.

Her mother was staring at her, half cross that Cecily appeared to have fallen asleep, half worried by her pallor.

"For pity's sake, child, do you have a fever?"

Cess shook her head and allowed her mother to lead her to the back of the line shuffling out into the soft evening light. Outside, Sir Edward was distributing coins to the villagers. Drax Mortain had mounted his horse and was gently stroking his hawk. Cess could not help staring at him. Something about him mesmerized and repelled her in equal measure. His eyes flickered over the crowd, unseeing and uninterested, except when they alighted on Amelia.

"A purse for the poor?" asked Sir Nathaniel, holding up a velvet bag heavy with coins to Sir Edward's son. Drax Mortain took the purse lazily and chucked a coin toward a gaggle of children. He tossed another some distance away, sending the children careering after it. Several fell and began to cry. He smiled slightly, amused by the chaos he could create. Cess glanced at Sir Edward, who looked unusually guarded. Drax continued lobbing coins and watched the children grow more hysterical, running screaming through the crowd, chasing the coins hither and thither, like starved birds at seeding time.

Only Cess and William did not join in. Drax noticed their stillness. William dropped his gaze, but Cess met his scrutiny and could not tear her eyes away. She felt her skin creep as his eyes moved over her body. It felt as though he was trying to remember where he had seen her before, although she knew they had never met.

Drax moved his gaze to William. When he noticed the boy was cripple-born, he gestured for him to come closer to receive a coin. Uncomfortable with the attention, William obediently walked forward with his arm outstretched, but just as he came within reach, Drax flicked the coin into the distance, with a harsh laugh, echoed by many of the villagers who were watching.

Instead of the dull ache of shame and anger that usually gnawed at her at moments like this, Cess felt as if she had been hit by lightning. Each wave of laughter was another bolt.

"No more!" she screamed inside, the sound bouncing painfully around her skull without means of escape. Before Drax could finish his bark of mirth, Cess had leaped backward and caught the coin. The crowd fell silent, shocked and fascinated by her insolence. Cess knew that if she pocketed the coin and gave it to William later, she might get away with what she had just done, particularly if she dropped a curtsy to Drax to show some humility.

I will not, she thought, surprised by her own defiance and wondering if her experience in the church had turned her mind. She walked slowly toward William.

"Cess," hissed William, "I don't want it. It doesn't matter!"

It did matter.

"This is yours," she said, pressing the warm metal into William's palm, willing him not to look or walk away from her and to stand firm. He took the coin, but Cess could see that he was unhappy with what she had done.

Suddenly the crowd came alive, hissing at her and whispering among themselves. The fury that had driven her drained quickly away and was replaced by a terrible sinking feeling. She looked around, but not a single face looked kindly at her or grudgingly admiring. Even William was limping away.

From the vaguely disdainful look on Drax Mortain's face, it was clear he did not deem her worth the effort of a whipping. Sir Edward mounted his horse and signaled the drummer to fall in and his retinue to follow.

Sir Nathaniel addressed Cess as he climbed into his saddle. "You will come to my office after the holy day, on Monday," said Sir Nathaniel. His icy tone left her in no doubt that she would not be poultry girl at Montacute House for much longer. She felt very small among the horses of the nobles as they rode away.

What had she done? Her mother could not earn enough to keep them from hunger. What had made her think she could stand up against the village and a nobleman? Maybe they were right—perhaps William's deformity and her own poor birth really were signs of God's displeasure—and she should keep quiet, as the parson urged, and show humility and shame.

Drax Mortain nodded toward Amelia, who approached the mounted noble gingerly. He dropped the velvet purse into her hand, and she smiled up at him. The look of triumph on her face added to Cess's unease. Then Drax turned his horse so close to Cess that she had to jump out of its way. The great white hawk flicked its head and she heard the tinkle of a bell. Such a pretty sound to accompany her disgrace.

Amelia slipped away from the crowd outside the church doors, even though she was enjoying the vicious gossip about Cess and William, and made her way to the parsonage, pausing to hide her May crown in some long grass. When she knocked, it was the parson, rather than a servant, who opened the door. His coat and hat were still in his hand, and he looked peeved to be disturbed.

"There is no need to clout the door so. What is it?"

Amelia did not answer but bowed her head and peeked up under her eyelashes with a look of innocence she had perfected over many years of getting her siblings into trouble.

"Very well, enter, but I must dine, for I have much to do this afternoon." He marched into the hall, where the servants had laid a trestle with a plain dinner of roasted poultry and fruit. He sat, without inviting Amelia to join him, and helped himself to small portions. After several minutes of absorbed chewing he looked up.

"I am relieved that you have removed your May crown. You may speak."

"Sir, I am troubled."

"If you're with child, take your troubles elsewhere. I can't waste time on low-life doxies."

Amelia reddened and pulled herself up to her full height. "Indeed not, sir. I am a gentleman's daughter. It concerns the dead boy found this morning."

Ignatius looked Amelia up and down, as if her appearance could vouch for the reliability of her information. "I see."

"It concerns my cousin, now estranged. Cess . . . Cecily Perryn."

"Go on." Ignatius picked at his teeth with a shard of chicken bone.

"I have seen her several nights leave her cottage and go into the woods on Saint Michael's Hill." Amelia's conscience was not overly troubled by this lie. After all, Cess was known to deliver requests from the villagers to Edith.

The parson looked nonplussed. "So?"

Amelia was surprised that the parson was so out of touch with his flock that he did not understand the significance of what she had just revealed.

"The woods, sir, on Saint Michael's Hill, are home to the crone Edith Mildmay."

"The witch? This is known?" said the parson, the color in his cheeks rising alarmingly. "Is Satan's working in the world of such small matter in Montacute that she is left undisturbed?"

Amelia was rather taken aback by the parson's reaction. Surely even he understood that many in the village thought Edith a wise woman and relied heavily on her medicines. "I know nothing of that, sir. But as you spoke of the dead boy in church today I thought it might be worth mentioning," said Amelia, looking her most sincere. "I saw Cecily mumbling furiously at Sir Drax Mortain after the service. She defied him most brazenly and, I think, was cursing him. Should he not be told what I saw and warned to take care?"

When Amelia emerged, she was pleased to find that her May crown was where she had left it. Putting it on carefully, she wondered whether her conversation with the parson would bring her the rewards she sought. Although this would be at the expense of her cousin Cess, it was clear the girl had no wit and was brought low already. She clutched the velvet purse that had so recently been in the hand of Viscount Drax Mortain. It was clear he was interested in her, but as her mother had often repeated, men sometimes needed a nudge in the right direction. She knew that boys and men fell for her as slugs for beer—why should it be any different if a man had a title? There was no one suitable for her in the village. She hoped her visit would provide the encouragement Drax Mortain might need. She heard the door of the parson's house slam, and ducked down at the sound of approaching steps. The parson strode past with a determined step, heading in the direction of Montacute House.

CHAPTER 5

He was taunting William," said Cess the following day, walking fast through the morning drizzle to keep up with her mother. Her arms held the meager bundle of damp kindling they had managed to collect in Stoke Wood. She was tired, having slept very little for worrying about what the steward would say to her on Monday morning. The fitful sleep she had managed was filled with strange dreams of shattered bones, broken teeth, and bruised flesh.

The bells were once again calling the village to prayer, but she and her mother had decided that they should avoid the Sunday service and the stares and disapproval Cess would attract.

"I don't care if he was murdering a baby, Cecily," Anne snapped. "You keep yourself out of the way when Their Lordships are around. We will both be in trouble for your stupidity. We are not loved in this village." She puffed air sharply through her nostrils, a habit Cess knew meant that her mother was very angry. "Now you will lose your place as poultry girl, and we will have scarcely anything to live on."

Cess felt heat rise in her face. She wanted to explain about the strange vision she had had in the church, which she was sure had prompted her defiance. She had thought about it a great deal, puzzling its meaning. But she kept quiet. Talking about such things would only add to her mother's worries. The same was true of the pendant hidden in her bodice. She had not even dared tell William about that.

The last time Cess had felt so desperate was when her grandparents had died of plague. Before their bodies were cold, her uncle Richard had told her mother "to leave and take your bastard with you." He had never forgiven Anne for having a child out of wedlock and bringing shame on the family. Cess and Anne were forced to move into a tiny cottage, not much more than an animal shelter, at the poor eastern end of the village. Used to the luxury of a brick floor and a box bed with sheets, the change had been humiliating. In that sorry place she grieved for her grandparents, whom she had loved with all her heart and who had loved her fiercely in return. They had protected her as much as they could from the circumstances of her birth, and few had dared to taunt Cess too cruelly while they were alive, although she hid from them many of the indignities she suffered.

Since their deaths three years before, life for Cess and Anne had become very hard. Had it not been for her position at the House, they would have starved.

She trudged in silence to their cottage and stooped through the doorway into the mud-floored room that was their home. It would seem like a palace if her behavior led them to be thrown into the street. A sour smell assailed her nostrils after the freshness of the rain-washed wood. Her mother had resealed the floor with milk a few days before. The room was gloomy, for a sheet of linen soaked in linseed oil hung over the window to keep out the worst of the rain.

Cess sat down on a low stool, her head in her hands. One foot kicked absentmindedly at the earthenware lid covering the embers in the fire pit. With each blow, a trickle of smoke escaped and floated up into the thatch. Against the far wall was their bed, a simple wooden frame strung with rope, on which rested a straw pallet. Although covered in a coarse linen sheet, the straw poked through like needles. Behind a low wooden partition that divided the room in half was their pig. A lean, unhappy creature, twitching in its sleep, it was almost the only part of her mother's inheritance that her uncle had allowed them to keep—the pig and a finely carved oak chest. In cold weather, their few chickens also gathered in this small space at night. Only at the height of summer was the cottage warm, and then the thatch kept it so hot the floor cracked.

"I'm sorry," said Cess to her mother. In the dim light, Cess saw Anne's face soften a little.

"I know you are, Cess. You don't like to see an unjust thing; you have always been that way. It hurts me to say it, but we cannot afford such principles."

Her mother moved to the chest. Although old, it was the only handsome piece of furniture they owned, and Anne had refused to barter it even when their bellies were painful with hunger. She picked up her stitching and sat on the back doorstep. Having had a child out of wedlock, Anne found it hard to get work, but she was occasionally given other women's mending. It earned her a few farthings.

The pig woke and leaned against the partition until Cess let it out. It pushed past her mother and went out into their small garden. Cess watched it from the doorway, rooting around for tiny scraps and straining toward the vegetables behind the wattle fence. After a while it gave up and flopped in the mud.

Cess thought of William's face as she had handed him the coin. His mother would be so cross she might forbid him to talk to her, which she had always wanted to do anyway. It was William's father who had insisted they allow William to choose his own friends, in gratitude for her saving their son's life.

"May I leave?" asked Cess, who could not bear to stay cooped up with her mother for long. Anne looked at her daughter doubtfully.

"I'll be careful," said Cess, interpreting her mother's expression. "Will you come to the great house later?"

"No, I will work."

Cess's mother stayed home during festivities, particularly the coarse revelries around May Day, with their emphasis on sex and fertility. The crude jokes that flew around at such times, about her having fallen pregnant unwed, were too much for her.

Cess kept her head down and walked a little way out of the village, through Hornhay Orchard, to the copse by the stream. So many trees had been felled, even in her memory, that this copse was all that remained of a large wood that had stretched from here to the village of Tintinhull, several miles to the north. She knew the land was needed for crops, but still it saddened her to see so many mighty trees toppled and sawed up for timber. William told her she was foolish to feel for trees when so many died of plague and hunger, but she could not agree with him.

He was sitting, hunched against the rain, on the steep bank of the stream where they always met if they had no other arrangements. As she approached, she knew he heard her footfall, but he did not look up. Cess crouched on her haunches a little way from him, pushing leaves around with a stick. It was several minutes before she spoke.

"I'm sorry."

"You should be." The anger in William's voice shocked Cess more than her mother's had. She had hoped he might be secretly proud of her for standing up against the cruelty of others.

"I could not bear for him to taunt you."

"You made me a laughingstock more than I am already. That I

should need a bastard girl to protect me! If you had left well alone no one would have noticed, but now everyone is shouting after me 'Cesspit's baby! Cesspit's baby!'" William's anger was deeper than she had ever seen. Whatever her intention, she had joined the ranks of those who had hurt him.

"William, I am sorry for what happened; I never meant any harm to you. You are my true friend."

William looked at her as he struggled to his feet, his eyes brimming with tears of fury. "A real friend would not have used me to make her point."

Cess's eyes widened. How could William think she would use him? She was so surprised that she could find nothing to say and watched mutely as he limped away.

The rain stopped during the afternoon, and as evening fell, the crescent moon, little more than a fingernail, could be glimpsed through scudding clouds. Cess pulled a shawl over her head and joined the other villagers in the breezy darkness, walking toward the great house. They were shouting and laughing, excited about the entertainment to come. No one had seen fireworks before, and it was rare for new things to come into their lives.

After William had left, she had felt furious with him for not understanding what she had done and why. Surely it was obvious that she had wanted to defend him, to show others that he deserved respect? But as the shadows around her lengthened and the owls hunted, she had calmed down and tried to picture herself in his place. She understood that by assuming he needed someone else to defend him, she had not considered his feelings. She realized that her fury was as much about her own humiliation at being fatherless as it was about William's crippled foot.

She slipped unrecognized through the crowd, anxiously looking everywhere for her friend. At last she saw him, pressed up against the fence that divided the villagers in the orchard from the gentle-folk, who were strolling across the bowling green and admiring the lawns and formal gardens close to the great house, their cloaks and wide skirts whipped about in the breeze. She stood next to William for a while, willing him to feel her presence and accept the unspoken apology that it implied, but he was too busy craning his head in the direction of the house, worried he might miss even a moment of the spectacle. In the deepening darkness, the pale stone of the house glowed.

"Have you ever seen so much glass?" asked Cess, looking at the diamond-pained windows aglow with a thousand candles. Although William's home was well built, with a second floor and a chimney, it was his mother's constant complaint that they had no glass and had to light candles even by day when bad weather forced the shutters closed.

William turned reluctantly, peering under the shawl to verify that it was indeed Cess. Before he could reply, the loudest noise they had ever heard made them both yell and cling to each other in terror. It ripped at their ears, and they were blinded by a profusion of bright-colored sparks shooting into the night sky. All about them villagers screamed and ran across the orchard, some toward their houses, others toward the woods.

"The Devil is come!"

"It is the Last Day!"

"The sky is ripped. Help us, Lord!"

One after another came great bangs and crackles as the night was filled with shards of color. William and Cess cowered behind the fence in terror, peering through the wattle to see what was causing the terrible noises.

"They're not frightened," shouted William into Cess's ear as he realized that none of the noble guests were running away or screaming, but laughing and pointing at the sparkling flames.

"They're fireworks!" shouted a gaggle of stable boys and grooms toward the backs of the fleeing villagers. "They will not kill you! The Queen herself loves them!" They laughed, enjoying their superior knowledge gleaned by talking to the men from London in charge of the display.

"Fireworks," breathed William in awe, standing up and gazing into the sky. His thirst for all things new and clever was rarely satisfied in the village. "These must be the *explosions*," he said, captivated by the sight. "I must find out more." William was determined to question the stable boys until he had every ounce of information they could give him, but he hesitated. Despite being furious with her, William still possessed the manners to know that it would be discourteous to leave Cess alone.

"Yes, of course," Cess said hurriedly, once she had realized why William was waiting. "I shall go to Edith. No one will notice with these *explosions*." Although she too was riveted by the whistling, booming lights bursting overhead, she knew it would be some time before she had another opportunity to slip away unnoticed.

Another firework filled the sky with burning colors, the wind blowing some of the sparks into the shrieking crowd. A kaleidoscope of hues illuminated William's awestruck expression, and without thinking about it, Cess darted forward to plant a kiss on his cheek. The surprise in his face was chased away by a closed, dark expression. He would not forgive her easily, she saw. He pulled back, nodded stiffly, and walked away.

Turn around, she pleaded silently. *Make a face, give me a sign that you forgive me*. But he did not. Cess felt little bits of her heart being ripped out as he went. He was the only person in the village who loved her, as a brother or as a man for his wife she was no longer quite clear, but now she had forfeited his affection through her own hotheadedness.

Sadly, she pulled her shawl closer around her face and pushed her way to the edge of the crowd and through the orchard to the servants' drive. A few stragglers were rushing up the drive, but the Borough was deserted. Cess paused a moment, unnerved by the earsplitting bangs and the lurid splashes of color that made the familiar street look eerie and unreal. She walked quickly through the Borough, past the shuttered shop fronts. No candlelight winked anywhere. As she turned into Middle Street she came to an abrupt halt and stared into the distance. She could have sworn a pale shape flashed across the end of the lane by the church. It looked like a ghost.

"Must have been an owl," she muttered, forcing herself on. Where Middle Street met Bishopston, Cess removed her clogs and ran barefoot through the darkness. The fireworks continued, but the bangs were growing fainter. The lane wound around the base of Saint Michael's Hill, past the track to Abbey Farm, then struck out westward.

As Cess passed the track, she stopped short. A horse and rider were walking up it, and flying beside them was a huge white bird. Cess watched as the man reached the farmhouse and kicked the door without dismounting. The dim light that spilled out when the door opened confirmed what Cess had already guessed. The visitor was Drax Mortain.

A few moments earlier and she would have met him in the lane. Knowing that his business might be short, and that the high, dense hedgerows would trap her in the lane until she reached the far stile, she ran on, wondering what Drax could want with the owner of Abbey Farm. It seemed unlikely the great noble would pay Nicholas Joliffe, a farmer too fond of his drink, the honor of visiting without good reason, especially at night and while a great fete was being held at Drax's father's house.

Cess did not hear the sound of hooves over the fireworks and her labored breath until they were almost upon her. She could not run faster, and the hedge was too high to jump. She threw herself instead at the foot of it on the dark side of the lane and wriggled under as far as she could. Hawthorns tore the skin on her arms and legs, and the brambles dug into her flesh like a thousand claws. She covered her face with her arms and pushed her bare feet farther into the punishing barrier so that her pale flesh would not catch the rider's eye. She lay motionless, despite wanting to groan with the pain of the sharp stones that dug into her ribs and the nettles that stung her.

A piercing whistle made her jump. The horse was coming to a stop so close she could smell its hot coat and the leather of the saddle. She was sure it would sense her fear. It took every ounce of resolve not to cry out when the animal began nuzzling her, pushing her to stand up.

"Bess!" growled Drax to the animal, pulling sharply on the reins. "What are you playing with?"

Cess's heart dropped to the pit of her stomach. He would look down and see her. She tensed herself for the crack of a whip, but instead caught the soft sound of flapping wings. The great white hawk had come in response to its master's whistle.

"My beauty," whispered Drax to the bird. His voice was full of fondness. She could hear him stroking the hawk's feathers and making little crooning noises.

"You did well," Drax said softly, and with only the quietest tinkle of its bell, the hawk flew away. Drax kicked the horse and urged her on.

Once the clatter of hooves had faded, Cess rolled slowly out of the hedge, gasping in pain. Her bare flesh was covered in nettle welts and thin, bleeding scratches. Even under her clothes she could feel the damage the long thorns had inflicted.

She walked onward until she reached the last stile. A small wooden bowl had been left beside it. Pulling off the linen cover, she saw that the bowl was filled with fine golden honey. Although tempted to taste it, she knew for whom the gift was intended and covered it again so that it would not spill as she carried it. She crawled over the stile and pushed her way into the forest.

As the unofficial messenger between the village and the wise woman, Cess often visited Edith, but never before at night. Moonlight barely filtered through the thick canopy of leaves, and she found herself banging into low branches and tripping on roots. The ground rose steeply and the way was treacherous and slippery with patches of mud. Cess found the going difficult, especially carrying the bowl of honey in one hand.

The fireworks stopped, and soon all she could hear above the wind in the trees was the call of owls and the distant barking of a dog in the village. An occasional night creature scuttled through the undergrowth nearby. Cess breathed as quietly as she could, afraid to wake the spirits of the hill. Like all the village children, she had been told the story of Saint Michael's Hill as soon as she had the wit to understand it; village children were threatened with a night alone on the mount if they misbehaved. Faeries, hobgoblins, and unquiet spirits were said to inhabit it, and no villagers ever went there, except Cess. In the days of King Alfred, the abbot in Montacute's priory had dreamed that a miraculous holy crucifix was hidden at the top of Saint Michael's Hill. The villagers at the time dug where he directed, and a piece of black flint engraved with a crucifix had been discovered. A chapel was built atop the mount and became a place of holy pilgrimage. The monastery grew rich and powerful, dominating the village and surrounding areas. But God deserted the hill when King Henry VIII destroyed the monastery. Now only Edith lived there, and Cess was the only villager who knew where.

Out of breath and muddy, Cess found the clearing she sought and crossed it to reach a wooden hut at the far side. The shutters were closed, but chinks of candlelight escaped under the door. As she approached, she was surprised to hear not one but two female voices singing in harmony.

O song of nighttime, clothe my heart,
O fire of day, protect my soul,
O light of moonshine, play thy part,
And glorious sunshine fill my bowl.

The voices repeated the verse, like a monk's chant, rhythmic and mystical. Cess did not want to interrupt, so she sat with her back against the hut and fell into a trance so deep that she did not notice when the singing stopped. She jumped like a March hare when a hand tapped her on the shoulder.

"Cecily, I hoped you would come," said a tall woman with prominent cheekbones, who looked with concern upon the dazed girl. "You are hurt? What has happened?"

"Edith, I heard your beautiful singing," stuttered Cess, as if waking from a long, deep sleep. She pulled herself up and embraced her friend. As her muscles relaxed, she realized how anxious she had been since the experience in the church and all that had followed.

"My sister is with me," replied Edith.

"Sister?" said Cess, surprised. "I did not know you had a sister."

Edith did not reply, but noticed the bowl of honey as she turned to go back inside. "Did you bring this?"

Cess took a moment to answer, confused by Edith's revelation. "It was at the last stile," she said, bending to pick up the honey.

Edith sniffed the contents of the bowl. "Delicious! It will salve your wounds. How did you get them?"

"I had to hide on the lane." Edith did not ask more. She knew that Cess took great risks in coming to see her. As the older woman stroked her fingers over the scratches and bruises on her face, Cess saw the love that brimmed in Edith's eyes. A warmth more blissful than that of any fire flowed from her. Cess knew she was lucky to know Edith.

Cess noticed that her friend looked different. Instead of her normal skirt and bodice, she wore a long, hooded cloak made of fine stuff. She had let down her wiry gray hair from its customary coif. Cess had never seen an older woman with her hair uncovered before, except her mother when she combed it. The effect was unsettling, almost as strange as seeing Edith naked.

She followed Edith into her shack, where the atmosphere was stifling after the clear, cool night air. Herbs had been placed on top of the fire in the central pit, and their pungent smell made Cess giddy. There were only two small lanterns to see by, and it was several moments before she perceived another woman in the smoky gloom. The woman's head was bent to the fire, and she rocked slightly from side to side. She did not look up at Cess but threw some small buds into the flames, which popped loudly as the heat touched them. When the last bud flamed briefly and burned out, she slowly raised her head, and Cecily stared. The face smiling up at Cess was the woman in her vision.

"It is good to meet you, Cecily Perryn," said the woman, observing the cuts and welts on Cess's skin without comment. "My name is Alathea Woodeville. Come, sit beside me." Cess noticed that Edith had not introduced her guest but that Alathea had taken the lead, even though this was Edith's home. This would only happen if the visitor was of a much higher rank, but Alathea wore the clothes of a goodwife.

Her face was delicately pretty, her smooth skin framed by wisps of pale blond hair. But from this fragile beauty came a gaze of such strength and directness, boring into her very soul, that Cess could not lower her eyes, even though she wanted to. She sensed this woman could see all her secrets, and she squirmed as she sat beside her.

"I am Edith's sister," Alathea explained with a smile, although it was no explanation at all as Cess was sure Edith had no sisters. "I came yesterday to celebrate the Festival of Beltane with her."

Taking hold of Cess's rough, chapped hands, Alathea's smile

faded. "I come also with a warning of danger," she continued, nodding at Edith, who came to sit on the other side of Cess. Strangely, although Alathea spoke of danger, Cess felt safe and tranquil in the presence of these two powerful women, as if this were truly her home.

"You have heard, perhaps, of the boy found this morning and the disappearance of others over these past weeks?" continued Alathea.

"I have," answered Cess.

"The boy appeared to have died of the sweat, but we believe it is man and not nature that lies behind the death and disappearances. We fear great evil has been unleashed and that sorcery is involved."

"Why are you telling me this?" said Cess. "I know nothing of man's plagues or of sorcerers."

Alathea appeared to consider her words carefully before continuing. "The evil threatens us all, everyone in the country, but it hovers closer to you than to others, Cecily," she replied. Cess pulled her hands away, shocked by Alathea's strange prophecy.

"Closer to me? What do you mean?" The questions tumbled out of Cess's mouth. She felt Edith's arm move protectively around her.

"You are in greater danger from this evil than I was when the villagers sought to take my life," said Edith. The fear Cess saw in her friend's face unnerved her. Cess was astonished that practical, clever Edith should be talking of "evil" just as the parson did.

"Evil?" repeated Cecily. "You mean, witches?" she asked, not knowing of anything else that could be so described.

"Not witches," replied Edith firmly. "Witches do not involve themselves in such practices. They work only for good."

"For good? Making people ill and putting disease in their cattle!" cried Cess, shocked at what Edith was saying.

There was a long pause before Edith spoke again.

"Do you think I would do those things?" she asked.

"Of course not," Cess answered immediately. "But you are not a witch."

Edith moved to face her young friend and put her hands on Cess's shoulders. She looked Cess straight in the eye, and without hesitation she replied. "Yes, I am."

CHAPTER 6

Sir Edward Mortain felt unusually satisfied as he stood on the terrace of Montacute House and looked out. The fireworks had been tremendous, and his guests were now strolling toward the ornate banqueting houses that adorned the two corners of the lawns farthest from the house. There they would enjoy sugar treats of marvelous invention, like a marzipan swan with jeweled eyes and real feathers. They could spear sweetmeats with their own silver sucket forks, a new fashion that was taking the court by storm; each guest had received one as a gift, engraved with their initials and the Montacute crest. His generosity and wealth would be in no doubt.

Many of the guests had been speechless when they toured the house with him earlier in the day. The great hall on the ground floor, at least twenty-five paces long, with its beautiful plaster friezes and elaborate stone screen to divide it from the passage beyond, where the hundred or more servants ate and where grand banquets would be held; the great chamber on the second floor, his private domain with its internal porch to keep out drafts, and a chimneypiece of white stone that reached to the ceiling, where he enjoyed after-dinner dancing with the most elevated visitors; the top-floor gallery, the longest in the country, had caused a particular stir. How his guests had laughed when he told them that he liked to take his horse up there to ride when it was wet out. Looking through the huge glassed windows at the rolling countryside beyond, all of which he owned, he allowed himself a moment's pride. The walls were hung with recently finished portraits of his forbears (made to look much more illustrious than they had been), and only the picture of his wife and seven children, all of whom were now dead except Drax, had created a moment of discomfort. When he had announced during the feast that Queen Elizabeth herself was intending to visit, the guests had shouted and clapped their approval, for Montacute was a home splendid enough to welcome a woman whose love of magnificence was legendary.

Sir Edward saw his son striding from the stable block across the lawn to greet two pretty women. He wondered why he had needed to visit the stables during the feast. His smile faded. Drax had been in Montacute for a month already, and he felt no closer to him than when he arrived. All his attempts to draw him into intimate conversation had been politely rebuffed or steered in the direction of safer subjects, such as the intrigues at court or the preparations for the Queen's visit. He wanted to build trust between them, but all he felt was suspicion, on both sides.

Sir Edward sighed deeply and slowly descended the shallow stone steps to join Drax. He was not prepared to give up on his son. Not yet.

He nodded at his guests as he passed but did not invite them to join him. He was missing his beautiful wife. After her death he could hardly bear to see Drax, who reminded him of all he had lost. Only when his son had behaved so violently that there were rumblings against him in the county had Sir Edward been forced to take notice. He had sent him to board with a tutor near Windsor, where some sense could be beaten back into him. Their estrangement had continued even after Drax was called to court.

Now, at the end of his fifth decade, having outlived many of his good friends, he felt a strong desire to bring Drax back into the family. What had his ambition been for, if not to pass its fruits on to the generations that would, he hoped, follow?

Drax ushered his companions into the banqueting houses, and Sir Edward wondered again why it was that his son had agreed to come to Montacute now, when all previous advances had been ignored. Sir Edward suspected there was more to it than simply to ensure his inheritance. He knew from his spies that Drax was recently betrothed. To engage himself without his father's consent was against all the rules, and Sir Edward had been furious when he first found out. However, he had held his tongue, intent on improving his relationship with his son. That did not mean, however, that he intended the identity of Drax's bride-to-be to remain a mystery.

"My lords and ladies!" Sir Edward beamed as he entered the crowded banquet. The room hushed. Only the most important nobles in the country, and gentry of Somersetshire, had been invited, and this small banqueting house held the most select of these. Every head was bejeweled or sported a velvet cap dripping with precious stones or alive with peacock feathers. Doublets were pinked, embroidered, trimmed with gold lace, or sewn with silver eyelets, and kirtles and overgowns were lined with silk or taffeta shot with gold or silver thread, ornamented with crystal beads or strings of pearls. In every ear and on every hand were rings wrought of gold set with gems, and necks were draped with chains of office or strings of pearls the length of a bridle. The room was bursting with the wealth and power of the land, its brilliance reflected a myriad times in the diamond-paned windows on all sides. Sir Edward considered it a safe place in which to pursue his son. A little gentle ribbing was sometimes necessary.

"Today I introduce to you not only my house"—a cheer went up—"but to someone else of lofty and handsome elevation: my son!" Another cheer, a little hesitant. Drax was already a known, though mysterious, figure at court. "And just as a house is in need of an owner, a good man is in need of a wife!" Louder cheering, more confident now that the guests had an idea of what their host was getting at. Several of the unmarried women giggled together or looked coyly at Drax through lowered lashes.

"Montacute House will one day be yours," said Sir Edward, looking at his son, "but before I die, give an old man an inkling of your betrothal plans so I know who to come back and haunt!" Again, raucous laughter. Sir Edward knew how to please a crowd while getting results. Drax bowed to his father and smiled broadly. Only someone who knew him well would see the cracks in his jollity, and no one in the room knew Drax well at all.

"Father," replied Drax, outwardly suave, "surely you should be thinking not of death but of love? You have built the most beautiful house in the land, perhaps the world, but you rattle around it alone. So may I propose a toast? For my father . . . a wife!" The crowd whooped and cheered at the clever joke-spinning of father and son. All assumed the good-natured banter was rehearsed. Only father and son knew it was not and that Drax had cleverly evaded his father's questioning and driven another wedge between them.

CHAPTER 7

Cess sat motionless in the little shack. The fire warmed her face, but her back was cold and stiff. She could not look at Edith.

"All this time I thought you were a healer," she said quietly. "I defended you against the parson and the villagers who spoke ill of you. I helped you with your healing work. Now you are telling me that I was a fool. You are a . . ." Cess could not say the word. Only think it. Witch.

"Please, Cess, do not be angry with me. It is forbidden to talk about our craft to someone not from a witch family until they are thirteen. I did not want you to know until I could explain it fully. I thought you might be frightened away by the nonsense the parson speaks." Cess could tell Edith was speaking the truth. Edith loved her and would do nothing deliberately to hurt her. But her diminishing anger was replaced by fear. If Edith and Alathea really were witches, what did they want from her?

"We are revealing ourselves now so that we can help keep you safe," said Alathea. Cess frowned deeply. The women's warnings of danger seemed misplaced. The dead boy in the crypt had nothing to do with her.

"Alathea is our witch queen, Cess," said Edith in a quiet but urgent tone. She poked the fire and put on more sticks, making sparks fly up. Alathea sat back, allowing Edith to introduce her properly to Cess. "She is the most powerful witch in this land and has foreseen that we will defeat the evil we face only if you live." Cess shifted uncomfortably. It had not occurred to her that she might not live. In the glow of the fire, Edith's face was patched with dark shadows that made her look rather frightening. "Alathea comes from a sighted family that traces its heritage back to long before the Bible was written. There are such families across the country whose bloodlines are very ancient and powerful. Their members are born with the power to see ahead of time. Many can also communicate using thought alone. Other witches learn these skills in their covens, and now we ask you to learn them too. To save your life."

"You see ahead of time?" asked Cess, incredulous.

"Not as clearly as Alathea," said Edith, nodding toward her friend, "but well enough to save my skin when the villagers tried to burn me alive. It is a common enough talent, only people do not recognize it. Think of the dreams you have, foretelling the sex of unborn children and seeing where objects are hidden. Those are *scrying* dreams. With practice you can do it while awake."

"I have other dreams these days," said Cess hesitantly. She turned to Alathea. "I saw you in one."

"I know," replied Alathea. Cess stared. She wanted to like Alathea but found her unnerving. "That is why you braved the darkness to come here tonight, as we hoped you might."

"We called your spirit to us, to cast a protective spell over you after Alathea saw you in her scrying," explained Edith gently, "but we had not realized how close the evil had come. In your vulnerable state you felt it too, and were rightly terrified."

"Why am I closer to it than others?" asked Cess, not at all sure she wanted to know the answer.

Alathea sighed. "I am afraid we do not know. Scrying is not exact—the things I see are often strange or unconnected and unclear—but do not ignore our warning, Cecily," she said with such solemnity that Cess felt the hairs on her scalp tingle. "Has anything out of the ordinary happened in the last day or two?"

"Yesterday morning," said Cess immediately. "I saw a face, watching me from the great house. And in the coop I found this." She pulled the pendant out of her bodice and passed it to Edith. Edith caught her breath sharply when she held the pendant toward the lantern and saw the woman in the painting. She handed it to Alathea.

"Where did you find it?" asked Edith.

"Under a hen. Do you know who it is?" Cess saw that Edith was weighing up what to tell her.

"It is the Countess of Montacute, Sir Edward's wife, now passed into spirit. I helped in the delivery of her children. This crest in the painting is hers, a raven on a white stag. The raven is the bird of prophecy—she chose it herself."

"The white stag is a symbol of good fortune, isn't it?" asked Cess.

"Nowadays, yes. In the past it symbolized the need to go on a quest to avert doom."

Cess swallowed. Her excitement at finding the pendant was fading.

"This was hidden in the coops, you say?" Edith asked. Cess nodded. "Then someone must have placed it there for you." She frowned. "The threat Alathea has seen was from a living being, not one passed into spirit." Edith took the portrait back from Alathea and looked at it again. Cess noticed her rubbing her mouth with her fingers, something she did when she was worried or deep in thought. She handed the pendant back to Cess.

"Beware of that pendant, despite its beauty. It may hold the power to harm you. In our craft we have certain laws or principles that have been observed to be true. The Law of Contagion states that any object that has been in contact with a person will maintain that contact through the ether until it is ritually cleansed. Your pendant will thus maintain contact with Lady Mortain even though she is dead." Cess remembered how it had burned her skin outside the church. But she was not ready to give it up. Since finding it she had gazed at the portrait whenever she was alone. Now she had a name to go with the face.

As she put it back down her bodice, Alathea pulled a small, very sharp black dagger from a leather pouch tied to her belt. Cess moved away in alarm.

"You have no need to fear me, Cecily, and never will have. It was your birthday yesterday and this athame is my gift to you."

Cess hesitated. It was a strange gift.

"It is one of the witch's tools and will provide powerful protection. It is fashioned from obsidian—see the light coming through the edges?" As Alathea held the knife to the fire, the blade seemed to flicker and move with the flame. "This knife can increase your strength when you use it for a correct purpose. It was given to me when I turned thirteen and has never been entrusted to another person until now."

"Thank you, Goodwife Woodeville," said Cess, taking the knife gingerly.

Alathea laughed, a rich, warm sound. "You need not be so formal with me. After all, we have already seen each other. Call me Alathea." Cess smiled back at the pretty woman, who looked far too normal to be a witch queen.

"It is late and you will have to go home soon," Edith said as she smeared a little honey onto Cess's cuts and scratches with a dock leaf. "I shall make you a purse for Alathea's present and a healing syrup for the cordwainer's boy, who is sick; it must be his mother who sent the honey. Can you leave it by their door in the morning?" Cess hesitated. She would be agreeing to become the go-between for a witch. On the other hand, she was the only means by which the villagers could contact Edith for her cures.

Edith did not press Cess for a reply, but when she had finished she stood up to put the honey on a high shelf, and pulled a long linen apron from a peg on the wall. She poured cups of warm milky caudle for them all, and spooned pottage into a wooden bowl for Cess, who was always hungry. While Cess ate, the two women worked together to concoct the sick boy's medicine. From leather pouches, sacks, and clay pots Edith pulled a root, a bulb, a pinch of powder—garlic, sage, and marshmallow. From the drying herbs that festooned the roof beams she broke a twig, stripped a leaf, pinched out a tip—mint, Saint John's wort, and elderberry. Cess marvelled at Edith's knowledge of the secrets locked in every plant, tree, and fungus in the forest. All were put into a small iron pot with water from a covered bucket. Edith then sat beside Cess with a piece of worsted to sew while Alathea stirred the concoction, moving her lips as she did so.

"Are you casting spells?" whispered Cess to Alathea.

"I am," replied Alathea cheerfully. "They are prayers to bring health, just as you have heard your parson utter." It was true that the parson prayed for people and even for cattle and the apple crop sometimes, although reluctantly, for he would have preferred the villagers to concern themselves with sin and repentance. "We cast spells to heal the sick, help the brokenhearted, strengthen those in trouble, or to find things lost. A true witch does not harm others, our services cannot be bought, and we seek to work with Nature, not against it. We do not believe in a Devil as Christians do," said Alathea.

Cess watched the women carefully. Had she missed clues that they were witches? Marks, deformities? But no warts disfigured their

faces; their limbs were intact. Edith had no cat, fowl, or animal familiar at all. She did not mutter curses and, as far as Cess knew, had
never wished harm on anyone.

"Do you believe in God?" asked Cess, regretting her question
the moment it left her mouth. To deny God's existence would con-
demn Edith and Alathea to Hell, and Cess did not seek that, however
amazed she was by Edith's revelation.

"We believe in a God and a Goddess," Edith replied. "For us, the
divine is male and female. There are as many male witches as female."

"Men? I have never heard of that."

"There is little of truth that you will have heard about witches,
for we have to keep our secrets well," said Alathea. "We are now
hated in the land, where once we were honored and revered. There
will come a time when witches will return."

"But do you fly on a broomstick?" asked Cess, her eyes wide with
interest.

Alathea chuckled, and Edith broke into her characteristic laugh,
a guffaw followed by small noises, like hiccups. "Oh, Cecily!" Edith
wiped her eyes with the sleeve of her smock. "We use a broom for
sweeping, like everyone else. We worship in a circle, made fresh each
time, and we sweep it clean with brooms, that is all." Edith bit off
the thread as she finished her sewing and handed the purse to Cess,
who placed the sharp black knife inside it. With the long strings she
tied the purse round her waist, between the layers of her kirtle and
smock.

"We can talk more as we accompany you home," said Alathea,
standing. She took Cess by the shoulders, and Edith came to stand
beside her. Cess felt her legs tingling the way they had in the church
as the women stared into her face.

"You have heard things tonight of the deepest secrecy. The
knowledge is a burden that you too must now keep safe and never
reveal to anyone."

It was easy for Cess to agree; she did not want to see these women hang.

"For your own safety we beg you to improve your scrying and learn silent speech," Alathea continued, "but we cannot help you unless you swear allegiance to the coven. This will make you not a witch but a novice. You will learn the craft, and when you are ready, you can be initiated. If you do not want to join us when you finish your novitiate, you do not have to."

Cess felt a wave of panic muddle her thoughts. Her heart told her to trust Edith and Alathea, but since her earliest days she had been told that witchcraft was evil and no one should dabble in things forbidden. Pictures filled her mind of women hanging, her mother weeping as she was dragged away, the villagers looking smug as if they had known all along that she was a child of the Devil.

"Stop! You will frighten yourself with such imaginings," said Edith. "Follow your heart. Then you will find the courage you need." Edith bent down to the iron pot and strained the syrup through a piece of loose linen into a jar with a clay stopper. Cess thought back to the previous morning when she had wished so hard for her life to be different. Here was a chance for it to be so. Edith bound the stopper to the jar with yarn and held it out to Cess.

Cess took it. "I will do as you wish," she said quietly, praying as she did so that she had not just signed her death warrant. Both women smiled broadly.

"Let's go outside," said Alathea, taking her cloak from behind the door. Edith removed her apron, covered the fire, and doused the lanterns. Cess pulled her shawl over her head and followed the women as they walked out into the cool night. The moon was low and the breeze had passed on with the clouds, leaving the air still and radiant with stars. They moved to the middle of the clearing where Alathea directed them to hold hands. Then she spoke:

You who seek me, the Goddess,
Know that your seeking will avail you not
Unless you know the mystery;
If that which you seek you cannot find within you
You will never find it outside you,
For I have been with you from the beginning
And I am that which is attained at the end of the desire.

"A witch's power comes from within," said Alathea to Cess. "She must come to know herself, listen not to slander or praise, but seek to appear truthfully to herself and others. Though we are human, every part of us is divine."

A thrumming started in Cess's hands and arms and rapidly spread through her body until she was buzzing like a hive. Inside her chest she felt her heart open, like a daylily in sunlight, to receive the gifts Alathea was bestowing upon her. The women dropped hands and placed theirs on Cess's head. Alathea covered Cess's ears and Edith, her eyes.

Your ears are stopped but now you truly hear.
Your eyes are blind but now you truly see.

The vibrating intensified to such a pitch that Cess felt the contours of her body explode, and suddenly she no longer existed as before. There was no division between herself and the universe around her. She could hear great beasts calling in the oceans and stars exploding above, the thump of three beating hearts and all of the people on earth, the scrambling of ants through the grass, the worms beneath, the breaths of sleeping creatures, the creak of sap rising. There was a myriad of faces, people she had never met; some lingered and smiled at her, some slept, some were born. She felt as if she were soaring miles above the earth, able to look down yet still be a part of it. The fears she had about becoming a novice evaporated in the bliss and power of the moment.

Edith and Alathea removed their hands, but Cess did not open her eyes. She did not want to break the spell. The women were content to stand sentinel beside their young charge until she was ready to come back.

The moon was almost gone. Cess walked carefully behind Edith, who knew her way well enough to walk the track blindfolded. Cess's heart still beat rapidly with the excitement of what she had felt in the clearing.

Edith stopped for a moment to study a silver birch by the side of the rutted path. A flat patch of moss lay in the crook of a branch, and Edith pushed her nose right into it and sniffed. "This is good," she mumbled. From the purse at her waist she pulled a little black dagger, similar to the one Alathea had given Cess. As if asking permission of the tree, she stroked it gently, then carefully removed the moss with the blade, and slipped it into the small hessian bag that always hung at her side.

They walked around the hill in companionable silence until they were near the bottom, where the track was almost flat as it crossed the base of the hill behind the village.

"Shh. Keep still," Alathea whispered suddenly. "There is someone nearby." Cess snapped out of her dreaminess.

Suddenly Alathea pushed Edith and Cess sideways, throwing her cloak over all three of them. A few seconds later, Cess heard footsteps, heavy and a little unsteady. Whoever was walking was panting hard. She heard the crunch of dried mud under the pliancy of Maytime leaves as hard-soled boots tramped along. The footsteps were coming straight toward them. Something sharp pressed against Cess's side. It was her dagger. She pulled it from the purse and clenched it in her fist. The footsteps passed so close that the bush they were hiding behind was all that separated them. Once she judged the person had moved off a few measures, Cess lifted the corner of the cloak. A tall, well-built man was shouldering a heavy sack with some difficulty. His hair was so pale it glowed, even in the scant moonlight. He was not from the village.

"A poacher," whispered Cess. "That must be a deer he has in there."

"We must go. I sense evil," said Alathea urgently.

"We can go the other way, through Lossell's fields," said Cess.

"We will accompany you as far as we can," said Edith.

They soon reached the edge of the forest. The women could go no farther for fear Cess would be seen with them.

"Take this," said Alathea, pressing a small metal object into her hand. Peering closely, Cess could make out a five-pointed star in a circle. "It wards off evil, so keep it close. Show no one." The women kissed Cess and melted back into the darkness.

CHAPTER 8

Wake up! Wake up! Anne Perryn! Cess Perryn!" Cess jumped up still asleep and fell off the straw platform of her bed. She groped in the darkness and pulled back the bolt of the door.

"Where is William? Is he with you?" shouted Peter Barlow, his anxious face harshly lit by his flaming torch. The sockets of his eyes were black, while his jaw and cheekbones were bright, like a skull.

"No," replied Cess, wide-awake now. It was pitch black outside and she guessed she had been asleep only a short while.

"He did not return from the great house. Has he been with you?" Peter questioned.

"We met briefly but we were separated," replied Cess cautiously.

"When did you see him last?"

"He was talking to the stable boys about the fire-sparks."

"Fireworks? You did not see him when you walked home?"

"No."

Peter Barlow stared at Cess as if he suspected that she was hiding something. Her heart was beating in her chest so painfully she felt it in her throat.

"If you see him, tell him to come home at once." Peter turned, the flame of his torch roaring as it sliced the air.

Within minutes the village was alive with rumor and fear. Doors banged, dogs were baying, and men's voices called to each other as a search party gathered to hunt for the boy. Cess heard their tramping boots as they passed by her cottage. She felt her way back to the palette and lay beside her wakeful mother until a faint lightening of the sky between the missing slats of the shutters told her it was nearly dawn.

Mother and daughter dressed in silence, both aware that Cess had returned home very late from the fireworks. Both knew where she had been, but neither wanted to talk about it. Anne knelt beside the fire and began to pray. Cess joined her, not knowing who to pray to, but needing to do something. It was hard to concentrate, and her thoughts kept leading her to the man in the woods.

"I am here, Cess." It was Edith's voice. Cess jumped and her eyes snapped open, looking about for her friend. The voice was real and close by. Her mother opened her eyes and looked at Cess.

"Why do you jump? What ails you?" she asked.

"Nothing, Mother. I must have dropped asleep." To Cess's amazement, it seemed that Edith had heard her prayers and was answering. Cess closed her eyes once more.

"William is missing!" Cess's body flooded briefly with emotion, like a blush, an echo in her body of Edith's reaction to the news.

"Think of him," came Edith's voice. "Help us to see where he is. You know him best." Cess was shocked by how clearly she heard Edith. Was this really happening, or was lunacy overtaking her? She kept her eyes wide open for a few moments, deeply unsettled.

"Do not be afraid, Cess. We might be able to help him."

Gingerly, Cess closed her eyes again. It took a little while for her to move her thoughts past the events of the previous day. Picturing his angry face made her shy away, but she tried again. She remembered the last time she had seen William—his delight at the fireworks and his care for her safety despite his hurt. She was just beginning to smile at the memory when her vision darkened. There was a narrow door, locked. She faltered, then walked through it. William was there, she sensed rather than saw. He was freezing cold and burning hot, shaking and gasping.

"William! He is in pain!"

"Child! Child!" said Anne, alarmed. "What are you saying? Are you ill?" She shook Cess until she opened her eyes, and helped her to the stool. Cess rocked herself beside the fire, appalled by her vision. She knew Edith had felt it too, though she did not know how she knew.

"You look like you've seen a ghost," said Anne.

Cess tried thinking of all the possible reasons William might have stayed out, hoping against hope that her vision was wrong. "God's death!" she exclaimed suddenly, jumping to her feet and grabbing her cloak. "I have to see the steward," she gasped. The news of William's disappearance had made her forget Sir Nathaniel's order.

She banged the thin wooden door behind her and set off quickly along the slippery track. Almost immediately, drizzle drenched her face and seeped into the rough cloth of her cloak. Saint Michael's Hill was lost in mist, but to her left some bedraggled sheep huddled among the twisted trees in the orchards. Their cottage was a few measures beyond the village, as if disowned, although the first dwellings she reached along the track looked hardly more prosperous. Tufts of straw and mud bristled in large patches where the plaster had dropped off the walls, and lay where they fell, like cracked ice, the occupants too tired to sweep outside as well as in. Rags had been stuffed into warped shutters that were so ill-fitting they would barely keep out vermin, let alone draughts. Puddles had formed around the front doors in the grooves made by passing feet.

The smell of smoke drifting through thatch grew stronger as she came into the village. Most people would be breakfasting or already at work, and the routines of the day seemed little different than normal. More women were standing around gossiping than usual, probably about William, and the men from the search party were straggling home to start the day's toils. Even for a missing boy, work could not be stopped. Without work, there was no food. The cord-wainer, the rope makers, the bell founder, the flax dressers and linen weavers, the cooper, pewterer, glovers, and even William's father the blacksmith, would continue as normal, while William, even as she walked to her own place of work, might be just a few fields away, overtaken by a sudden illness.

As she neared the Barlows' smithy and cottage she could hear wailing coming from within. A group of women stood outside the door, heads close together, talking fast. At the sight of Cess they fell silent. Then one slipped into the house and the wailing stopped abruptly. She felt her heart slow as she walked on.

"Stop, Cecily Perryn!" barked a shrill voice, hoarse with crying. Margaret Barlow, William's mother, was marching toward Cess, her face alight with hatred.

"Come here!" she half shouted, half croaked, while the eyes of the women around her grew wide in anticipation of the scene to come. Previously Cess would have meekly obeyed, but something had changed in her. She stood her ground.

"I said, Come here!" screamed Margaret, ignoring the women trying to comfort her and help her back inside. "What have you done with my son? You have bewitched him! Where is he?" Spittle gathered at the corners of her mouth, and her hair was wild where she tore at it.

"William is my only friend here, Goodwife Barlow," said Cess, her voice far calmer than her feelings. "I would give my life to save his."

Margaret was too angry to listen. "We will search you," she shouted, jabbing her finger toward Cess, "me and these goodwives here. We will strip you naked and find the Devil's mark on you, just see if we don't." Cess stumbled backward, away from the gesticulating woman, but bumped into more goodwives who had gathered around her. They pushed her forward, and Cess pulled her cloak tighter. She looked desperately for a way out of the tightening corral.

"Be quiet, woman! Your temper does not help us," shouted Peter Barlow, who had heard his wife's threats as he rounded the corner of the cottage. He threw his spent torch by the door, looking worried and exhausted after his night of searching. "Cess has already shown us that she would save William's life. Let us not curse a soul until we know what has happened." He towered over his wife, stonily indifferent to her ranting, until his presence forced her inside. Then he waited by the door until the other women had dispersed. Cess quietly thanked him as she walked on, receiving a curt nod in return.

"Come in!" Cess felt so sick, she stayed put. Her legs, trembling like willow branches, refused to carry her forward. The manservant gave her a mighty shove, and Cess almost fell into the room. Sir Nathaniel Davies was engrossed in some papers, and she braved a quick look around his chamber. The room was square and tall, paneled in wood, and lit by a large window. The steward was seated at a long wooden table behind neat stacks of rolled manuscripts in wooden racks, vellum-covered ledgers, and several fine quills. A huge amber seal, elaborately mounted in gold, lay beside him with a bundle of red sealing-wax candles. Cess looked closely at the seal. It carried the Montacute crest, a large hawk with a dead rabbit in its claws. Cess felt like that rabbit, and her stomach churned so loudly she knew the steward must be able to hear it.

"Crowther," said Sir Nathaniel so suddenly, Cess jumped.

"Sir," replied the manservant.

"Tell the apprentice to clear the room above the last stable block by tomorrow. We will need it to store the fireworks for the Queen's visit, so make sure there are no horses below it. And send the chief groom to me."

The manservant bowed, leaving Cess alone with the steward. When she looked, his eyes were upon her. Tossing his quill upon the table, he indicated that she should come closer.

"It was my intention to have you flogged and sent from the charity of this house." Cess noticed that the steward did not address her by name, as if she were as lowly as the cattle and the sheep. Her mouth was so dry that her tongue stuck to her teeth.

"However, you are spared in this instance." He seemed to want to say more, but shook his head in annoyance and waved for her to leave. Cess could tell this had not been his decision. Someone more powerful had ordered him to treat her kindly. She was mystified as to why this should be, but overjoyed at her reprieve.

"If you please, sir . . ." she said in the humblest voice she could muster, although she knew that to speak at all was impudent, once he had dismissed her. The steward ground his teeth at the malapert he saw before him. "I am most grateful for your mercy . . ."

"As should you be. Now go."

But Cess remained where she was. "Sir, may I take the hens to market myself now that I am thirteen?" The steward looked as if he was about to explode. A thick vein at his temple pulsed alarmingly. "I can get a better price for the birds than the kitchen boys, knowing them as I do," Cess said quickly. She also knew that many of the boys who had disappeared had been taken from Yeovil, where the market was held. If she could get there, she might discover something that would help in the search for William.

The steward narrowed his eyes and bounced the tips of his fingers together as if beating time to the stream of suspicions he had about the impudent wretch before him.

"Come back with one penny less than you ought, and you or your mother will furnish what we are owed. Do you understand?"

Cess curtsied deeply and fled the room.

"Not the brown kirtle, Mother. I'll look as shabby as that cousin of mine. The green one," ordered Amelia, brushing her hair furiously as her mother pulled clothes from the chest. It was not much past dawn, but ever since a boy had come from Montacute House with a message from Drax Mortain, the two women had been running about as though their gowns were on fire.

Amelia finally descended the stairs dressed in her new green bodice and kirtle with a separate yellow skirt panel tied into the front with matching yellow and green ribbons. She had borrowed her mother's Spanish farthingale to make the skirt stick out, bell-like, at the bottom. Her new sleeves were tied on to the bodice with green cords and were slashed to show yellow material beneath. Her fair hair was loose around her shoulders. Her mother had wanted to frizz the front, but Amelia refused, judging that Drax Mortain would be impatient. The boy had insisted that she should reach the house as soon as possible after sunrise. She wore her best girdle and slung from it a fine silver pomander, an embroidered purse, and a small steel mirror.

"You are a beauty," her mother said proudly as she finished lacing the sleeves to Amelia's bodice. "I knew he was bedazzled by you!" she whispered in her daughter's ear so the boy would not hear.

Amelia did not reply. She knew it would take more than beauty to win Drax Mortain. She strapped her wooden pattens over her best leather boots so they would remained above the mud and make her taller.

"Who will chaperone you?" called her mother as Amelia left the house, pulling up her hood against the drizzle. "Shall I?"

"No, Mother, he has called for me only," said Amelia. Her mother did not know that Amelia had provoked this meeting through her scheming. Amelia suspected her mother might not approve of bringing a relative, even a shameful one like Cess, into disrepute. Only she understood how her plan would ultimately lead to her parents being delighted with her.

The Perryn compound, at the southern end of the village, was quite close to Montacute House. She hurried after the serving boy, who was already turning on to the servants' drive.

"This way?" she called to him. "Are we not going to the front door?"

He did not stop, but only turned his head to reply, "His Lordship told me to take you straight to the knot garden. This is the quickest way."

"In this damp?" she questioned, but the boy just shrugged. Amelia supposed Drax Mortain to be one of those men who were happy only when out of doors, but she was disappointed not to see the great hall of Montacute House or the famous long gallery. She had only been in the grounds once, in the dark, for the fireworks. She comforted herself with the thought that the gardens would be a prettier backdrop for her charms.

They passed the sties on her right, with orchards beyond where the pigs could hunt for windfalls. The kitchen gardens were to the left, protected by high wattle fences and wicket gates. Beyond those, in the distance, she could see what looked like chicken coops, where she supposed her miserable cousin spent her days. Before her began the formal lawns that led to the western front of the house. Amelia tried to think what she would say to Viscount Drax. It felt like a flock of blackbirds was inside her, beating their wings to get out. She was so nervous she could smell the strong tang of it at her armpits.

Amelia followed the boy through an archway in the clipped yew hedges and saw Drax Mortain in the far corner of a knot garden, seemingly studying the intricate interweaving patterns made by the low box hedges. He looked up as she approached, making no move to meet her, his eyes taking in every detail of her form.

"Maid Perryn." He bowed, waving the boy away without a glance.

"My lord," replied Amelia with a well-practiced blush. She sank into a deep curtsy, giving Drax Mortain the opportunity to take her hand to draw her up again. He did not let her go but led her toward the maze beside the garden. Amelia remembered well when cartloads of large yews had been brought through the village for the maze. There had been much gossip about the expense. She never guessed then that she might one day walk through it with the earl's son.

"Are you frightened of mazes, lest you never emerge alive, or will you accompany me in? I thought it good for us to enjoy some privacy," he said. Amelia had never been in a maze, but was not wholly ignorant of their purpose. Her father, a dour, puritanical man, had scorned them enough for her to know that they must be for pleasure.

"With you as my guide, my lord, I will have nothing to fear," she said with a perfect mix of trust and coyness. Drax smiled for the first time. Amelia could not tell if he enjoyed her or found her laughingly naive, for his smile gave nothing away.

"It seems I must thank you, Maid Perryn," said Drax Mortain, leading her into the maze as if into a first dance, "for alerting me to the mumblings against me of a supposed witch. The parson was most prompt in delivering the warning to my father's steward and thence to me. We will strive too, of course, to discover what happened to the dead boy."

Amelia flushed slightly, delighted at how well her plan had worked. She only hoped Drax Mortain did not consider her foolish to think that he would care a jot that a bastard peasant girl was muttering a few spells.

As if guessing her thoughts, he continued. "Witchcraft can be very powerful, even if performed by the young. Has she a witch's mark or familiar?"

Amelia hesitated. She had spun the tale about Cess to give Drax Mortain the excuse to summon her, not to start a full-blown witch hunt. However, despite the seriousness of his questions, she could not help thinking that he was enjoying her discomfort, teasing her.

"No, my lord, although Cess is not so young—she has just turned thirteen."

"Ah, a good age." He smiled again, looking into her face for much longer than was necessary, then guiding her under a low arch, causing their bodies to touch. Amelia was flustered. She wanted his attention, but when she got it she felt scared and utterly unsure what to do with it. Although fifteen, and quite grown-up, she felt reduced to a child in the presence of this nobleman who had seen at least thirty summers.

"And how came your cousin to meddle in such practices?" asked Drax.

"Cecily is estranged from the rest of the family," Amelia said, choosing her words with care. Her cousin's shame might reflect badly on them all. "She is fatherless, my lord, with no strong hand to guide her," she went on, acutely aware of Drax's hand clasping hers.

"Is she pretty? Does beauty run in your family?" he asked, stopping to run a finger along her jawline and push back a stray curl. Amelia felt like an idiot, blushing all the time, but she had no experience of such flirtation. When the village boys got cheeky she just slapped them.

"No, she has freckles," said Amelia with finality, then added, "but, my lord, you can judge for yourself. It was she who defied you outside the church on May Day. See how she rewards your generosity?"

Drax pulled up short. "That wench?" he said, seemingly genuinely intrigued by Amelia's story for the first time. His expression clouded with concentration. "I thought I had seen her before some-where," he mused to himself. Amelia allowed his thoughts to be elsewhere for a brief moment as they walked on, then she stumbled on an imagined tree root.

"Oh, forgive me," she said prettily, squeezing his hand. Drax's attention was once more all hers. His wealth, his power, his title, and his interest in her made her feel heady, as if she had drunk too much cider. On his horse outside the church, with his hawk, surrounded by men-at-arms, he had looked like a hero in a story. But up close he became a man, who wanted as much from her as she wanted from him. His bald brow was unsettling, like a baby's in an aging face. She could see the deep lines in the skin around his mouth, and a couple of his teeth were black. His lips were plump, the bottom one especially so, and the idea he might kiss her with them made her squirm, from pleasure or disgust she could not quite say.

"And why would you wish to warn me of your cousin's ire?" he said as he raised her face with his hand under her chin, and bent down so close she could feel his breath. Amelia's prettiness was usu-ally enough to convince people that she was honest, but clearly Drax would need flattery and flirtation too.

"My lord, I have heard that curses can make a man ill, even to death. How could I stand by and not warn you?" she said in a voice husky with sincerity but with a look that she hoped left no doubt that she herself would be happy to bewitch him.

Drax stared, still standing so close that Amelia could smell the lavender water used to wash and iron his undershirt. He eventually released her gaze and pulled something from a pouch on his girdle. He took Amelia's hand and placed the object on her palm as he whis-pered into her ear so closely that his lips brushed her cheek, "I hope you reward generosity more pleasantly than your cousin."

Amelia felt her stomach turn, understanding perfectly what was meant by his words. On her palm lay a large ruby pendant on a chain of gold links. Its deep color was clearly visible, even in the gloom of the maze. Amelia caught her breath.

"May I?" Drax asked, picking the chain off Amelia's palm and passing the chain over her head. He ran his fingers over the naked skin above her bodice to ensure the chain lay well on her chest. Then he lifted her face and kissed her.

CHAPTER 9

As Cess entered the kitchen yard she noticed that the horses were already being led between the shafts of two market carts. She grabbed her skirts, threw her heavy clogs into them, and ran barefoot to the poultry yards. If she missed the cart, her plan would be ruined. She felt the heavy gold chain and pendant bounce a little inside her bodice.

Cecily skidded to a halt by the coops and grabbed two large wicker baskets from the narrow hut where she kept her pails and brooms. With deft speed she filled one with eggs, padding them well with straw, and into the other she pushed the birds to sell, crooning softly to soothe them. As she struggled back toward the kitchen courtyard, a movement made her look toward the gardens. There was a figure standing just inside the maze, her head tilted slightly back as if laughing, or smiling at someone out of view. She was too distant to hear, but Cess could have sworn it was her cousin Amelia.

Lack of sleep is making me see things, she thought, shaking her head. When she looked back, the girl had gone.

She staggered into the kitchen yard and placed her baskets carefully beside the back of the second cart, looking about for someone to help her lift them onto the footboard. The cart was already loaded with people and produce, but there was just enough space for her. The servants in the yard and the cart ignored her or shot her dirty looks. After a few minutes the clerk of the kitchens emerged, squinting in the pale morning light and clearly irked at having to interrupt his hectic schedule.

"Why are you here?" he barked.

"The steward says I may take the birds to market," Cess replied. Out of the corner of her eye she noticed the other servants were listening to their conversation.

"Perhaps he did not know that I have always sent a kitchen hand with the hens. There is no need to change the arrangement."

Cess blanched. "Sir, it is the steward's wish." To challenge the clerk was dangerous, but she had no choice. She must go to Yeovil.

"No one will travel in the cart with you. The produce must go to market, so you need to be gone."

Cess looked around. It seemed that every servant in the household had gathered to watch her humiliation. She felt her courage waver, and only her fears for William drove her on.

"May I not go at least to where the lane meets the Yeovil road?"

"You may go to where my boot meets your arse!" he roared.

Blushing furiously, Cess picked up her baskets and stumbled away from the laughing crowd. A kitchen boy ran to take them from her, but she snarled at him like a wild animal, cornered and hurt. "I am the poultry girl!" she spat. The boy recoiled and looked to the clerk for support. He shrugged his shoulders and marched back inside.

Cess struggled down the servants' drive, angry and frightened that fingers were already pointing at her over William's disappearance.

Her outburst outside the church would not have improved her popularity. The Montacute carts trundled past her, but Cess did not falter despite every bone and muscle aching with the weight of her load. If she could make it to the end of the drive and along the Borough, someone else might stop to pick her up.

Six carts passed, but their occupants pretended not to see her. Eventually, Cess sat by the side of the lane and did not even bother to look up at the sound of wheels squelching toward her in the muddy ruts.

"What are you sitting there for?" Farmer Joliffe had pulled up his horse and was peering down at her. He looked badly bruised, scratched, and even more disheveled than usual.

"Waiting for a ride to market," she replied.

Joliffe eyed her. "You can come with me, if you wish," he said eventually.

"Thank you," she said simply, and was grateful for his help loading the hens and eggs. The farmer grunted in pain as he moved.

"Did you come too close to the horse, sir?" she asked quietly with a sympathetic nod at his bruises, not sure if Joliffe would welcome conversation or not.

"Aye," he replied grimly. "A noble steed." Cess pictured Drax Mortain entering his farmhouse the night before, and ceased her questioning. She knew that Joliffe's reputation was worse than her own. He had been a popular young man until a fight he was in before Cess was born led to the death of another villager. No one witnessed the brawl, and Joliffe had been too drunk to remember much. There was no trial, but many of the villagers considered him guilty. Since that time he had kept his own company and taken increasingly to drink.

As children, she and William had played on the fields around Joliffe's farm, digging up interesting rubbish from the old priory middens. Joliffe had caught them repeatedly and quite often chased them away in a drunken rage. At other times he would give them apples or cheese and tell them to come back whenever they wanted. He even asked after her mother, which had surprised Cess; no one else did.

They traveled in silence, lost in their own cares. The drizzle stopped and a light breeze brought some sunshine and scudding clouds with it. At the last milestone before Yeovil, the track was churned from farm carts bringing in early spring greens, bitter skirret roots, peppery Alexanders, and wild garlic, the meager crops of early May. Others carried willow cages of pigeons, ducks, and geese, and braces of woodcock. Cess saw round cheeses, sides of salted bacon, and fish under wet linen cloths, and barrels of cider. Pigs and cows were being driven to their pens in the marketplace by young boys, and there were a few early lambs bleating anxiously as they wobbled their way to town. Cess looked at the women and children crouched by the side of the route with threadbare clothes, their feet wrapped in rags. Many held up their hands. "Money for bread? My children are dying for want."

Cess's eyes grew wide with pity as she saw the scrawny little babies tied to their mothers' chests with patched scarves.

Once inside the walls of the town, Cess was overwhelmed by the medley of new sights and sounds. So many people crushed together, houses with two or even three floors, many with glass windows.

"Gardyloo!" goodwives shouted as they threw the contents of chamber pots out of overhanging windows into the street below. Joliffe pointed out his favorite inn, the Red Lion, which had four floors, fine black timbers, and painted plaster walls. Although it was not as grand as Montacute House, Cess was amazed that ordinary people were allowed in. Whole streets were dedicated to one trade—Shoe Lane, Baker Street, Rope Passage, Tanning Way, Fishmarket, the butchers in the Shambles. The stench from the tanneries shocked her nose and mingled with the cattle dung and human excrement flowing freely in the street. As they passed a pomander stall, the sharp scent of oranges sweetened the air for a welcome moment. Ribbon Passage, aglow with rich colors and precious metals, made her long to run her fingers through the silken cords, ribbons, and baubles hanging up for sale. She longed to be there with William.

The streets nearest the market square were so crowded that Joliffe was forced to clamber down from the cart and lead the horse, swearing and shouting at people in his way.

"This'll do," he said shortly, tethering his horse to one of the posts that ran around the edge. He helped Cess unload her two baskets, and together they unhitched the cart and lowered the back end. A half-dozen sacks slid to the ground filled with early crops from his farm.

"Poultry's over there," said Joliffe gruffly, nodding toward the farthest corner of the market. It was the most he had spoken since Cess mounted the cart. "You'll find it." Then he heaved two sacks onto his back and walked off.

Cess stood still for a few moments while she gathered her courage. She had never been in such a crowd, never crossed a busy marketplace, never had to reply to the hawkers and sellers begging for her to buy their wares. Keeping her gaze ahead with what she hoped was a worldly-wise expression, she struggled through the tightly packed stalls. The sun-warmed odor of feathers mixed with the acid tang of droppings drew her on; her nose could lead her to poultry even when the odor was mingled with those of earthy vegetables, squealing piglets, and ripe cheeses. As she emerged from the stalls, she walked into a blizzard of down. A gaggle of women squatting on short wooden stools were plucking birds and gossiping. Cess walked nervously toward them. The oldest and plumpest turned to measure her up.

"Who are you?" she inquired. Cess saw that the woman had not a single tooth in her head.

"I . . . I come from Montacute," stammered Cess, worried that these women would turn her away.

"Sit there if you wish," said the toothless woman, indicating an empty stool but never pausing from plucking the bird she held firmly between her knees. It was screeching. The woman laughed. "This one has no complaints. Done nothing but sit in my loft eating curds and grain." The bird had a large hole in one foot, its edges ragged and blackened, where it had been nailed to the floor while being fattened.

Without thinking, Cess took out one of her hens and stroked it on her lap.

"A petted hen don't get you more money," said her neighbor, shrieking with laughter. Cess wanted these women's help, so she quietly replaced the bird in its basket. She smiled along with the goose plucker, making small talk until it was safe to bring up the subject she was really interested in.

"You must be worried coming here. I heard some boys had disappeared."

The woman plucked and tutted in time. "Aye, it's an awful business."

"It's the work of the Devil," piped up another woman.

"Do they only disappear at night?"

"Yes, always in the dark," said the goose plucker, whose work seemed less arduous now that the bird had fainted, "and it's never the rich folk, oh no, just the poor ones. Two of the swineherds disappeared, *poof*, just vanished. As if we don't have enough to deal with, what with the prices these days."

There ensued a general lamentation about last year's failed harvests, the wet and cold weather, the price of everything, the taxes on candles, who of their acquaintance had died and of what, and much besides, so that Cess could ask very few questions. She realized that her plan to come to Yeovil had not been well thought out. Having never left Montacute before, she had had no idea that Yeovil would be so large.

She opened the basket of eggs, remembering that she had to sell her produce as well as find out about the missing boys. The kitchen hand got a halfpenny a dozen for the eggs, so she had to do better.

"Three farthings a dozen," she called out, smiling at those who hovered to look. "And the birds are fat, reared on the Montacute estate. They eat as fine as His Lordship!" she cried out, encouraged by the smiles and laughs that greeted her banter. To her surprise, she discovered herself to be a natural hawker. By midday she had sold all the eggs and all but one bird.

"Could I leave my baskets here a while?" Cess asked of the toothless one. The woman nodded cheerfully, Cess's silver tongue had brought business to them all.

Wandering among the market stalls, Cess remembered what the women had said about the swineherds. If the missing boys were poor, it was worth starting at the livestock pens, where the neediest boys worked. She followed the sounds of cattle to the corner of the market that led onto the London road. The pig pens were outside the square, a little way along the road. They were not much larger than those at Montacute House but heaved with animals belonging to many different smallholders. A painfully thin boy, a little older than Cess, was scratching the back of the pig nearest him with a stout stick. He looked her up and down as she approached.

"How now," he said with a smile.

Cess smiled back.

"How do you remember whose beast is whose with so many?" she asked.

"I know pigs better than I know my own family."

"Do you live in these parts?"

"A little north. Why you interested, big nose?" he said with a cheeky grin.

"I didn't mean to pry. A friend of mine went missing last night from Montacute way. I thought he might have come here," said Cess.

"A runaway?"

"I hope so. Rather that than taken."

The boy nodded, his smile fading. "I don't go out after dark these days," he said. "I knew two of them as has gone. They wouldn't have scarpered. They was taken, for sure."

"Where were they when they disappeared?"

The boy looked at her, surprised a girl should be so curious. He eventually jerked his head along the road.

"There's a wrecks' shack down there and a tavern, a real shit hole, the Hog's Head. They'd got their wages, which God knows ain't enough to eat with, but they boasted they was going to get drunk, get women, and taunt beggers . . . It's not my idea of fun, which is why I'm still here. I saw them head off that way. Never came back."

"A wrecks' shack?" asked Cess, mystified.

"It's where vagabonds and beggars shelter," he elaborated.

"Did you tell the magistrates?"

"Hah!" barked the boy. "A pox on them. The likes of them don't speak to the likes of me! They don't reckon we have enough brain to know anything useful. Wouldn't tell them anyway—what would the boys' parents think if they knew their lads was spending their pay on ale and whores?"

Cess saw his point. "Is this the only road to London?"

"Yes, and I've been here since before dawn. What's your runaway look like?"

"He's a bit taller than me. He has a . . . bad foot."

"Nope. I'd have spotted him if he'd limped this way. Never leave my post, not even to open my bowels." He grinned, and Cess turned her head away from the pigs and the foul-smelling muck they were wallowing in.

"How far is it to the tavern and the wrecks' shack?" asked Cess, looking down the road.

"Not far, but you're a girl," he said, looking her over again. "If you go alone, they'll think you're one of the doxies. I wouldn't bet a farthing on your getting back here in one piece." Cess realized he was probably right. She would ask Joliffe to go with her after the market. He seemed well acquainted with Yeovil's taverns.

On the way back to the poultry corner, Cess asked every stall-holder she passed if they had seen a boy like William, but none had. She was bitterly disappointed not to find out more, and felt the day had been wasted except for her success at selling. She had made more money than her predecessors ever did.

"You're a lucky one!" exclaimed her toothless neighbor, without a trace of jealousy as she packed away her stool.

"Maybe it is you who brings me luck." Cess smiled back. It was a wonderful feeling, to be liked.

"I'll buy that last bird off you," said the woman. "Reckon it'll make good chicks."

As the church bells rang out for evensong, the last of the stalls was being dismantled, and the dust boys swept the square. Cess watched them picking over their sweepings for anything edible or valuable before chucking the rest into a large dunghill in one corner. She took her empty baskets back to Joliffe's cart and stowed them carefully. Making sure that she was not observed, she untied the purse from under her skirt and placed the day's takings inside. She heard the coins chink against the pentacle and athame. She replaced the purse and checked that the necklace and ribbon were still lodged safely in her bodice. Then Cess waited for Joliffe, impatient to ask him to accompany her to the tavern the boy had talked about. She might yet discover something. As long as they did not spend too long there, they would be able to reach Montacute before the moon set.

Her backside was numb from sitting on the cart, and evensong was almost over by the time Joliffe staggered up to her. Dusk had already fallen.

"Here you are." His words were slurred, and Cess could smell the drink on him. She wondered, crossly, where else he would expect her to be.

"Farmer Joliffe," she asked directly, "will you come with me to the eastern end of town? There is a tavern there where I might find out something about the missing boys. You know William Barlow did not return to his home last night?"

"I heard the commotion. It's your friend, eh? What tavern?" he asked, swaying on his feet so alarmingly that Cess wandered if he would even make it to the London road, let alone protect her when they got there.

"The Hog's Head," she replied.

"What?!" Joliffe exploded, covering her in a light mist of beery spittle. "Take you to that den of filth! Do you have brain fever? Never."

"But I need—"

"I am a man with a bad reputation, missy, though I do not deserve it. If I took you to that damned louse pit and anything happened to you, which it probably would, I would never forgive myself, and no one else would forgive me either. And even if we went, which we won't, you wouldn't be able to believe a word anyone said because it's as much a nest of thieves and ne'er-do-wells as you will ever see." Cess had never heard Joliffe say so much, and it was clear he was speaking from experience.

"So are we to return home?" Cess inquired, disappointed.

"Home? That miserable hellhole? Of course not! Here there is drink and merry fellows aplenty. At home there is nothing but dark looks and tutting. No, lass, while I am here I like to enjoy the pleasures of the place."

"But where will we sleep?" asked Cess, worried that her purse might be stolen if she slept in the open.

"Sleep?" said Joliffe, a little puzzled. "I don't know that I do a lot of sleeping when I'm here. I lie beside the cart a little while before setting off back to the farm. You can sleep in the cart if you wish. We'll be off before dawn."

The idea of sleeping in an open cart alone, or with a drunken man, was not appealing, but since Joliffe was already staggering off to another inn, there was no need to reply to his offer. If she was not back at Montacute House by dawn, they would think she had run away with the takings, but if she tried to reach the village in the dark she risked being attacked by cutpurses, breaking an ankle in the deep potholes, or at the very least losing her way.

She looked around her. The once-bustling square was now empty save for a few vagabonds and ragged children who were searching every inch of cobbles for a scrap of food or a dropped penny. She couldn't sleep outside, but she dared not spend a single farthing on lodgings in case the steward found her out. It was almost dark, so she walked back down the street by which they had entered the town. The shops were boarded up, but she could see candlelight winking through the shuttered windows above, and hear the sounds of the families that lived there. Now that the market and evensong were over, all the goodwives of the town were at home, cooking for their families. She was aware of being the only woman on the street, other than a couple of brightly painted prostitutes who stood at the corner of a narrow, dark passageway. Groups of apprentices loitered about, staring and clicking their tongues at her as she passed.

There was a commotion up ahead, and as she rounded the corner she saw a group of men outside the inn Joliffe had pointed out, the Red Lion. The brawl was blocking the road, so Cess slipped silently through an arch to her right, into a busy courtyard. Servants, stable boys, and clients moved purposefully about the yard in all directions, feeding and watering the horses, fetching straw and firewood, hurrying off to slake a thirst, slopping out and sweeping. In one corner a knife grinder was sharpening the inn's metal tools by the light of one of the many lanterns that hung from metal hooks set into the walls.

Stables formed the whole of the right side of the courtyard, with room for fifty or more horses. To the left were the brew house, bake house, wood store, and other outbuildings. The privies, the usual shack over a pit with a plank on which to stand, were in the far left-hand corner. The far wall was high, and beyond it she could see only trees. There was a door in it, which opened as she looked. A well-dressed and handsome young man let himself into the courtyard and locked the door behind him. He walked confidently toward the back of the inn, which formed the fourth side of the courtyard, where a few steps led up to a door. On either side of the door were more lanterns. The boy was slim, tall, and aware of his good looks.

Just as he reached the bottom step, the door flew open and a stout woman in a large white coif marched out, shouting at the top of her voice, "Jasper! Jasper!"

"Here, Mother," replied the boy, wincing slightly at her yells.

The woman looked down. "There you are, noddle! Where have you been?" The boy did not reply. He looked Cess over briefly as he bounded up the steps and disappeared inside. The woman made to follow.

"Mistress, excuse me," called Cess as she walked up the steps. "May I sleep in the stables, ma'am? The cart I am to ride in is delayed till the morrow. I can wash pots or do any chores you wish in return."

"Do I look like a woman without servants to you, girl?" said the woman, glaring down at Cess. "Why would I let a wench under my roof who has never crossed my path before? Be gone!" She was about to slam the door when the thunder of many horses' hooves trotting on cobbles filled the air, and a cavalcade of liveried horsemen rode into the courtyard. Cess counted sixteen men, most of whom wore green-and-white-striped belted tunics, with the Tudor rose prominently embroidered in gold and red. Four were not in uniform but smartly attired in velvets and brocade.

"Greetings of the most excellent Master of the Queen's Scouts and Harbingers, here by order of Her Royal Majesty, the Queen Elizabeth, God bless her soul!" announced the rider at the front of the cavalcade. "We need room and board this night, mistress. Pray fetch the tavern owner." The shiver of excitement that had spread across the courtyard at the sound of the Queen's name amplified severalfold as it reached the innkeeper. She pushed out her considerable bosom, patted her orange wig, and smiled around the courtyard for all the world as if she were the Queen herself.

"I am mistress of this tavern, sir, since my beloved husband's demise. I am Mistress Makepeace, and you and your men are welcome. The better kind of person is often to be found here at the Red Lion as we run the most select establishment in the town, to be sure." This admirable self-promotion was drowned out by the clatter of breastplate and sword as the men dismounted. She took no offense, too delighted at the prospect of such fine company, and curtsied low as the scout and his outriders tramped past, somewhat stiff and bow-legged from their long ride.

"You," said Mistress Makepeace, eyeing Cess, "if you want board this night, you can help in the kitchens. We shall need another pair of hands. You may not enter the dining and drinking rooms under any circumstance, is that understood?"

"Yes, ma'am," said Cess, dropping a curtsy.

Cess was put to work washing trenchers in cold, greasy water. The only light in the scullery came from a few evil-smelling, pig-tallow candles that guttered and smoked blackly enough to make her eyes sting. She worked without rest until well after midnight and was dropping with fatigue when Mistress Makepeace stormed in for what seemed like the hundredth time. Her fancy clothes, more sumptuous than a woman of her status was permitted to wear, were decidedly disarranged. Instead of yelling for more food or ale, she announced that she was retiring to bed and ordered the stable boy to bring straw for Cess's bed.

"The cook has left bread and dripping on the table," she said, popping her head into the scullery before she swept out. When her daughters burst in moments later with the last pots to wash, they also looked flushed and disheveled. Their clothes too were finer than anything the village girls wore. There were no stuffs in brown or thick gray wool, but bright colors, stripes, and silky materials that showed off their figures. No village girl would ever wear a neckline as low, or a hem as high, as these girls did. They were babbling in excitement. By their conversation, Cess thought they must be a little older than her, for they seemed to think of nothing but romance.

"Did you see the captain's fine cape? Has ever a man so handsome been in Yeovil!" enthused one.

"Yes, sister. The guard by the fire. He has better looks, I swear, and has spoken such sweet words to me all night. He says the Queen will make a progress in our county, and he will return with her and come for me! At least I will marry one of them, to be sure."

"Sweet words, sister? He did more than whisper with you, I saw! His hands were in your bodice as if he had lost his cap in there!" The girls howled with laughter, clearly as excited by ale as they were by fine uniforms. Without glancing at Cess, they snuffed out the candles and left.

Cess wiped her hands on the coarse linen apron Mistress Makepeace had tossed her way at the start of the evening. Her fingers could hardly move, and the skin on her hands and arms was red and sore. She felt her way into the main kitchen. The fire had already been raked and covered, so it provided no light and little warmth, but the moon was up and shone into the room just enough for Cess to see her way to the pile of straw that was her bed. Too tired to care what she slept on, she kicked off her clogs, folded the apron to make a damp pillow, and pulled her cloak over her as a blanket. It was not long enough to cover her entirely so she chose to have warm feet and cold shoulders. She started to think back over the events of the day, but was asleep before she'd got very far.

She awoke with a start. She did not know how long she had been asleep or what had roused her. For a few moments she lay very still, totally at a loss as to where she was. Then she heard a noise and saw candlelight flickering on a wall. Taking a deep breath to steady her nerves, it slowly came back to her that she was in the kitchen of the Red Lion Inn.

The noise came again. A vessel, probably a clay pot, being scraped along wood. Cess raised herself on one elbow, being careful not to make a sound. If the inn was being burgled, she did not want to get hit over the head. Then there came another noise of someone moving a stool and standing on it. More pots being moved. Cess dared to raise herself enough to peep over the top of the rolling table. Balancing with one leg on the stool and the other kneeling up on a narrow trestle was the boy she had seen earlier. He had placed a single candle pricket precariously on a high shelf and was looking in all the pots stored along it. There were at least thirty.

Suddenly his foot on the stool slipped, and the boy came crashing down out of view behind the table, still holding a small pot. He swore richly but under his breath. After a few minutes, when he had still not got up, Cess walked around the table.

The boy was sprawled on the floor looking quite content, for all the world as if he were on the green sward in the sunshine. In one hand he held the pot, in the other, the lid. He was chewing with his eyes shut like a cow with its cud, humming quietly. Cess supposed that whatever was in the pot was supremely delicious.

"Are you all right?"

The boy leaped several feet in the air, quite a feat from a supine position. "Jesu!" he yelped.

"I'm sorry, I did not mean to startle you," said Cess, jumping back herself in the face of the boy's reaction.

He stared at her, his chest rising and falling as if he had run the length of the town. "I saw you earlier. What are you doing here?" he demanded when he eventually regained his voice, obviously much vexed.

Cess noticed, even in the dim light, that the boy's lips and teeth were black. She was sure they had not been earlier.

"I've been working in return for my board. The mistress told me I could sleep here."

The boy looked Cess up and down, in a way she thought rather rude, before turning his attention back to the little pot. He dug his fingers in again, taking out a pinch of soft black threads and popping them in his mouth. Cess knew what it was as soon as she saw it. It was a drug that could only be bought from an apothecary. Strong and supposedly possessed of powerful medicinal qualities, which was why Mistress Makepeace would store it in her kitchen, it was said to be hard to give up once tasted. Some of the wealthier craftsmen in the village used it, by chewing it or putting it in pipes, setting light to it and sucking in the smoke. When the traveling apothecary came to the village, it was always his most successful ware.

"I haven't seen you around here," the boy said, but without appearing to find that fact interesting.

"This is my first time in Yeovil. I come from Montacute, ten miles distance at least—"

"Montacute House?" asked the boy.

"You know it?" said Cess warily, unwilling to reveal too much about herself.

"Of course. Doesn't everybody? My mother wishes to place me there after my schooling. She thinks if I am found a position, it will be my passage to court," he explained with a short, harsh laugh.

"Do you not wish to go?"

"It would be better than school." The boy shrugged. "What kind of man is His Lordship? Scholarly, or a man for amusements?" he asked, clearly judging the latter to be the best. He had a wad of the drug in his cheek and was leaning against the trestle, observing Cess as if she were a horse or a brace of coneys. It felt to her as if he was weighing up whether she was worth his attention.

"He seems a kind man under his grand exterior," she said, "and I imagine there is plenty of distraction to be found there. . . ." she continued, eyeing the pot in his hand. The boy looked at her out of the corner of his eye, his curiosity piqued by her lack of deference.

"It's best if my mother knows nothing about this," he said, indicating the pot. "She's against tobacco and only keeps it for when the plague or the sweat come." He bowed his head to acknowledge that Cess deserved his respect in return for her silence. "I am Jasper Makepeace." He bowed lower, with exaggerated gallantry.

Cess hesitated. No one had introduced themselves to her before with such formality. She dropped a tiny curtsy and replied, "Cecily Perryn."

The moon, drifting through the night, now skimmed the side of Jasper's handsome face. He had large, pale eyes with heavy lids and long, thick lashes like a girl's; a fine, straight nose; and a wide mouth with lips curved like an archer's bow. His hair fell to his shoulders in soft waves.

"Won't you sit?" he invited Cess, for all the world as if they were nobles in a grand house. She moved back to the hearth and sat cross-legged on the floor. She saw him smirk at her lack of airs and graces as he brought the stool for himself.

"What position have you at Montacute House?" Jasper asked.

"I am poultry girl. I brought the eggs to market."

"Why have I not seen you before? It is often I who goes to the market if my mother can't."

"I turned thirteen two days ago. I asked to come."

"Ah, seeking adventure."

"Not really. My friend has gone missing and I thought I might find out something about him here."

"A good friend? Run away?" Jasper's questions came fast. She wondered what interested him more, William's disappearance or her relationship to the missing boy.

"He could not run far. I think he was taken," Cess replied, almost in a whisper. Just saying those words made it more real, and she did not want it to be true. Jasper said nothing. It was clear to her that he saw no need to concern himself with her friend.

"Do you hear anything about those who have disappeared?" asked Cess.

"Yes, indeed, all the gory details. The regulars know my mother likes to be entertained," said Jasper, taking a last pinch and reluctantly putting the lid on the tobacco pot. Cess could well imagine that Jasper was also not averse to gossip.

"When did your friend go missing?" he asked, yawning rudely and clearly wanting his bed.

"William. His name is William. He was last seen yesterday evening, Sunday, just after dark. I found out today that at least two of the missing boys were taken from the east end of the town, near the wrecks' shack. If I can discover who took those boys, it would lead us to William. If he has not been taken but run away, he might have to take shelter in the shack. I want to go there but cannot alone."

Jasper snorted. "I admire your optimism, but many have been looking already, and nothing has been discovered," he said, getting up from his stool and walking with it round the rolling table. He used it to kneel up on the trestle and push the pot back on the shelf from where he had taken it. Cess rose and stood between Jasper and the door.

"Good night, Cecily Perryn. I hope I shall always buy my eggs from you," he said with exaggerated flattery, trying to walk round her.

Cess thought fast. "Please take me there now. I must return to Montacute at first light."

Jasper's astonishment was plain. "Don't be ridiculous. It's too dangerous. If the people stealers don't catch us, we will be set upon by thieves. People are hungry." Yet he did not turn away. Cess saw that her plea had seized his attention. She sensed excitement at the thought of prowling the streets, hunting for a missing boy.

"No. I cannot," he said decidedly. He tried to push her aside, but Cess resisted. She felt desparate. If he left, she had no chance of finding William that night. Jasper needed to be persuaded. . . . "If you will not help, I cannot promise my silence."

Jasper grumbled continuously as they walked quickly eastward toward the poorest quarter of the town, keeping close to the buildings and choosing the widest streets so that the moonlight would allow no one to lurk unseen. He had insisted that Cess wear an old cap and cloak of his to cover her hair, and a battered pair of boots: two boys out at night would arouse less suspicion. The boots were so large she had stuffed them with some of her bedding.

"It's not proper. You behave like a man, not a girl. My sisters would never be caught dead out at night like this, chasing after some boy. . . ." he moaned, to Cess's deaf ears.

"There," he said, stopping suddenly.

A hundred yards away, Cess could just make out the faint glimmer of candlelight through shutters. As they neared, she saw a dilapidated two-story building leaning alarmingly to one side. A sign hung above the door, but the paint had peeled too much to tell if it showed a hog's head. The decrepit tavern was still open for business, although, as they passed an open shutter, they could see that most of the clients had fallen into a stupefied slumber among the cups on the tables. It had not occurred to Cess that the people she wanted to question would be too drunk to make any sense at this late hour.

Jasper was wearing an "I told you so" look, so she walked on toward the byre that lay beyond the tavern outbuildings. Cess guessed that this had to be the wrecks' shack. One side was open to the elements, and it had so many holes in the roof and plank walls that Cess was sure the occupants would be as wet inside as out when it rained. Strange noises wafted out of the darkness. To Cess it sounded like a herd of unhealthy cattle snoring, shuffling, sneezing, and coughing. The smell was startling and noxious. Cess had confronted that smell before, when passing sheep left to rot in the fields, calves born weak and abandoned to the crows, or injured deer half-eaten in the woods. She recoiled into Jasper as she looked into the byre.

In the moonlight, she could just discern that the place was packed with the very poorest human creatures, wearing rags, some half naked, some with the protruding bellies of the starving. It was hard to believe that some of them were still alive. Most slept fitfully, but a few looked up at Cess and Jasper with empty, hopeless faces.

"God be with you," started Cess uncertainly. "I am searching for my friend who is missing."

There was no response at all, but before Cess could say more, Jasper stepped forward, impatient to be finished with this business. As he opened his mouth to speak he retched and had to turn away. Cess was feeling increasingly guilty for making him bring her here. Jasper held out his hand to her. In it were a few farthings. She took them gratefully.

"There is a reward for anyone who can tell me about my friend," she said, holding up the coins in the moonlight. Instantly the mood in the shack changed. Bodies stirred. People sat up and stared.

"His name is William. He has lived thirteen summers"—Cess paused, wondering if it would help or hinder her search to mention William's clubfoot—"and he has a rounded foot that limps." A low muttering in response to Cess's description gave her brief hope.

"Have you seen or heard of him?" she continued.

"Maybe, but my tongue cannot eat itself, can it?" said a reedy voice.

Cess held out a coin. The thinnest arm she had ever seen whipped out of a bundle of filthy rags, grabbed the coin, and retreated, like a frog catching a fly.

Cess waited. "What do you know, then?" she prompted, growing impatient.

"Nothing," the voice replied.

Jasper pulled Cess away from the byre. She swiped at the tears of disappointment and anger that pricked her eyes.

"Don't cry," said Jasper, surprisingly gently, considering how she had treated him. "When you return to Montacute, he might be there." He put his arm around her shoulders.

Because he was comforting Cess, his guard was down. When the blow came, he fell sideways with no more than a gentle grunt. Cess did not have time to scream before the sack came down over her head and darkness engulfed her.

CHAPTER 10

It was still dark, but the forest was noisy. Edith woke with a start. Rooks were cawing when they should have been silent. She went to the door and saw a badger running across the clearing in the moonlight. The animal stopped and looked directly at Edith before continuing on its way. It was a warning.

She pulled a large sack from the corner where it had stood since she had first arrived in the forest, packed and ready for just such a flight as she was to make now. She threw a few extra items into the sack: a cooking pot, some provisions, the velvet bag she kept under a stone in a dark corner, bunches of dried herbs that hung from the rafters, her cloak and staff. Her movements were so quick and precise that the striped back of the badger was not far ahead of her as she fled across the grass and plunged into the forest. She heard the men approaching. Not voices, they were trying to catch her by surprise, but a crackle in the undergrowth, the stirring of a branch and the flapping of birds' wings. She could hear the men's jumbled thoughts. Their fear.

Edith did not stop to look back. As she disappeared into the darkness, a dozen men entered the clearing armed with heavy spades and smithy tools. Led by Ignatius Bartholomew, they crept toward the shack. The parson indicated that they should surround the small building in case Edith tried to give them the slip. On his signal the men began pounding on the walls and door with their tools, intent on smashing the little building to kindling.

"Witch! Where is he? Where is William? Witch!" the men were screaming, working themselves into a frenzy. The door gave way after a few blows. It had no lock. The men ran inside and looked into every pot, bag, and chest. They threw everything outside, upturned the pallet, and checked the floor for a trapdoor.

"She is not here," said the parson through gritted teeth. The others did not hear him as they continued their frenzied destruction.

"SHE IS NOT HERE!" he shouted. "Someone must have warned her." He spoke with cold fury. Frustrated that their search had turned up no evidence of Edith's witchcraft or of William, the other men pushed and hammered at the walls until the hut collapsed. They jumped on whatever they could, splintering planks into short, useless lengths, so that it was beyond repair. The parson picked his way through the remains of the hut with great care, as if they stank or might explode. He walked away in the direction of the village. The other men looked keen to continue their destruction, but they reluctantly followed him.

Dawn was approaching, but the forest around the clearing was unusually silent. A place of peace and sanctuary had been violated, and Nature was not blind to that.

CHAPTER 11

As the first rays of sun lapped over the rim of the earth, Cess was shaken out of the sack onto a damp, cold stone floor. The first thing she noticed was the smell, so thick and putrid she did not want to breathe. Perfumed smoke was coming from a couple of braziers, but it could not cover the hideous odor of putrefaction that thickened the air. Her eyes watered. She tried to move, but her ankles and wrists were tied.

On the floor beside her lay Jasper, also trussed with ropes. His eyes were open, but his mouth was gagged with a length of grubby cloth darkened with blood that had oozed from the wound on his head. Looming above them were three men, each holding a lit torch. They wore black robes to the floor like priests. One had a leather satchel strung across his body, his neighbor grasped two long metal rods, one sharp, one with a tiny scoop at the end, and the third held a cloth. It looked like a gag, intended for her, but instead of putting it on they were staring at her.

Cess could feel saliva collecting in her mouth, and her head was swimming. She turned from Jasper and was sick until her sides hurt. A flaming torch was thrust toward her, and Cess cowered, terrified the men were going to set her alight. Far from being disgusted by her vomiting, they gawped all the more and began a rapid discussion in a language Cess did not understand. They appeared to come to a decision and hurried out of the room, one leaving his torch in a wall bracket before shutting the door behind him.

As soon as the men had gone, Jasper and Cess struggled to sit up. Their arms were tied behind them, so it was difficult. The torch flames made deep, jumping shadows, but there was enough light to make out that they were in a vaulted cellar or crypt, low and square. Two stone-and-brick pillars supported the ceiling, and the walls were brick-lined and dripping wet. It appeared to be a very ancient place. Nearly all the plaster had long since dropped off, and the walls sagged and bulged in places. The stones on the floor were uneven, and some were entirely gone, revealing bare earth. Puddles gathered in the depressions. There were no windows, and the arched doorway was narrow and low.

"They will not be gone for long," Cess whispered to Jasper. She was desperate for a drink to swill the vomit from her mouth. "Are you all right? Your head is bleeding." She was painfully aware that it was she who had led them to this place. It reeked of death. Jasper grunted through his gag and thrashed around, struggling to untie his bonds. She shuffled toward him and felt for his ropes, aware of how she stank of vomit and fear. The warmth and weight of him against her back was comforting.

Despite tugging hard, she could not loosen the knots that held him. The dagger that hung from his girdle had been removed. They sat back-to-back in silence, lost in the horror of the place. Cess shut her eyes and tried to picture what Edith would do.

"I have a knife!" she blurted out in the excitement of remembering the athame. "In a pocket beneath my skirts," she continued in a whisper. "I don't think they will have taken it. They seemed appalled by me for some reason." Cess noticed Jasper gulp, and she wondered whether he also felt sick or whether he was unsure about putting his hands up her skirt.

"It's between my smock and kirtle. Go on," she urged, hearing voices in the distance. "It is to this side." She struggled onto her knees and pushed her right hip toward him. Jasper managed to get his joined hands under her kirtle and, with much writhing, to reach up and fish the knife out of the pouch. His hands were shaking so much it took a few attempts to saw through Cess's ropes. As soon as her arms were free, she cut through Jasper's bonds and those still around her legs. Jasper pulled the gag from his mouth.

"Argh!" Jasper moved his jaw and tentatively dabbed at the sticky lump on his head where he had been cudgeled. "God's breath, the smell!" he said, gagging as he rubbed his stiff, bloodless legs and wrists. He struggled to his feet and began to feel around the walls, but almost immediately tripped over something. He swore like a fishwife.

"Take the torch," Cess suggested.

"You have told me what to do enough for one lifetime," snapped Jasper. Cess's cheeks burned. She longed to be at home with her mother, William by her side, and Jasper someone she had never met. "Who the devil were those men? They looked like priests in those robes," he said, moving over to the door to examine it.

"Or monks. What tongue did they speak?"

"Spanish or Italian or something. It wasn't French."

The door was very old but still sturdy, made of thick wood, reinforced with metal bands, and with a narrow viewing window cut into the upper portion too small for Cess to fit her hand through. There was no lock, but it would not open, so it was latched or bolted from the outside. Cess had a nagging sense that she had been there before. She recognized the smell, although it had been much fainter, as well as the darkness and the fear. Leaving Jasper to work at the door, she looked around the room to see if there was any other way out. She found the lumpy sack on which Jasper had tripped, and bent to open it. The sack came away in her hands. It was only covering what was underneath. She sucked in her breath with horror and let out a low, stricken groan.

Jasper turned at the strange sound and looked down at Cess's feet. There was a body, almost unrecognizable as such, it was so bruised and bloodied. The flesh was black, streaked blue and garish yellow, and it had cracked and burst in places. It was only identifiable as a young man by the clothes. The lips were pulled back in a tortured grimace to reveal teeth broken by the force of the shaking the poor creature must have suffered.

"He's alive," Cess gasped, kneeling down beside the shivering body. The boy tried to speak, the breath rattling in his throat, and spittle gathering at the corners of his mouth. Cess pulled off her cap to dab his mouth and knelt close to the blistered face, stroking his hair away from his burning forehead. The boy's limbs began to shake violently, and Cess held him.

"It's all right, it's all right," she said soothingly, asking him his name so that he would know, even in his fever, that he was not alone. Suddenly Cess understood why she felt she had been in that ghastly place before. It was what she had seen when Edith told her to think of William. The door, the darkness, the stink. She groaned again and held the boy more tightly to her.

"Jasper," she whispered, taking her eyes from the boy for a moment to peer into the dark recesses of the rooms, "are there others?"

Jasper grimaced and walked carefully toward the darkest end of the cellar. "There are two more," he said, shaking his head meaningfully as he walked back over to her, not wanting the boy to hear that they were dead.

"Do either have a curled right foot?" But even as Cess spoke she knew Jasper would not find William there. He was not dead, she was sure of it. But she was equally certain that he was close by.

"Not that I noticed," reported Jasper.

The boy in Cecily's arms began mumbling in his fever.

"I should not have gone," he whispered, eyes staring, unseeing. With each word spoken the boy winced as if a hot poker was being forced down his throat. "Whores and drink, I will go to hell!" He lunged at Cess, trying to pull himself up. He scrabbled desperately, crying out, then collapsed back onto the stone floor. His chest caved inward, empty, and did not shudder again with the effort of bringing in new air.

Although many people Cess had known were dead, including some she had loved deeply, none had been in her arms at the moment life left them. The boy's face was wet with her tears as she laid him on the ground. She pulled the sack over him and would have stayed there a while but for Jasper pulling her to her feet.

"He's in a better place now than we are," he said. "We have to get out." He pulled her to the door.

"No guard, and it's latched, not bolted," he muttered, craning his neck, "but I can't see anything to lift the latch with. We will have to surprise whoever comes in and stab them with your knife."

Cess did not object to wounding her kidnappers but doubted Jasper's plan would work if more than one entered at a time. She picked up her athame. "Try lifting it with this," she said. Jasper poked the knife between the door and the frame but it was too thick to reach under the latch.

"I have some money," she said, patting the purse beneath her skirt that held the market takings. "Could we bribe them?"

"I don't get the feeling they're in this for money," said Jasper.

Her purse held one more hope. She found the pentacle Alathea had given her and began sawing at it with her athame.

"What is that?" said Jasper, his eyes narrowing.

"A good luck charm from a friend," she replied lightly, pulling the metal straight and bending one end up a little. It was exactly what Jasper needed to lift the latch. He poked the metal through the narrow gap, shaping and reshaping it, swearing all the while under his breath. At last, the latch clicked upward.

The mumble of voices grew louder as they pushed the door and edged out into a dark corridor. Like the cell, it was of brick, vaulted, low and narrow. The only light came from an open doorway, much larger than their cell door, ten paces to their right. Between them and the doorway were two more cells, whose viewing windows revealed a faint red glow. To her left, Cess felt a wall of slimy rock. The corridor was a dead end, the only escape past the open door. Cess gripped her athame tightly.

They crept along the corridor, pressed against the wall. As they reached the first viewing window, Cess peered in. William was close by, she knew it. Jasper gripped her arm and pulled her head to his.

"We take no one with us," he breathed. "If William's here he'll be dead or dying by now. We'll only get away if we're on our own." He gave her a hard look before turning and creeping closer to the open door. Cess could not help but look into the next cell. By the light of a single tallow candle she could make out the shape of a body. Unusually, it lay on a pallet. Her heart started to thump even harder. It was William, she was certain.

Fumbling in the dark, Cess raised the latch and slipped into the cell. As she neared the body she saw that the face was swollen and unrecognizable. She pulled at the oily covering sack, and her hand flew to her mouth. One foot was curled.

"William," she whispered, kneeling beside him and stroking back the hair plastered to his face with cold sweat. He was breathing, but his eyes were rolling about in their sockets, and a trickle of blood from his nose had congealed on his cheek. Cess dropped her athame and put her arms around him.

"William . . . It's William," she whispered urgently to Jasper, who had followed her into the cell. He did not even glance at the pallet but jerked his thumb angrily in the direction of the door.

"We must help him," she whispered desperately.

Jasper stared at her then stalked out of the cell without looking back.

Cess felt panic rising in her chest. She could not move William alone. She rested her head on his chest and tried to think clearly.

"I will find help and come back for you."

As she spoke, William's eyes stopped rolling and focused on her. He winced as a smile cracked his swollen lips. "Cess," he mouthed, his throat too dry for speech and his eyes still moving unnaturally. "I came to find you. On the hill after the fireworks . . ."

"What have they done to you?"

"They scraped me . . . They gave the illness to me," he whispered.

"William . . . I am so sorry," she said. She meant for everything. For catching the coin, for arguing with him, for not coming sooner, for not being able to help him now she was here. His eyes reached her face and he struggled to speak, as if to reassure her that every-thing was forgiven, but the effort was too great and he sank back into oblivion.

A part of her wanted to stay wrapped around him. But a louder, more insistent voice was telling her she must get out while she still had a chance. She pushed the ribbon he gave her, still warm from her body, under his shirt. He might find it next time he came around and know that she had been there and would come back.

She picked up her knife, closed the cell door carefully, and caught up with Jasper. The voices from inside the room were excited or angry in their foreign tongue. Jasper gave her a sharp look, as if to gauge her mood. Cess was miserable to leave William, but she could see they had no hope of rescuing him by themselves.

"Latin . . ." he breathed into her ear. Despite the turmoil Cess felt inside, she could not help being a tiny bit impressed by Jasper's skill in languages. "They are talking about you. They won't touch girls because—"

Suddenly they heard footsteps coming in their direction, and a man was speaking, in English. Cess and Jasper were hidden by the door that opened into the corridor.

"It has endangered everything for which we are working." Through the gap between the door and frame she saw two figures pass into the room. The first seemed to be wearing a fine coat, and the second, a plain gray cloak. He was tall with pale blond hair. With a shock, Cess realized it was the man she had seen in the woods.

Through the crack Cess could see into part of the room. It was well lit by torches and good quality tallow candles, although the walls and vaulted ceiling were in as poor repair as elsewhere. She could see one end of a wide table, around which sat or stood several men, all wearing long well-worn black robes, and talking at once. The blond man let them speak as he removed his cloak. Underneath, he wore the simple hose and sleeveless jerkin of a laborer. Cess judged the clothes to be a disguise, for the man was clearly in a position of authority over the others. Eventually he raised a hand for silence.

"One of those I caught last night was a girl?" The man spoke with the confidence and accent of a gentleman. Although he used English, it appeared that the men understood him or whispered to their fellows if they did not.

"She was wearing a boy's boots and cloak, Father Garret," said one of the men, with a heavy accent, who had been in the cell.

"You must proceed regardless," said Father Garret. "Although it is against the precepts of our order to touch women, the prohibition is lifted in this instance. The sooner she is scraped, the sooner she will fall ill and her presence no longer unsettle us. After all," he said, smiling with his mouth only, "we are interested to see the effects of our work on a woman."

Several of the monks muttered angrily, others nodded, but Father Garret raised his hand again until they fell silent. "There are other matters to discuss," he said brusquely.

Cess moved so that she could see more of the room and bent down a little so that Jasper could look over her head. There were two long tables and benches and at least eight or nine men including Father Garret. On the tables were miniature braziers containing glowing coals, over which stood a variety of glass and ceramic dishes and flasks on tall metal trivets. In some simmered different colored liquids, while others had boiled down to a powdery substance. Some had flasks with downward pointing spouts that dripped into small pots and dishes. There were jars containing metal skewers like the monks had carried in the cell, and small vials of what looked like blood. It reminded her slightly of Edith's medicine-making tools, though far more exotic and expensive.

"I was disturbed while disposing of the last body," said Father Garret, without a trace of remorse for the death or the discovery of it. The muttering that followed was silenced with a look. "The villagers found the corpse on Saturday morning," he said with a note of contempt. "Thus, we must be more cautious than before. No one is to leave the cellars until our task is complete. As our Holy Father in Rome has commanded, nothing must jeopardize our task to rid this country of its Queen and her heir and bring the true, Catholic faith back to these forsaken shores."

Cess thought a firework had gone off in her head. She stared at Father Garret. Had she misheard? He had just spoken treasonous words, words that could see him hanged, his guts cut out of his body while he was still alive, and his head spiked on a pole on London Bridge.

It took a few moments for her to realize that the other man was speaking, in a thin nasal voice, as if he had a runny nose. "My lord sends thanks for your great work and prayers for your success."

Cess shifted her position again but could not see the speaker.

"He wishes you to know that the Queen's household has confirmed that she will arrive before the end of this month." Murmuring broke out again. The man shifted his position, and Cess could at last see him properly. He was short and thin-boned, with patches of red skin around his nose and by his earlobes. He looked weedy, as if he had been poorly fed as a child and was sickly as an adult. His fine green coat, intended to disguise his poor physical presence, accentuated it. His eyes bulged, as if someone held him by the throat. He moved, and Cess saw that there were hanging sleeves attached to the shoulders of his coat. He was wearing the uniform of a page.

Suddenly Cess remembered where she had seen him before. It was he who had been shooing the villagers away from his fine livery outside the church on May Day. "That man," she whispered to Jasper. "He's part of Lord Montacute's retinue." Jasper looked shocked. "If we can see the crest on his sleeves, we'll know which lord he works for."

"Time is short, but we must achieve our aim," Father Garret said firmly.

"But we have not yet perfected putting the illness into the body in food or drink," called out someone out of Cess's view, in broken English. "We need more—"

"We are close," said Father Garret, cutting off the speaker.

"What of the boy who resists?" asked another. For the first time, Father Garret's self-assurance looked strained. Cess saw the page look at him, eyebrows raised.

"The boy is an exception and has the Devil's mark," said Father Garret, as if that explained everything.

"One has not died?" the page asked. The silence was thick with accusation.

"All have died but him."

"Why does he live?"

Father Garret hesitated, and one of the seated men interjected, "It is possible he has had the illness before and survived. This sometimes gives the body strength. Or he is protected by God."

The page narrowed his eyes. "Or by the Devil?" he said. "Let us see this boy." Monks began rising, causing the glass and ceramic dishes, bottles, and flasks to clink as the workbenches were jostled.

"Bring your instruments for the new arrivals," ordered Father Garret. "I will scrape the girl myself if your scruples are too great."

Cess and Jasper realized at the same instant that if they did not cross the doorway immediately it would be too late. They leaped across the patch of light and did not wait to find out if they had been seen. Running as fast and quietly as they could, they came to a junction with another passage. The only light came from the right, so they ran that way, full tilt into a robed man. He cried out as he fell, and Jasper and Cess leaped over him. Rounding a corner, they came to a dead end. Cess looked desperately for a way out. If they were caught, she knew they would not escape again.

"Here!" said Jasper. To one side bricks had been removed from the wall, and there was a faint suggestion of daylight coming through a wooden panel above. She scrabbled up, knife held in her teeth, terror forcing her on, but the panel would not shift however hard she shoved against it.

"Hurry," whispered Jasper. "They're coming!"

"It won't open."

Cess desperately ran her hands around the edge of the panel and felt a short length of cord. She pulled and heard the welcome sound of a click on the other side of the board. Pushing hard, she clambered out into a large, square, stone building, whose upper walls were pierced with hundreds of small holes between which bristled wooden perches. The air was filled with the cooing of hundreds of pigeons, and the floor was crusty with droppings and littered with broken perches.

"Cess!" Jasper was pulling himself up toward her, but someone stronger had him by the leg. The look of terror on his face made her fly to him as if her own life was at stake. She threw herself to the ground, reached through the hatch, and stabbed wildly at the hand that held him. The robed man yelled in pain, releasing Jasper, who scrambled up as if the Devil himself was in pursuit. Cess caught a glimpse of another face staring up. It was the bulging-eyed page.

Before anyone else could climb through the trapdoor, Cess slammed it shut and jammed a broken perch above the latch to keep it closed. She could not fathom why the tunnel led to a dovecote, but there was no time to think about it. The feeble wedge would soon give way. They ran toward a small door and listened carefully before looking out.

"It's just a field," said Jasper, surprised because dovecotes were usually close to large houses or farms. Cess was even more astonished than Jasper, but for different reasons.

"The priory!" she mumbled, more to herself than Jasper.

"You know this place?" asked Jasper. Cess nodded. They were standing in the ruins of Montacute's priory, once a thriving monastery, which owned hundreds of acres of land, farms, and woodland. The ancient dovecote and massive gateway were all that remained intact, and even these were obscured by the bushes, ivy, and trees that had grown in the fifty years since it had been closed down by Henry VIII, Queen Bess's father. The land had been acquired by Lord Montacute's father, and some of it, including the ruins, was leased to Nicholas Joliffe. There had long been rumors about the monastery gold being buried in the fields, and it was said that there were secret tunnels running from there to Saint Michael's Hill and Montacute House. No one really believed the stories, but they were diverting for children.

"Come, I know where to go," said Cess as she ran out of the

dovecote, across the field, and plunged into the trees. Without cap or scarf, she tried to push her long hair into the neck of her borrowed doublet.

"Where are we going?" asked Jasper as he tried to keep up.

"This is Montacute, my village," Cess replied. "There's only one place I can think of that's safe." She nodded her head towards Saint Michael's Hill. "Up there." She could not take this unknown boy home. The man from Sir Edward's retinue had seen her, and if he remembered her from outside the church, they would soon search her cottage.

Cess glanced back at Jasper and saw that his face was white. She stopped and waited for him to catch up.

"There is someone who can help us," said Cess, trying to sound reassuring. Jasper was only a little older than her, and now he was a fugitive from a murderous sect who seemed intent on high treason, accompanied by a girl he barely knew, who carried a symbol of witch-craft on her.

"Up here?" Jasper asked doubtfully, puffing uphill with difficulty.

"She is my friend and I would trust her with my life," Cess explained. "She might have an idea what those men are doing."

They had finally reached the clearing.

Cess stopped dead.

The scene before her was so unexpected that it took several moments before she could comprehend it. Where Edith's hut had once stood was a heap of smashed wood. Her friend's belongings were strewn across the clearing, broken or ripped. The damage was so great Cess thought at first some natural force was responsible, a freak wind or ground shake. As she walked closer she could see that Nature would have been less thorough. Even Edith's few clothes had been torn to shreds, and stinking patches of yellow showed they had been pissed on. The villagers had done this. This sanctuary of peace and health had been violated beyond repair.

Cess sank to the ground, too shocked to cry or speak. Jasper sat heavily beside her.

"I am sorry," said Cess, unable to look at him.

A noise close by made her stop.

Out of the corner of her eye, Cess caught a movement. At the edge of the clearing a cloaked figure stood half-hidden behind a tree, watching them.

CHAPTER 12

She was not on the cart? Why not?" Sir Nathaniel Davies inter-
rogated the kitchen hand, who shrugged. The steward was taxed that
morning; he had to list every improvement that needed doing in the
House before the Queen arrived, as well as informing Sir Edward of a
worrying development that one of his agents had discovered. Coming
down the main staircase to the great hall, he had glimpsed the kitchen
boy in the screens passage beyond. It jogged his memory that he had
not received the market takings from the poultry girl.

"So how did she get to market, boy?" he continued.

"We saw her arrive with drunken . . . Farmer Joliffe, sir," he stammered, regretting now that he had joined the crowd who refused to
let Cess ride with them on the cart. He had even tried to take the
hens from her. It had not occurred to any of them that the steward
would care what happened to her.

"Go to the cottage of Anne Perryn and ask after the girl's whereabouts. Now, boy!" Sir Nathaniel pressed his lips together, irritated

by the boy's evasive answers and the disappearance of the poultry girl. "The Queen will be here within the month," he proclaimed to the army of servants who were rushing about clearing ashes, sprinkling fresh herbs, and cleaning the precious glass windows. "Is this how you wish to greet your sovereign? With dirt and sloth!" he barked.

"Trouble, Nathaniel?" asked Sir Edward, who had been observing the scene from the top of the stairs.

"Sir," said the steward with a smart bow, abashed that his bad temper had been witnessed, "I have some pressing matters to report. May we speak in private?"

"Why have you sent after the poultry girl?"

"Sir, she is late and has yet to give me her takings."

"Is that usual?"

"I have had no previous complaints about tardiness, but she went to market yesterday for the first time, and I fear the money may have turned her head. But I have urgent news of another matter—"

"Turned her head?"

"She will be flogged, my lord. But I must speak of . . ." Again the steward could not finish his sentence, for Sir Edward raised his hand for silence.

"Walk with me."

Nathaniel fell in step with his master as he turned and mounted the stairs that led to the great chamber. Sir Edward spoke quietly but with a firmness that reminded Nathaniel of his place: great, but not so great as His Lordship.

"If you receive no word of the poultry girl by sunset, I wish you to go in person to Yeovil to find her."

Nathaniel was too astonished to reply. This girl, whom he had never once noticed before May Day, was becoming the bane of his life. "Yes, sir. May I also speak of an urgent matter?"

"Nothing is more important than this," said Sir Edward as he retreated into his chamber and shut the door behind him, leaving

Nathaniel wondering what it was about this poultry girl that nobody was telling him.

After banging on the door for several minutes, she was answered by a bleary-eyed Joliffe. When at last he was able to focus on her, Anne saw a look of astonishment cross his face. A long, silent moment passed between them before Joliffe spoke, in a voice barely louder than a whisper.

"What do you want?" he said, making no move to ask Anne inside.

"Cecily has gone," stated Anne simply. "I hear you took her to market?"

Joliffe frowned and gave a slight nod.

"Did you bring her back?"

"No."

"Why not?"

"She did not return to the cart in the morning. I thought she had traveled with someone else."

Anne tried hard to control the panic she was feeling. "Did she meet anyone?" A terrible thought had occurred to her. Had Cecily run away with William? A lame boy and a penniless illegitimate girl would need to find work or to beg. Doing either without permission from their own parish would bring them to the attention of the magistrates, who would send them to debtors' prison or back to Montacute to be flogged.

"I saw her little and don't know where she lay her head."

"You did not come back in the evening?"

"No," he said with mounting irritation. "This morning."

"Did you forget her?" asked Anne, bold in her fear.

Joliffe's face, always ruddy, turned puce. "Forget her? I helped her out when everyone else refused to let her ride on their cart!" He slammed the door in Anne's face, but she stayed rooted to the spot, thinking what to do. When they had courted, Joliffe had been the most handsome man in the village. His family was as prosperous as the Perryns, owning large tracts of farmland and leasing more from the Montacute estate. He was handsome and warm and had pursued Anne with a romantic vigor that had been the envy of her friends. His only vice, and that a common one, was to drink too much on feast days. Anne had never believed that he could drink so much that he had killed his own friend in a brawl. He would have loved her all the more for her faith in him, she knew, but she never had the opportunity to show it. Something had happened too awful to think or speak about, and their romance had been just one of the victims.

She was not too proud to beg Joliffe to return to Yeovil for Cess, but she knew he would refuse. She walked away with quick anxious steps, lowering her head and pulling her shawl over her face.

CHAPTER 13

ecily?" said Edith, pulling back the deep hood that hid her face. "Are you ailing? What brings you here on a workday, and who is this?"

Cess threw herself into the older woman's arms. "They caught us in Yeovil . . . me and . . . This is Jasper . . . They threw us in a cellar . . . It's all my fault William's there. He came to find me. It's monstrous what they are doing . . . The boy died . . . Jasper," she said, trying to collect herself, "this is Edith Mildmay."

Edith nodded a hello and held Cess until she quieted. "You will tell me all. But now we must hide." She looked around the clearing as if she could see for miles through the thick forest. "You are being followed."

Edith moved quickly, ignoring the ruins of her shack, and plunged into the woods, followed by Cess and Jasper. After a few minutes she motioned them to stop beside a rocky outcrop. Moving to one side she felt about on the forest floor until there was a click.

Cess watched in astonishment as Edith lifted out a square of earth to reveal the top of a ladder leading down into darkness. She gestured for Cess and Jasper to climb down, and followed them, quickly closing and bolting the trapdoor.

The ladder was only about twice Cess's height, but the shaft was so dark she had to feel her way down. She felt strange breaths of warm air on her skin. Once her feet were on hard ground she stepped to one side and waited for the others.

"Where are we?" Cess whispered.

"In a tunnel," said Edith as she felt about for two small rush torches and lit them. She pushed them into rusty metal brackets. Cess could just make out the walls, which were in parts brick but mainly stone and bare earth interspersed with wooden props, the ends lost in darkness. A ledge was cut into one side, on which was a thin straw pallet. There were niches for candles and Edith's few possessions. The rock and earth floor was wet with puddles, and an irregular drip of water echoed across the cheerless space.

"This is a wider part. One way leads up to the chapel on Saint Michael's Hill. The other to the ruins of the priory and on to Montacute. They used to connect with the old great house, but I don't know if they still do now the house has been rebuilt."

"They look ancient. Are they safe?" asked Jasper, eyeing a wooden prop that was sagging under the weight of earth above.

"They've been here at least three hundred years, built by the monks of the priory and the nobles at the old house. I don't know if it was the Mortains then, but it might have been. They wanted to worship on Saint Michael's Hill where a miraculous crucifix was found, but the Norman lord who took over this part of Somerset built his castle there and stopped them." While she spoke, Edith led Cess to the ledge and indicated that she and Jasper should sit. Cess was exhausted. "So the family and the monks dug beneath him to the chapel. The tunnels were only used for about thirty years and forgotten afterwards, except in the stories parents told children and by my family, who have always collected a very special fungus down here." Edith lifted the lid from a small pile of ashes and blew on them until they glowed.

"But if the tunnel goes to the priory, that is where the boys are being killed, where William is, in the cellars. We are not safe here." Cess's eyes were huge in the torchlight, full of terror at what she had seen and what she feared ahead.

"The entrance to this tunnel is well hidden in the crypt of the priory, linked to the cellars by a short passage, but we must be mindful to talk quietly, for sound echoes strangely down here. Anyway, there is no other sanctuary for us hereabouts," said Edith matter-of-factly.

"We heard the monks talking," said Cess.

"Monks? Are you sure? They are usually men of peace and learning," said Edith.

"We think they were monks or priests. They wore long black robes and spoke in foreign tongues and some used Latin. Except the leader, that blond man we saw in the woods, whom they call Father Garret. He is an English gentleman. They are planning to kill the Queen and her heir."

"To kill the Queen?" repeated Edith. She stared at Cess, shocked.

"And murdering those boys has something to do with it," added Jasper. "They want to return the country to Catholicism."

Edith nodded gravely. "These men hold extreme views, I have heard of them. They are trained on the Continent and smuggled into England. The majority of Catholics in this country are law-abiding people, wanting only to practice their faith without persecution. They are as much afraid of the radicals as everyone else, if not more so, for their murderous plots make all Catholics appear to be enemies of the Queen. It is a sad state of affairs."

"These men have all manner of glass jars and flasks, and William said they scraped his skin and gave him the disease," said Cess, frowning deeply in a way that made her look much older than her thirteen years. Deep in thought, Edith distractedly handed them each a meager cracked lump of greasy cheese and a wizened apple from a small barrel. Jasper took the poor fare with distaste.

"I do the same with the pox, of course," said Edith. Cess noticed that Jasper's eyebrows shot up, appalled. "To prevent deaths, not cause them. A weak amount of cowpox prepares the body, which then does not succumb to the deadly smallpox," she explained. Jasper looked unconvinced.

"I am proof," said Cess, leaning toward Jasper and showing him a scar on her wrist. "Edith tied a linen thread round my wrist that had been steeped in pus from a pox-ridden cow. Although I felt unwell for two days, when I later caught smallpox I was hardly ill."

"These monks' experiments must be to prepare a deadly dose of the illness to give the Queen," said Edith, almost talking to herself. "Whereas I make a disease weaker before I give it, it sounds like they are making it as strong as possible. And no one will look for a killer because she will appear to have died of natural causes. Cecily, this is the evil that Alathea and I have seen." Cess saw Jasper look between them with such an appalled expression she almost felt sorry for him.

"There was a man amongst them from Montacute, a page. We could not see whose crest he wore, so any lord could be behind this," Cess told Edith.

"Or several," warned Edith. "And William? He has the sweat?" she asked as she put a metal trivet over the coals and balanced a kettle on it.

"Yes, but he has not died of it," said Cess. "If these tunnels go to the cellars, can we get him?" she asked with a bravado that failed to disguise the terror she felt.

"I'm not going near that hellhole again," muttered Jasper, sniffing suspiciously at the cheese before shoving it all into his mouth at once. Cess looked at him pityingly. He had obviously never known hunger, or he would be chewing each tiny morsel for as long as possible.

"Do you have any tobacco?" he asked with his mouth full.

Edith shook her head, looking concerned that someone so young would be yearning for the drug. She rummaged in a bulging sack beside her and pulled out a stick, a hand's length, to which a few silvery leaves still clung. "This is sage. Chew it. It will quell your desire for tobacco."

Jasper took the twig reluctantly but began chewing it as soon as he had swallowed his cheese.

"Father Garret said William was alive because of his clubfoot," said Cess. Edith snorted.

"It's not because of his foot," she said.

"Oh?" said Jasper acidly. "They are not entirely foolish. They said that if it wasn't God's protection, it might be the Devil's." The silence that met Jasper's words was as thick as the darkness. Cess saw Edith's smile fade, but she looked sad rather than angry. "How is it you had a pentagram in your purse?" he said to Cess. "And what did you mean by saying you 'saw' this evil? No simple healer can know that people are coming before they are in sight, or would consider taking on the hellhounds we saw in the cellar. I know what you are. You're a . . . a . . ." he could not say it. The word "witch" would not come from his mouth. "Are you one too?" He stared at Cess.

"You dolt!" she said, anger flaring at this spoiled boy's rudeness. "Edith's skills owe nothing to the Devil, and they have saved many lives."

"Answer me," he said quietly.

"What does it matter?"

"What does it matter! Are you soft in the head?" he said, jumping down from the shelf, red-faced and furious. "Thank you for your hospitality, Mistress Mildmay," he said to Edith abruptly, bowing slightly and ignoring Cess, "but if you would be so kind as to give me a drink, I will be on my way."

126

"You can't go, you'll be caught," Cess blurted out.

"Do not worry yourself on my account, Maid Perryn." His exaggerated formality was infuriating. "I can look after myself, especially if you are not with me."

"You will let them kill the Queen and William and any other innocent person and do nothing?" said Cess, standing to face him. "You're a selfish wretch!"

"We are a boy, a poultry maid, and an old woman. What exactly do you expect us to do?" he spat back, his face inches from Cess's.

Jasper was rude and infuriating and she wished she had never met him, but she did not want him to go. They would be even more alone without him. It occurred to her too that he might betray them if he really suspected they were witches. Cess saw Edith reach into a pot beside her and fish out a clay cup of small beer, which she handed to Jasper. He gulped it down.

"I wish you luck," he said quietly, handing back the cup and moving toward the ladder. "Which way when I reach the top?" Neither woman answered. Jasper looked furious, but Cess could tell he was frightened. She could not blame him. She was too.

"Jasper, a plot to murder the Queen is not a trifling matter," said Edith grimly. "Whoever is behind it is ruthless, dedicated, expertly organized, and well funded. They have everything to lose if discovered, so they will stop at nothing to make sure they are not. You and Cess know too much. Their first priority will be to find you and to kill you both."

"I shall ask my mother to send me to a tutor far away," retorted Jasper.

"You can go to Land's End, but they will not rest until your tongue is stilled," said Edith. "If you stay, at least you have a chance to defeat them. If you leave, you are alone."

Cess felt a stabbing guilt at having drawn Jasper into a situation awful beyond their wildest dreams. He hesitated, foot on the bottom rung of the ladder, then sighed and slumped back mutely beside her. Edith refilled his cup and he took it without thanks and threw the pale liquid into his mouth.

"There is greater chance for *you* to escape," said Edith, turning to Cess, "because you will have the protection of our brothers and sisters as we try to find safe passage for you, probably north." Cess chewed slowly on her apple. If she fled she had more chance of surviving, but she would not leave Edith and Alathea to fight alone. She knew there was only one path she could take. She had to try and stop the killing. Anyway, she had promised William that she would return for him.

"I will stay, Edith," she said. Edith's voice rang clearly in her head.

"You are a brave lass. As Alathea has foreseen, you are needed in ways we cannot yet fathom in order to defeat this foe." Then she spoke aloud, yawning deeply. "I must rest and you should too while you have the chance. Tomorrow we will make plans, when we are fresh after sleep. If you decide to stay, Jasper, you will be very welcome. There are blankets by the tunnel mouth."

"But what about William? We can't just leave him with those monsters," said Cess, sure she would not be able to sleep while William lay in the priory ruins.

"Being caught ourselves won't help him, and he won't die of the disease if he hasn't yet. We must get help and devise a plan that will work. Wake me if anything happens, and respond to no one except Alathea." Jasper was struggling to hear, staring from one woman to the other as if they each had two heads. Edith, white with exhaustion, settled down on the hard ground beside the hearth with a sigh. Cess fetched a blanket and tucked it around her friend.

"It will soon be night," said Cess, thrusting another blanket at Jasper. "I hope you will stay till the morning at least." She crouched to put the lid over the embers and, with her back to Jasper, pulled the miniature of Lady Mortain from its place. It was rubbing a sore patch on her chest. She ripped a corner from a worn blanket in which to wrap the pendant, and put it in her purse. She was no closer to solving the mystery of why it had been put in the coops, but she wished heartily that she'd never taken it, for nothing but trouble had happened since.

Drax Mortain walked his horse silently through the breezy orchards, pushing her into a gallop only once they had reached open fields. It was past midnight. If he avoided the village, he would be unlikely to encounter anyone. The moon was high and gave ample light as he crossed the Parkway, Abbey Meadow, Broad Calfhay Mead, the Curtles, and finally rejoined the coach road that ran along the base of Saint Michael's Hill to the west. He soon reached the other side of the mount from the village, at the start of a disused track that wound its way up to the ruined chapel at the top of the hill. It was the only way a horse could reach the summit.

The track was treacherous with deep holes and ruts, and Drax slowed the horse to a walking pace. Soon trees blocked out the moonlight, and rider and horse had to feel their way along. It was disorientating circling their way upward in darkness, and he soon lost any sense of where they were in relation to the village or the summit.

"Whoa, whoa," said Drax gently to his horse, who was spooked by the intense darkness and the wind in the trees above her. She whinnied in distress as her hooves slipped on the deeply rutted mud. Drax cursed as his cloak caught on branches. "Damn Paget! I told him this was a madcap idea." Drax pulled up his horse and tethered her to a tree. "Wait here, Bess, wait here." He stroked her muzzle briefly, then swore again as he began the rest of the long climb on foot. His leather riding boots were too thin-soled to be comfortable, but at least his gloves allowed him to cling onto branches to keep upright over the steepest places. He had argued with his page to choose somewhere within easier reach. Having climbed the mount as a boy, Drax knew how difficult it was. The hill had been abandoned to Nature back then too, but Drax had never worried about the sprites and demons said to inhabit the place. He had rather hoped he would encounter ghosts so that they might tell him about his dead mother and siblings. These days he would rather have avoided the mount with its memories, but Paget had insisted that the place was sacred and would lend power to their work. His page had discovered that an old hag now lived on the hill, but that she kept to herself and would not trouble them.

Sweating and breathless by the time he reached the summit, Drax Mortain found the chapel yet more dilapidated than when he had last seen it. Perched on the roof, which was nothing but rotting beams, was his hawk, Mexica. He whistled and she swooped down to his gloved left hand. Drax brought her up close to his face, and she rubbed her beak against his cheek, nuzzling his ear and nipping it gently. He stroked the length of her back, feeling her spare body under the carapace of feathers. He liked her smell—warm hay, slightly dusty—and the weight of her on his arm. He would not say he felt happy—happiness was for fools—but he felt alive.

Before he reached the battered door of the chapel, it was opened by his page. A pale, thin-boned man, Bartram Paget looked even slighter in his loose livery. He wore hose and boots slightly too expensive for his purse, and had a number of annoying mannerisms, such as talking about anyone of rank as if they were a personal friend, that would have caused Drax to dismiss him had Paget's skills in sorcery not been so great. Paget was the seventh son of a seventh son whose powers were acknowledged even among the loose circle of London gentlemen and nobles who used sorcery. His rise, however, had been hampered by a lack of breeding. That had changed once Drax Mortain made him page, and Paget had now made social connections that were as useful as his sorcery. Paget had shown his gratitude by placing his skills at his master's service, and as a result, he shared intimacies with Drax that no man of his station would normally be allowed.

"Paget," said Drax.

"Your Lordship," replied his page, his bulging frog eyes observing Drax carefully. He had little physical strength, but he made up for it by being well-informed. He remained bent double in a deep bow as the nobleman swept past and entered the chapel.

"Let us begin without delay," commanded Drax, aware that he must return to the great house before anyone missed him. He removed his riding cloak and seated himself on a broken column. Paget bowed again, then reached into his doublet and retrieved a small pouch containing ten tiny ivory dice. Moving closer to the light of a small lantern, he squatted carefully, taking care not to dirty his hose, and threw the dice. Squinting to see the dots in the half-light, he arranged the little cubes according to the number they displayed. Drax craned his head to see, and leaned closer. His page flinched and moved, almost imperceptibly, a little further away.

"What do they mean?" asked Drax impatiently.

"Have you been crossed, my lord?" asked Paget, his eyebrows raised melodramatically.

"Somewhat," replied his master. "Nicholas Joliffe, that drunken oaf who leases Abbey Farm, defies me."

"He refused to relinquish the lease early?" asked Paget.

"Indeed, despite some quite forceful persuasion," said Drax icily, kneading his hands together.

"The dice tell me you have met one who will become a great adversary, greater than you have yet known. It is someone with whom you have had a powerful connection, many summers old."

Drax was surprised. He had expected resistance from his father but not from any other quarter. Joliffe was a stubborn, ignorant fool with a long-standing grudge against him, but a great adversary? "No matter. Continue," he commanded, irritated by the prediction. "As well as implementing the curses, I need you to locate the papers my father has hidden."

Paget hesitated. "My lord, you are sure you wish to proceed?" Drax's frown deepened. "We use our darkest powers to make this magic, and now those two children have escaped and one boy is not dead. Perhaps we are not yet ready," continued Paget. "I have seen this curse used just once before, and it had more strength than foreseen. Such malediction cannot always be controlled once it is unleashed."

Drax stared unpleasantly at his page. "Your courage fails you, Paget?" he sneered. "Or is it more money you want, to recompense you for the loss of your soul?" Drax threw a heavy purse at Paget's feet.

"It is not money I seek, sire," said the page, picking up the purse nonetheless and calculating its weight in his hand. "It is to do my duty. To warn you of the strength of the malevolence we call upon."

"Get to it, man, and stop bleating. There is nothing about your sorcery I fear. Proceed!"

Paget bowed and opened the leather panniers he had brought with him. He removed two straw fith-faths and a glass bottle. He gave the dolls to Drax to inspect. Although made of rough straw, they were surprisingly detailed. One was of a woman with reddish-gray hair. When Drax looked closer he could see that the hair was real.

"Whose hair is it?" he inquired, fascinated by the doll.

"Hers."

"Hers?!" he exclaimed. "How is that possible? Your sauce bodes well for your sorcery!"

Paget bowed his head in recognition of the compliment. "The magic would not work without something of the living person embedded in the fith-fath."

Drax took up the other doll, of a dark-haired man.

"And in this?"

"Nail clippings."

Drax nodded slowly, impressed by Paget's ingenuity.

"Once I have circled the flames six times, you must submit the dolls to the flames," said Paget. He opened the small glass bottle and threw half the contents onto the flames. A terrific hiss and spitting was accompanied by a bitter smell of burning alcohol and perfume. The rest he poured carefully over the dolls as Drax held them. Once covered in the dark liquid, Paget took the dolls and placed them close to the blaze.

He started to sway, breathing deeply. Eyes closed, he mumbled incantations and quickly became intoxicated with his sorcery. Drax Mortain watched with wary curiosity this preened figure strutting and swaying like a drunken kingfisher. He seemed to struggle for a moment as if a great weight threatened to pull him over, but then he regained his balance and stood still. He twitched and jerked, then began his dance again. Paget intoned louder and louder, higher and higher.

"Now!" he cried.

Drax threw the dolls into the fire. For a few moments they lay in the white heat, untouched. He looked at Paget, who was staring at the fith-faths with unbroken concentration. As he nodded, a single flame caught the red hair of the female doll. Soon both were burning whiter than the heart of the fire itself until they were gone. As the last piece of straw dissolved into ash, Drax glanced at Paget, seeking confirmation that the task was complete, but his page stood motionless.

"What saw you?" barked Drax, impatient with Paget's silence.

"All you need and more," breathed Paget, his face ashen.

"Good. We can speak at the house" said Drax, pulling on his cloak and walking to the door. "Come, man. The fith-faths have burned. The sorcery was successful."

"It is true," said Paget in a whisper. "None can stop it now."

CHAPTER 14

Jess blinked. Again. Were her eyes open? It was black.

"Edith?" No reply. Panic tightened her chest. She had never been in such complete darkness before, or such silence. She clapped her hands to make sure she could hear, took a deep breath, and tried to calm her galloping heart.

Groping around, she felt the fire lid and lifted it. She blew toward the warmth, and a slight red glow showed her that her eyes were still working. She found Edith's tinderbox and lit a torch. Edith was sleeping by the hearth, and Jasper on the thin straw pallet on the shelf.

It was impossible to tell the time of day. Quietly, she climbed the ladder and unbolted the hatch. As she lifted it, the smell of wet leaves and bluebells seeped in. The urge to throw wide the hatch and run around the clearing was great, but she peeped quickly at the sky and bolted herself inside again. Who knew who might be standing by the hatch.

The sun was up, its rays checkered by storm clouds. They had slept for a long time. Cess's stomach growled and she drank a cup of small beer to slake her incredible thirst. Trying not to disturb the others, she picked up some rushlights from a pile on the shelf and put them in her apron, which she tucked up into her girdle. Wondering what to do with the coppers chinking in her purse, she looked around for a small herb pouch and eventually found one in a niche by the ladder. She put the coins in and hid it in a sack of lavender stalks.

"What are you doing?" asked Jasper, sullenly. Cess jumped. He had been watching her from the pallet.

"Those are my takings from the market."

"Why are you hiding them?"

Cess shifted uncomfortably.

"As it's only you, your friend, and me here, I can only assume you think I might take your coppers. Be assured, Maid Perryn, it is beneath my honor to steal from a pauper child."

Cess sucked in her breath at Jasper's rudeness. "Indeed? Although stealing tobacco from your own mother is not?" she retaliated.

Jasper snorted. "That's different," he said, stretching his arms above his head and sitting up.

"Some might say it was worse."

Jasper was peering at Cess as she moved about the dark space. "What are you doing?"

"I'm going exploring," she replied, heading into the tunnel that led downhill, toward the priory cellars and Montacute House.

"What! You really are soft in the head. They'll catch you."

"I don't think they'll be expecting me." Cess ducked into the tunnel.

"Wait!" he called. "Is this your solution? To get yourself killed?"

Cess did not wait nor reply. She stumbled into the dark tunnel, stooping, for it was low. The ground was flat for a few paces but suddenly sloped downward so steeply that she found herself slipping and skidding out of control. All she could see was within the small pool of light cast by her smoking torch, not enough to prevent her banging her head painfully against the rocks, tree roots, and wooden props that protruded into the narrow tunnel. The oversize leather boots that Jasper had insisted she wear in Yeovil were useless on the mud.

"Wait!" Jasper cried as he crashed into view behind her, limbs and torch flailing.

"Jesu!" panted Cess as he caught up with her. "Just send a note to tell the monks we are coming!"

"If the monks are close enough to hear me, we're in trouble," he countered.

Cess was secretly pleased that Jasper had followed her. It was good to have some company in this underworld. "So, are you staying?" she asked, trying to control her descent.

"Until I can safely leave," he muttered back grumpily.

They half fell, half clambered downward for some time before the tunnel flattened out. Still crouching low, they carried on in silence, keenly aware that the tunnel was connected to the priory. After a while, an opening appeared on their right.

"Which way?" asked Jasper.

"I think that must lead to the priory crypt," Cess whispered.

"Let's not go there yet," whispered Jasper. "I do not wish to visit those fine gentlemen until we have at least some chance of escaping or killing them." Cess nodded. She walked on, but Jasper pushed past her. Cess opened her mouth to protest but realized it was futile to argue with this boy who had come first his whole life.

Their progress was slow. The rotten wooden props that held up the roof and walls of the tunnel sagged dangerously under the weight of earth that pressed against them. In some places the props had rotted and the tunnel was partially blocked with fallen debris.

"One good shove and these props would collapse," said Jasper quietly. Cess tried to stop herself thinking about being buried alive or trapped to die a slow and painful death from cold, thirst, and hunger. As they waded through black pools, she prayed that the black rats that infested the village did not breed in these tunnels. Jasper cursed the damp penetrating his expensive leather footwear and soaking his hose.

"Are we going up?" Cess whispered a few minutes later. The earth beneath her feet was dry again, and a few paces later they stood on ancient warped planks. They walked a few paces until their torches showed that the roof of the tunnel had collapsed. Besides earth and wooden props, however, there were flagstones among the debris, sharp and clean, newly cut.

"There's a gap," said Cess, noticing her torch flare in the slight breeze that came through. "Let's clear it a bit and see if we can squeeze through."

Jasper looked doubtful, but he wedged his torch between the tunnel walls and the pile of rubble and set to work beside Cess, widening the gap. It did not take long. The roof fall seemed quite recent and the debris was not firmly compacted.

This time, Cess handed Jasper her torch and scrabbled up in front of him. As she reached up she was surprised to find space above her head instead of solid earth. But no daylight. Puzzled, she stood upright on the fallen heap.

Jasper handed up her torch, and Cess held it over her head. In the wavering light she could just make out a small, bare room with a door in one corner and an unusually narrow staircase in another. There was a plain wooden candle box near the door but no other furniture at all. Part of the floor had collapsed into the ancient tunnel. The architect and builders of Montacute House had obviously not been aware of the tunnels' existence.

Cess bent down to Jasper. "It's a room. You'll need to give me a leg up."

Jasper scrambled up beside Cess, leaned his back against the tunnel wall, and intertwined his fingers to make a stirrup. Cess stepped into it and heaved herself up as Jasper pushed from below. Once up, she lay flat on her stomach, feet pointing away from the hole, and reached down. Jasper handed her his torch, which she lay flat, then let him pull on her arms like ropes until he could reach a foot over the lip of the floor and lever himself into the room. They picked up their torches and looked about.

"There's nothing here. It's not a storage room," noted Cess, opening the box and finding candles and prickets.

"This door has a lock, and it's new. We can't get out this way," said Jasper, running his fingers over the wood.

"Let's try the stairs, but we'll use a candle," said Cess.

"Beeswax? Does His Lordship have money to burn?" asked Jasper. Cess shrugged. It did seem strange. In the House they used best-quality tallow candles made of sheep and cow fat, the first skimming, so they were white and burned quite cleanly. She sometimes earned an extra halfpenny or penny by helping to polish and degrease the many candlesticks, and knew they used beeswax only when the finest visitors came to dinner.

They pushed a candle onto the little spike of the pricket and lit it, then carefully extinguished their torches against a wall. Jasper held the candle aloft. The stairs were narrow, and Cess steadied herself carefully as she climbed. They were halfway up when they heard a voice so clearly that both froze. It was the voice of a gentleman. Cess peered wildly into the gloom below to see if someone had entered the little room, but it was empty. Jasper looked back at Cess, anxiety puckering his forehead. They tiptoed to the top of the stairs.

They were in a long, narrow stone-and-timber passage, just wide enough for one slim person to move along. Here and there pinpoints of light streamed through holes in the wall. Cess looked through the nearest one, about the width of the tip of her little finger, and stared in amazement. Sir Nathaniel Davies was standing so close to her that she could see the hairs protruding from moles on his face. She had to resist the urge to curtsy and lower her head. After a few moments, Jasper pushed her aside. Cess put her lips right against his ear and breathed into it.

"Lord Montacute's steward."

Jasper stood back to let Cess have another look. When the steward spoke, they both jumped slightly, for his voice was as clear as if he were beside them.

"You left London on Monday?" he asked, beckoning someone to come closer. Into Cess's narrow field of vision stepped a messenger boy whose plain riding clothes were thick with mud. A battered leather satchel was strung across his chest.

"Aye, sir."

"You must have ridden through two nights to reach here so quickly."

"Aye, sir." Cess could see the boy was drooping on his feet, eyes barely open.

"Go to the kitchen for food. The stable boy will show you where to sleep." The bedraggled boy nodded and moved off as if already dreaming. Sir Nathaniel remained seated and held the letter over the flame of a candle. Words appeared down one edge of the parchment that had been invisible before. He frowned deeply as he read the letter, rolled it up, and stood. Although he walked out of her view, Cess could hear his footsteps and the sound of the heavy wooden door opening and closing.

She edged carefully along the hidden passage to the next pinpoint of light and found herself looking into the great hall. As she watched, Nathaniel walked through it. Two blue-clothed servants, sweeping out rushes and spreading sweet fresh ones on the floor, stopped their work and bowed as he passed. Cess was unnerved at being so close to people without them knowing.

"These must be spy passages. Lord Montacute must have built

them into the house to spy on his visitors and servants. I have heard of such things," Jasper whispered.

Cess had never heard of such a thing and was glad she worked in the poultry yards. With a lurch in her stomach she remembered that she no longer did work there and was unlikely to ever again. There had always been rumors among the estate servants and the villagers that Lord Montacute was one of the Queen's spymasters. Cess felt a little shocked to find such direct evidence that the hearsay was true.

At the end of the passage they came to another narrow staircase. They climbed it to the first floor and a similar hidden passage, only this time the passage was so low that they had to bend double to pass along it. When they looked through the first spyhole, they saw why. It ran along the top of the wall, above the level of the doors into the chambers. The spyholes were angled downward, and elaborate hinges had been fixed to some of the panels.

"Concealed hinges," whispered Jasper to Cess when he saw them. "My mother has them for her safe box in the wall. The hinges are hidden so no one knows the panel can open. Our blacksmith could not do them. The goldsmith had to. Here is the catch." A tiny brass hook and eye kept the panel shut.

Looking through the first hole, Cess saw a bedchamber of such richness she could not have imagined it even if a king had been living here. The room contained a large bed, lifted high off the floor by its wooden base and turned legs so that rats and mice could not make it their home. At each corner of the bed was a tall wooden post, carved with intricate patterns of leaves and flowers, hung with curtains of green and gold silk. How secret and cozy it must feel in a bed with curtains closed around it at night, to keep out drafts and prying eyes. Several plump pillows were encased in fine striped cotton, and the coverlet was of quilted green velvet edged with gold silk. The whole room was paneled with oak, over which hung richly colored tapestries of hunting scenes. In the window recess was a carved oak table on which were several parchment rolls, sealing wax, quills, and an elaborate silver inkpot. There was a large clothes' chest and a strongbox strengthened with metal strips and a lock for valuables. Woven rushes covered the floor, and the summer fire in the hearth was laid but not lit. Around the fireplace was an impressive stone mantelpiece with the Montacute coat of arms carved into it.

She nearly missed them, but as she turned away, Cess spotted two eyes staring at her. She gasped, then nearly laughed aloud in relief. On a wooden post by the window sat the white hawk. She was looking at Cess as if there were no wall between them. The smile faded on Cess's lips. The bird looked cruel. Here was no lapdog that would lick its master's fingers. Its large black-and-gold eyes were as keen and cold as if it was soaring leagues up in the sky, watchful for the next kill.

"This is Drax Mortain's chamber," she whispered. "Sir Edward's only son. That's his bird. Could his father be spying on him?"

Jasper shrugged. "I don't suppose it's the first time a father has distrusted a son," he whispered back.

"The bird knows we are here," said Cess. As if it had heard, the hawk leapt off its perch and flew straight at them. Cess jerked back in fright, leaving the hole free. Jasper looked through just as the bird thrust in its talon. It scratched him a fraction below his right eye. The bird's massive wings beat loudly against the panels as it tried to hover, but within moments, the talon was retracted as the bird swooped back to its perch. It picked at its foot, looking at the wall with its head on one side, as if preparing for another attempt. Blood was smeared below Jasper's eye, and Cess scrabbled in her purse for something to stem the flow. She pulled the scrap of blanket away from the pendant and faltered. It was hot.

"What?" said Jasper. Cess shook her head and Jasper snatched the piece of cloth and pressed it onto the scratch to staunch the blood. "That bird will give us away if anyone comes into the room," he whispered grimly, dabbing at his lacerated face. "Let's go."

They carried on along the corridor, sometimes hearing voices behind the paneling so close that they dared not breathe for fear of being heard. At the end of the passage some steps led down to floor level. Here they found another set of hinges on a section two panels high. It would be possible to walk through it bent only slightly. As before, the panel was shut with a single hook, but beside the hook, a small hole had been cut and plugged again, to look like a knot in the grain. Cess saw that if someone inside the room wanted to open the panel, all he need do was push out the plug of wood and put a finger through to lift the catch. There was even a small wicker basket beneath the hole to catch the plug.

The peephole in the panel looked into a room several times larger than Cess's entire cottage. On one wall was an enormous mantelpiece carved from white stone, with lifesize statues in niches and pillars taller than her. A huge bay window in the wall opposite the spyhole had rows of coats of arms in stained glass along the top. Although she had seen the colored glass from the outside, she had never seen it from within and marveled at how the early afternoon sunlight was transformed into shafts of deep color that seemed to stain everything it touched but left no mark. The other wall she could see was covered from floor to ceiling in books. Cess had only ever seen two or three books in one place. To someone who could only haltingly read her own name, the idea that anyone could read so much was like discovering they could fly.

In front of the books was a long trestle table covered with a Turkish carpet. A large wooden writing box stood on the table with a multibranched candlestick beside it, and on the floor next to the trestle were several chests with locks. Two chairs with backs and velvet coverings stood around the fireplace, and several stools and benches were pushed against the walls. Two candles in holders stood on a wooden stool near the fire. All was still, other than the stormy afternoon sky outside. Through the windows Cess could see the rooks thrown around like ash from a fire. Suddenly they heard footsteps approaching, voices, and the sound of the outer, then the inner, door opening. Into her view walked Sir Edward Mortain, followed by Sir Nathaniel Davies holding the letter he had just received.

"It is from the informant at Whitehall. The list of those women who might be Drax's betrothed is inscribed in alum in the margin." Lord Montacute held out his hand and Sir Nathaniel put the rather squashed-looking scroll into it. Sir Edward went to the window to scrutinize it. When he had finished, he rolled the letter back up.

"And of those on this list, the one at the top is most likely?" he asked, sounding as if he hoped the answer would be no.

"Indeed, although if it is the Lady Arbella Stuart, she has entered into the betrothal secretly, for there is no talk of it openly. Certainly Her Majesty has not—"

"Yes, yes, I know that," said Sir Edward, raising his eyebrows. It was a habit Cess had noticed when he came to inspect the poultry yards. His eyebrows seemed to talk to save his breath. "But it would be an act of madness to betroth himself to Lady Arbella. They may be alike in age, and she is comely enough, but without the Queen's consent they'll be thrown in the Tower when it becomes public knowledge. Elizabeth talks still of making Arbella her heir and has spent much time considering an appropriate match for her. My son's name has certainly never come into the discussion." His Lordship looked worried and stared distractedly around the room.

Sir Nathaniel waited a while before speaking again. "Sir, there is more. I wished to tell you yesterday, but you gave orders instead concerning the poultry girl." The steward paused pointedly. His feathers appeared to be still ruffled at being sent after a lowly servant.

Far from looking contrite, Sir Edward turned on his steward. "You may be my trusted servant and steward, Nathaniel," he said quietly, but with such a threatening edge that it made Cess's skin prickle. "You may even be privy to the clandestine work I perform on our sovereign's behalf, but do not presume to think that you know everything that comes to my attention. Some of my orders may seem perverse to you, but everything is done for a reason." Sir Nathaniel visibly shrunk a few inches and bowed. Cess and Jasper stared at each other, and Cess moved aside to let Jasper look. "You said you had other information about my son?"

"Sir, yes. From our contact in Billingsgate, the servant in Vicar Harris's household. He saw a noble gentleman ushered into the house, his visit intended to be secret from all members of the household. From the description, the visitor could have been your son. Harris is a known Catholic, although he pretends to follow Elizabeth's church."

Cess pushed her way back to the spyhole; Lord Edward was her master after all.

"Drax? A Catholic? He appears to believe in nothing but himself," said Sir Edward, rubbing his neatly bearded chin, clearly perplexed. "He traveled in Europe when he was younger to improve his languages—could he have been drawn to the Catholic faith then and kept it hidden? It seems far-fetched to me," he mused. "Certainly he has never been connected to papists on English soil."

"Until now," said Sir Nathaniel solemnly.

"I will write to Sir Robert Cecil to have Vicar Harris brought in for questioning. Wright should conduct the interview. We must tread carefully, for if Drax's name is mentioned it must only be in front of men loyal to me."

"Could he have converted for his bride-to-be? I have heard said that Lady Arbella has become a Catholic."

"The poor girl has been accused of many things, including being unhinged," said Lord Montacute sharply. "Well, she would have to be, to become betrothed secretly to Drax."

"Has your son made no hint to you, sir?"

"I fear I do not know his mind at all," said Sir Edward, sighing. "It has been so many years since he has lived with me, and at court we are both so busy our paths rarely cross."

Cess thought His Lordship cut a lonely figure, despite his gold chains and fine clothes. Nathaniel Davies perhaps thought so too as he spoke in a cheery tone that did not quite ring true.

"Any ambitious young man will arouse suspicions, my lord. Perhaps your son is simply a victim of his success at court?"

Sir Edward looked at his steward so sternly that, although his back was to her, Cess could see him wilt further. "I am old, Nathaniel, but never take me for a fool. We both know full well that my son has come to stay for reasons other than honoring me during the Queen's visit. He is my only surviving child, but I am not blind to his, or anyone else's, faults." The steward bowed his head and began his backward exit.

"And what of Cecily Perryn? What have you found out about her?" Cess's heart shot up to her mouth, and she nearly coughed. Jasper turned to stare at her, obviously amazed that the master of a great estate, one of the most powerful nobles in the land, was asking after his poultry girl, and by name. Cess could barely breathe as the steward stopped his retreat and stood wearily.

"I traced her to an inn in Yeovil, but she left without being seen. The innkeeper's boy has also gone missing."

"They've run off?" exploded Lord Montacute with more emotion than he had displayed during the rest of the conversation.

Cess blushed deeply at the thought of being romantically linked to Jasper. First, she would never pick a conceited dolt like him. Second, what good reputation she had would be damaged beyond repair if gossip spread that she had run away with a boy.

"It seems unlikely there is any . . . romantic . . . link. I spoke to the boy's mother." Sir Nathaniel seemed to quail a little at the memory. "The girl washed pots in return for her bed and had never been to the inn before. Nothing has been seen of them since Monday evening. I felt it best to return here but have men making inquiries in the villages and towns nearest Yeovil. They cannot simply disappear." Sir Edward frowned deeply and dismissed Nathaniel, who looked grateful to leave.

For the rest of the afternoon, Sir Edward Mortain sat at his writing box, stopping only to call a servant to light the fire. From the peephole Cess and Jasper could see him up close, in profile. He sat with his back to the fireplace, facing the book-lined wall. His writing box was one of the most luxurious objects Cess had ever laid eyes on. Once opened, the writing slope was covered in intricately patterned gold-embossed leather. Lifting up the top part of the slope, Sir Edward had removed some parchment sheets. Under the lid of the bottom half of the slope she saw him unlock a compartment containing finished documents and a small money bag. In the base of the box were three drawers, the fronts of which were decorated with family crests and other pictures she could not quite see. One of the drawers contained sticks of red sealing wax and a ring seal; another, a small pot of prepared ink; the third, sand for drying the ink. From a long drawer in the side of the box, he pulled a fine goose-feather quill.

Starting a new letter, Sir Edward pulled out the drawer with the ink pot and felt carefully along the inside top edge. There was a tiny click, and the roof of the drawer space dropped. Sir Edward retrieved a small piece of vellum and spread it out carefully on the table beside him. It was covered in tiny writing, far too small for Cess to make out through the spyhole. Cess touched Jasper's arm and indicated he should look. When Cess looked again a few minutes later, Sir Edward was writing but looking at the piece of vellum over and over again.

"It's a cipher," Jasper breathed into Cess's ear. Cess looked puzzled, but neither dared to say more with Lord Montacute sitting just a few paces away.

The afternoon was already turning to dusk when Cess and Jasper gave up watching and slumped quietly against each other on the ground. They wanted to leave but dared not for fear of being heard. Jasper kept fidgeting, twisting the buttons on his doublet and nibbling at his lips. Cess guessed he was missing his regular dose of tobacco. She mimed chewing on a stick, and Jasper's eyes lit up as he remembered the sage twig in his doublet. They were almost dozing off when a slight noise in the room roused them.

Sir Edward had moved to the mantelpiece and was lighting the candles in a branched candlestick with a taper he had lit from the fire. Holding the candles aloft, he felt down the right outer edge of the fireplace until there was a grating noise. A small panel opened and he took a scroll from his doublet and tucked it inside, shutting the panel carefully afterwards. He left the room, carrying the candlestick. Cess noted how gray and lined he looked.

"I'm going to get that scroll," said Cess as soon as she heard the outer door close.

"What?! You don't even read," said Jasper. Cess lifted the gold hook, bent down, and entered the room. It was dusk now, but there was just enough light to see by. Jasper followed reluctantly. Once through, he pushed the panel back into place without latching it while Cess went to the mantelpiece. She ran her hands down the right side, which was carved with interwoven animals, birds, and plants. The details were so intricate that it was difficult to see where one plant ended and another began, or which was animal, which bird. Although she poked and prodded, she could not find the hidden cubbyhole.

"Jasper," she whispered, "come and help." But Jasper was busy with the writing box. He had seen the open ink drawer and dropped panel, and was carefully running his fingers around the inside edge where the drawer had been.

"In a minute," he said, then sighed with satisfaction as he heard a click and the secret panel dropped out. He took out the vellum square, unfolded it, and began to read.

Cess sat back and looked again at the carvings. Near the top was a white deer, which she recognized as one part of Lady Mortain's emblem. She looked to see if there was a raven too. She could see many other birds, but no raven. Cess was just thinking her hunch was wrong when she spotted an eye among some ivy. The bird had been cleverly disguised in the foliage. She pushed, and a panel, ingeniously hinged on a central pivot, opened with the faintest noise of stone on stone.

Jasper folded the vellum and pushed it inside his doublet. He carefully replaced the panel, closed the writing box, and walked over to see what Cess had found.

She reached into the cubbyhole and pulled out the scroll, which was tied with a narrow red ribbon. She then felt right to the back to make sure she had not missed anything. Her hand closed around a leather bag. She pulled it out, handed the scroll to Jasper, and whistled between her teeth as she opened the bag. It was heavy with gold sovereigns. She had never held one before, and now she had at least one hundred in her hand, more money than anyone she knew could hope to earn in his entire life. Jasper took the bag from Cess. He looked at her with unusually shiny eyes.

"This would be useful, wouldn't it?" he breathed.

"Yes, but we are not thieves," she said firmly.

Jasper was about to argue when they heard soft footsteps in the corridor and the sound of a door being opened, very quietly. Cess threw the money into the cubbyhole and pushed it shut. They dived under the table just as the second door opened, this time into the chamber.

Cess's heart was beating so loudly she could barely hear anything else, and did not want to swallow in case the person entering the room heard the sound in her dry throat. She and Jasper huddled to the back of the table, against the wall of books. The carpet covering the table was long but not quite to the floor. They could see the light change as the person lit a candle. The tiny sounds of the rush matting crunching underfoot told them roughly where the person was moving. When Cess was able to breathe again, she bent down and looked under the cloth from far enough back to allow no light onto her face. Although his back was turned, there was no doubt who was in the room with them. His scalp was smooth and he wore a gentleman's doublet and hose. It was Drax Mortain. Cess sat up again quickly. She dared not look longer, for some people could sense when they were being watched.

Drax was cursing under his breath. Cess guessed that he was looking for the cubbyhole, for why else would he hover around the fire for so long? Eventually they heard the scrape of stone on stone as the cubbyhole opened. She heard the purse being clinked, then thrown back in. She could hear more rustling, as if he was searching about inside it for something else. The scroll. Then the panel door was slammed shut and she heard Drax swear with quiet fury.

Then, to their horror, Drax walked to the table and sat down at the writing box. His beautifully embroidered slipper was nearly touching Cess's knee. She inched away, terrified, and prayed he did not shift his feet or cross his legs. If he did, they would surely be discovered.

Above their heads they could hear Drax opening Sir Edward's writing box. They heard the three drawers being pulled out and Drax's angry growling when he came to the lockable compartment. They could hear him poking something into the lock, but it did not open. Cess and Jasper jumped as he banged his fist on the table.

Drax pushed back his chair and started pacing up and down, occasionally coming to a stop in front of the box. Seeming to come to a decision, he huffed in frustration and thumped the chair back into the position he had found it.

"A pox on him," Drax muttered angrily as he walked away. They heard the sound of two doors opening and closing, but Drax walked so lightly that there were almost no footsteps.

They waited a while before daring to speak.

"Jesu, that was close! Who in God's name was that? He was obviously up to something," whispered Jasper, his eyes wide with fear.

"That was Drax Mortain, Lord Montacute's son." They both looked at the scroll as if it were a firecracker with its fuse lit. Slowly Jasper untied it, and Cess held up the edge of the carpet to allow some firelight to penetrate their hiding place.

"Can you read it quickly now?" asked Cess.

"It's some sort of list, in code. I can't understand it," said Jasper.

"Do you know anyone who speaks code?"

"It's not a language," replied Jasper as if talking to someone very stupid. "Code is when you write things down in a way that is impossible for anyone else to understand. So you would write a *b* instead of an *s* for example, but only you would know that the code for *s* was *b*, so only you could read it."

"I see," said Cess, not really seeing at all but annoyed by the way he spoke to her.

"But I think this is the cipher," he said, pulling the square of vellum from his doublet. "With this I should be able to read the scroll. If I make a copy, Drax might still come back and find the original, but at least no one will know we were here."

"Let's get away from here," said Cess.

"If we take the scroll, Sir Edward will know someone has been here. If he knows about the secret passages in the house, which he must, he might suspect someone is using them, probably his son. It will mean we couldn't use them again. Is Edith likely to have writing materials?"

"I doubt it." They both eyed the magnificent writing box. Jasper took a piece of parchment and quill from the box, and pushed them inside his doublet along with the scroll and the cipher. The small pot of ink he held carefully in his hand. As they moved back to the panel, a book on the shelves caught Cess's eye, for it had a picture of fireworks stamped in gold on its spine. Her stomach tightened as she thought of William and how much he would love to read it. He was still alive; she sensed it.

CHAPTER 15

Mexica slept undisturbed on her perch as Drax stood at the window, staring out into darkness unbroken by any lantern or moon. His anger mounted as every risky foray into his father's domain brought him no closer to the scroll. He had, at last, discovered its hiding place, but his father must have taken it to use. Drax had been tempted to take the writing box, but then his father would know someone was tampering with his things. Without that scroll, the last ten years of planning could come crashing down.

He took a deep breath and held it long enough for his head to clear. For the first time in many years he remembered when he first learned to do this. He tried to force the pictures from his mind but could not. He was a boy, looking into the coffins of his older sisters, Margaret and Rosalie, and his younger brother, Henry. He had not wanted to look, their bodies were ravaged by illness, but his mother was there, strange and furious.

"You must face death," she had insisted. A few days later, three more coffins. Edmund, seventeen, already making his way at court.

Little Elizabeth, six; and his mother. Rumors circulated later that she had committed the great sin of killing herself in her grief, but Drax refused to believe she had willingly abandoned him. He had wanted to die himself, and for a while it looked as if he would.

On the day of the last funeral he had held his breath until he fainted. He remembered how the servants had fussed around him, but his father had remained silent, oblivious to his son's suffering in the midst of his own pain. When he came around, his head was clear. For a while it made him feel better, powerful, that he could deprive his body of air, take himself away, and come back feeling stronger.

Unfortunately, he also learned that drink did something similar, and he had gone mad for a while. Something happened one night that made his father banish him to a tutor in London. But he did not wish to think about that. That was the old Drax that did stupid, violent things fired by alcohol and emotion. The old Drax was gone.

Even as he stood there, a powerful, strong man in his thirty-second year, he could hear the rhythmic thwhack of his tutor's whip on his backside. He would never forgive his father for sending him away, but would not waste time hating him.

My mother would be proud of me now, he thought, remembering his mother's smile but not how happy it used to make him. He had gained control over grief, his feelings, his heart. He could hear of, or inflict, death without a flicker of emotion.

You must face death.

He leaned his head against the cold stone mullions to clear the images of the coffins. He would get that scroll. He had always possessed an uncanny ability to find things, to know what people were thinking, to manipulate situations to his own advantage. His mother had called him her sorcerer.

A cold draught and a little cough made him spin round. Bartram Paget was halfway through the door.

"What is it, Paget?" Drax said gruffly.

Bartram moved into the room and shut the door behind him. "The girl who escaped from the cellars, I have just remembered where I saw her. It was she who defied you in front of the church. When I read the dice, I saw you had been crossed. Perhaps it is she who is your enemy."

"The girl?" Drax paused, turning the idea over in his head.

"The girl knows about the activities in the old priory and is wandering around the countryside unchecked. She is certainly our most dangerous foe at present," said the page.

"My father refused to dismiss her, despite her defiance. What is her name? Cecily, isn't it?"

"Yes, sir. And Maid Amelia has informed you that she is involved in witchcraft."

Drax Mortain snorted. "Amelia's accusations against her cousin are lies to attract my attention," he said dismissively.

"Although I do sense the presence of witchcraft," said Paget.

"People see witches wherever they look these days, Paget. A real witch is a very rare find indeed. First thing in the morning I will send dogs out to hunt Cecily and the boy. Get a piece of her clothing—we shall need it for the dogs to trace a scent—but go carefully; we don't want her mother running to my father."

"Shall I also use my own means to trace the girl?"

"Which are?"

"A prophecy fire, sir."

"Very well. Do as you will."

"Sir, if I may . . ." ventured Paget, wringing his hands. "If word reached Lady Arbella of your dalliance with—" he began, but Drax cut him off.

"Stop fretting. Amelia is a peasant, a pleasant diversion, and I am enjoying her company while I wait to be married. There's no harm in that." In an unusually friendly gesture, Drax took his page's arm and guided him to the door.

CHAPTER 16

The white face of Lady Mortain came close. She kissed Cess on the cheek with lips that were freezing cold. They left a shining mark that started to bleed. Cess stared down at her hands; they were holding the pendant but turning black as she looked, and blistering. Two dolls—no, people—burning, the stench of singed hair, red. A blade at her heart. A witch's tool. She was falling, burning, dying . . .

"Shut up!" hissed Jasper hoarsely, his hand clamped over her mouth.

Cess's eyes snapped open and she sat bolt upright, gasping for air and flailing her arms about as if scaring off crows. She had been screaming in her sleep. Edith removed the lid from the fire, and the deep red embers glowed in the blackness of the tunnel. Cess crawled close enough to feel the heat on her eyes, and she stared at the tiny movements of red in the firewood and the gray ash paths they left. Gradually, the details of her nightmare faded. Jasper lay back down and pulled the thin blanket up to his ears, sighing with impatience at having once again to endure the hard rock, the cold and the damp that his sleep had blocked out.

They had not been asleep long. After returning to Edith, Cess had told her all they had seen and heard, while Jasper, by the light of a spitting candle, had decoded and copied the scroll. He seemed to have accepted that his most likely chance of survival lay in fighting rather than fleeing. He had returned to the House alone to replace the scroll and cipher while Cess and Edith had talked.

"Cecily, most novices have a year to learn their craft before initiation; you will have less than a month. Alathea wishes your initiation to take place as soon as possible, if you choose to become a witch. You must learn the Goddess rune and take its meaning into your heart. It is the key to our craft.

> *You who seek me, the Goddess,*
> *Know that your seeking will avail you not*
> *Unless you know the mystery;*
> *If that which you seek you cannot find within you,*
> *You will never find it outside you,*
> *For I have been with you from the beginning*
> *And I am that which is attained at the end of the desire.*

"You have within you the world's wisdom. To look outside yourself for answers will not help, for you must believe in your own ability to become the Goddess, divine and human."

Cess's heart sank at how much she had to learn. Edith recited other long runes, chants, spells, the names of magical tools she would be given at her initiation, the order of the ceremony, the strange names of gods and goddesses, and showed her clockwise and widdershins dances and the correct way to draw symbols in earth, air, and water with an athame. The darkness in the tunnel made Cess sleepy, and she had no habit of learning.

"I know you think we ask too much of you," said Edith gently, "but this was the religion of your ancestors, so deep in your heart you already know what I am telling you."

Although Edith had not mentioned it again, neither of them was any closer to uncovering what secret power Cess held that would aid them in their fight. Cecily was an adequate novice, of unusual courage perhaps, but not yet displaying particular brilliance in the witch's craft.

There were other reasons Cess had barely slept. It seemed that every time she closed her eyes the face of Lady Mortain, or Drax's stare, or William's disfigured body, crashed into her dreams. Cess could work out the significance of most of it, but the pendant confused her.

"I keep dreaming of Lady Mortain and of burning dolls," she whispered.

"It might be best to return the pendant," said Edith quietly, who was lying sleepless on the other side of the fire pit. "And burning dolls? That sounds like fith-faths. Do they look like anyone?"

"A man and a woman," said Cess. "Maybe Queen Elizabeth and James of Scotland?"

"Or a boy and a girl? The sorcerer Alathea and I have scried has perhaps made fith-faths of you two. It is powerful sorcery and imperative that you master the art of closing your mind to it. Alathea and I and the coven can help protect you, but ultimately it will be up to you to keep him at bay."

Cess nodded. "Edith, what was Lady Mortain like?" she asked.

Edith hesitated before answering. "Lady Mortain came from a sighted family, although she did not know it, for the knowledge of her witch heritage had been lost several generations before. But I knew it as soon as we met. Perhaps it was that that blinded me to her true nature. She worshipped her husband and children, but as her sons grew, so did her ambition for them. She crushed the kindness out of her boys, encouraging ruthless self-promotion. I remember Drax Mortain being particularly loving as a young boy, a characteristic his mother at first encouraged but later punished. When she thought all her children were dead, she asked me for a draught to take her from this world, but I could not do it. I heard she found her own way." Cess saw a gray shadow pass over Edith's features, a complicated mix of emotions that included sadness, anger, and regret.

A low whistle from behind her made Cess jump.

"I thought *my* mother was difficult," said Jasper. He must have heard everything.

Edith managed to smile at Jasper's quip, and pulled herself to her feet. She climbed the ladder and briefly opened the hatch.

"It is dawn," she said, coming back down and stoking up the fire. "There is much to plan."

"Edith," said Cess, "this is the start of the fourth day since William was taken. I feel he is getting sick at heart and can't last much longer. I'm not sure how we can get him out unhurt, but I have thought of a way to destroy the monks' work."

"Why don't we just smash it?" said Jasper.

"Because you will almost certainly catch the disease if you are in the room when the vials are broken," Edith replied.

"In the house we heard Sir Nathaniel talking about the fireworks for the Queen's visit," said Cess. "Could we steal them to blow up the cellars?"

"Petards!" said Jasper, looking admiringly at Cess for the first time. "I know all about those. I used to make them—small ones."

"You made petards?" said Cess, disbelieving. "What did your mother say?"

Jasper looked sheepish for a moment. "She didn't know. Until I blew up the privy."

Even Edith stopped working and stared.

"Was anyone in there?" asked Cess, horrified.

Jasper burst out laughing. "Yes, a man wooing my mother. It was not long after my father died; I didn't like him."

"Was he hurt?" asked Cess.

"His bottom was burned, and his clothes were ruined because he fell into the cesspit. But we got him out before he drowned. It was his pride that was really hurt."

"Well, at least your education will prove of some use," said Cess.

"Indeed, I hope so. And perhaps you would like me to teach you the alphabet?"

Cess smirked. Jasper was rude, but she felt quite in awe at him for blowing up his mother's suitors, although she would never admit that to him. Edith threw some small yellow flowers into the pot and allowed them to steep for a while before pouring cups of steaming liquid for them all. "Chamomile tea, soothes the nerves. Petards might work," she continued soberly, "but they will take a little while to make. I have called the coven, but they cannot convene immediately, and I fear we must seize William fast or, as Cess has warned, it will be too late. Whoever seeks you at the House, they are sure to send out dogs. I shall make a mix of strong-scented herbs to put them off your trail. There is also the matter of food. There is none left."

The three sat in silence for a while, a little stunned by the tasks and problems that beset them.

Cess sipped her tea. "Perhaps we should visit Goodman Joliffe," she said. "He might give us food."

"Nicholas Joliffe?" said Edith, surprised.

"Who is he? Can he be trusted?" asked Jasper.

"I think so," Cess said, remembering the cart journey to Yeovil and the farmer's bruises. "He has something against Drax Mortain, to do with the murder he was accused of years ago. He is unlikely to betray us to his enemy."

Jasper took a sip of his tea and spat it out. "What is this evil brew?" he gasped, puckering his lips. He looked so funny that Cess laughed. "By the way, I think I have worked out why the scroll is so precious to Lord Montacute and to his son. It's a list of names, sorted by degree. Nobles and gentlemen at the top, yeomen and craftsmen last," he explained, taking a sip of small beer to rinse away the taste of the tea.

"Who are they? Why the secrecy?" asked Cess.

"I think they are his spies."

Cess had to admit that Jasper really was very clever. "So the rumors about him are true. He is one of the spymasters to the Queen."

"It seems so. His job is to discover plots against her life and keep her safe. He suspects his son is up to something, and from what we heard, his web of spies is working night and day to find out what. He is worried"—Jasper almost chuckled—"that the Queen's greatest enemy is hiding behind the spider itself."

CHAPTER 17

The night air was cool and damp. It must have been raining. Dogs had been baying around the forest all day, and so Cess and the others had not even dared poke their noses out of the tunnel. As she slid down the mountain, she had to hold on to branches and brace her feet against tree roots to prevent herself falling. It was only just dark. She could hear the noisy rustling of night creatures.

She felt light-headed and shaky. Her stomach growled. She had not eaten a proper meal since the day she left for Yeovil. As she walked, she sprinkled Edith's masking scent behind her and rubbed it into the wet leaves and rich earth of the forest floor.

The witches of Edith's coven were helping her, taking it in turns to keep watch day and night to protect her against the sorcerer who was pursuing her. Cess was able to tell when one witch finished a shift and another joined. Coven members lived as far as three or four miles away, but Cess could feel their presence as strongly as if they were walking quietly beside her.

As she came to the edge of the forest, she stopped. From this vantage point she could see for miles. The moon, a few days off full, gave good light and the clouds were high and thin. In the near field were rabbits. An owl was above and behind her, preening and hooting. She could hear but not see a she-fox two fields away. The windows of the House were dark. She was not surprised, for the main chambers were on the side she could not see. Jasper and Edith would be leaving soon to go there. She hoped her descriptions of the yard were good enough for them to find the correct stable and that it was not locked or guarded. There was still so much to do if they were to get to William.

She looked across the fields to her right. She could see Goodman Joliffe's farm. Through the slats of one shutter she thought she saw a glow, but it was too far away to be sure. The most dangerous part of her route would be crossing the lane that cut between the mountain and his farm. Beneath her, the village was dark; no smoke came from any of the roofs, and there were no human sounds. The dogs were silent, the pigs sleeping, the chickens roosting in their coops or beside their owners' beds in the ramshackle cottages and hovels.

Her mother's cottage was to her left. The urge to visit her, to whisper in her ear that she was safe, to kiss her and beg forgiveness for the trouble she had got herself in, was almost overwhelming. As she looked with longing at the cottage she knew so well, she felt her scalp prickle with fear. What was it? Her intuition was warning her of something her eyes could not yet trace. Then she saw it. The tiniest movement farther along the lane, between the church and the inn. Someone was edging down the lane, keeping to the shadows. Cess's already thumping heart sped up, and sweat prickled under her arms.

Before moving, she looked more carefully at the route to the farm. Nothing. As quietly as a fox, she moved inside the fringe of the forest until she was as close as possible to the fields that led to the lane. She crawled on her stomach across the rough grazing land between the trees and the hedgerows. Crouched on hands and knees, she stuck to the shadows, pausing frequently to listen. When she reached the lane, she squatted inside the hedge until her breath was silent. As her heart quieted she knew beyond doubt that she was not alone. The cloaked figure she had seen was now near the stile, walking toward her with light steps. Then she heard a voice. The figure was talking to itself as if to steel its courage. Cess cowered back as the figure walked so close to her she could smell its scent: lavender, fine wool, and fear. Although the cloak and hood hid the person completely, Cess knew immediately who it was. Amelia.

Her cousin climbed over the stile inches from where Cess hid. She walked slowly up the hill, still muttering to herself to keep at bay the fear of being out alone at night. As soon as Amelia had rounded the bend in the hedge, Cess took a deep breath, vaulted the stile, shot across the moonlit lane, and plunged into the shadows of Joliffe's track. She ran as swiftly as a frightened deer to the farm and hid until she got her breath back. She had been right about the glow from the shutters, but there were no voices.

Even in the dark, the place looked dilapidated. The courtyard was weedy where cobbles were loose. The barn doors were off their hinges, the well needed repairs, and the water trough beside it was leaking. The farmhouse, once a fine two-story building with a large chimney stack, now had broken or missing slats in the shutters and graying timbers.

Avoiding the front door, Cess crept to the back and tried the latch. It was locked. She was surprised—most people had no locks on their doors. She knocked very quietly. No reply. She knocked again and heard the noise of someone shifting in a chair and snoring. The snoring turned into a belch followed by swearing, and she heard the man inside heave himself to his feet. She tapped again.

The back door opened and a florid face stared down at her.

"What the . . . ?" Cess shot inside and waved at the farmer to shut the door quickly. He did so, staring at her as if a ghost had just entered.

"Your mother's near dead from worry about you," said Joliffe.

"You've seen her?"

"Aye, she accused me of leaving you in Yeovil," he said grimly, indicating that Cess should sit in the only comfortable chair. He leaned against the fireplace wall, still watching her closely.

"I'm sorry," said Cess. She sensed that Joliffe was prepared to listen to her. Here was another outsider, like herself. She explained briefly what had happened to her, William, Jasper, and Edith, and saw his face transform with every sentence, from disbelief to shock, outrage, and fear. As she described William's piteous state, he pulled up a stool and sat heavily upon it, his head in his hands. "It is hard to believe what I say, but I swear it is true."

Joliffe looked up at her and she saw that he did not doubt her. "That bastard," he said, hatred on his face. "See these bruises and scratches?" They had faded since Monday but were still visible. "A gift from Drax Mortain and his demonic bird to persuade me to give up the lease on this land. I couldn't understand his sudden interest in farming, but now I see it's because the priory cellars are just there." He pointed behind him and seemed to shudder at the knowledge that, even as they sat there, robed men were inflicting indescribable misery on their young victims just a few measures from his home.

"What can I do? Can we storm the place?" he asked.

"You and whose knights?" Cess smiled ruefully. Neither of them had many allies in the village.

"Peter Barlow?"

"It's not enough. But we are gathering people, friends of Edith, and then your help will be crucial. For now we need food and saltpeter."

Joliffe raised his eyebrows. "Saltpeter? Got time to preserve some meat?" he said, puzzled.

Cess giggled. "No . . . but I'd better not say more."

"As you wish," he said amiably, hauling himself up from the stool and trudging off into another room. He returned a few minutes later with a large sack and a trencher of bread on which was some butter and a wedge of cheese. He put the sack by the door, gave Cess the trencher, and poured them both a cup of ale from the sideboard.

"I doubt you can carry more than that. Come back when you run out. All the saltpeter I have is in the blue clay jar."

While Cess ate, Joliffe tied the top of the sack with a piece of twine he cut from a loop at his girdle. He then cut a second piece of twine, took a key from above the back door, and tied the string around it. He handed it to Cess, who put it around her neck.

"Let yourself in with that if you need to. I've got something to show you." He led Cess into a chamber that led from the main hall. In the far corner, to one side of the fireplace, he lifted the rush mats on the floor and showed Cess a small hole in the old oak planks. Joliffe inserted his finger and the board lifted. He pulled it out and showed Cess a dark space.

"This is the priest hole. Space for three, four at most."

"Are you a Catholic?" asked Cess in surprise as she stared into the tiny space and shivered in horror; it would be like hiding in a coffin, like being buried alive.

"My folks were. Devout. I lost my faith in God—" He stopped abruptly, glanced at Cess, and frowned. "Never mind."

He walked with her to the back door. "If I get a chance, I'll tell your mother I've seen you. If I can do more, you let me know. That bastard deserves to rot in hell."

"I don't know how to thank you for your kindness, sir," said Cess simply. Her face showed the gratitude she felt.

With the heavy sack over one shoulder, Cess was nearly in the forest when a foot shot out from some brambles and someone was upon her. Cess bucked and punched, managing to turn over, but a knife was held to her throat and she quieted. When she saw her assailant's triumphant face above her, she nearly laughed.

"Amelia! What are you doing?"

"Catching a witch's accomplice," she said. "I knew I could do what the whole village failed to do," she sneered. "Stealing food, I see?" she said, eyeing the bag Cess held. "Come with me—there's someone who wants to meet you."

Cess could tell from her cousin's superior tone that she meant someone important, like Viscount Drax Mortain. "No, Amelia, you don't know what's going on."

"Oh? On the contrary, I would say I am one of the few people who do know what's going on."

"You're wrong, Amelia." Although she wasn't sure how Amelia's play for Drax was progressing, it was the only subject she could think of that might stop Amelia in her tracks. "You're being a fool. I saw you with Drax Mortain in the maze. He's just playing with you."

Amelia stopped poking Cess with the knife and stared coldly at her. "What of it?" she said loftily.

Cess growled in frustration. She dared not tell Amelia anything of what she knew, for the little sneak would go straight to Drax Mortain.

"Anyway, how would you know he is 'playing' with me? What are you up to?" Cess said nothing. "Well, if you won't talk to me, I'm sure the viscount will loosen your stubborn tongue." Amelia jabbed the knife at Cess again, to force her down the hill, but took only two paces before finding herself pulled back. Her fine, new wool cloak was caught in briars. Amelia pursed her lips and clucked crossly at the damage the thorns were inflicting on a prized possession.

"Untangle me and don't try to escape, because I shall scream the place down and stab you."

Cess could not help admiring Amelia's determination. She carefully separated the cloak from the tiny thorns, taking her time so she could think. She had to get away.

"Where have you been hiding?" Amelia demanded.

"In the forest."

"You are with Edith?"

"No. Did you not know that the shack has been wrecked and she has been chased away?"

"Well, yes, I heard, but what of it? There are other places she can hide."

Cess looked at Amelia doubtfully. "I have searched all over and could not find her," she said.

"Hurry up!" snapped Amelia. "And you, I suppose, are too frightened to return to the great house? The money you earned at market turned your head, did it? All spent? A witch and a thief—what good company you must be for each other."

"I spent not one farthing, Amelia. I did not run away, I was taken like those boys who disappeared."

Amelia did not deign to reply to such obviously tall tales.

"I will make a bargain with you," said Cess, holding her ground. It was clear to her that Amelia was determined to sacrifice Cess in order to advance her cause with the nobleman. She could not help feeling sad that her cousin cared so little for the friendship they had once shared.

"You are in no position to bargain, dear cousin."

"Amelia, we both know that if we fight, you will be hurt too. I know things that could help you."

"I have no need of your help," Amelia huffed dismissively as if she were already mistress of the Montacute estate.

Cess looked skeptical. "You are a village wench, and Drax Mortain one of the most powerful men in the land. Don't you think it might take more than a pretty face to win him over?"

Amelia scowled. "What do you know about such things?" she replied scathingly.

"Edith taught me much," said Cess tantalizingly. "I know how to make heart philters that turn a man's lust to love."

Amelia was unable to disguise her interest, and Cess could tell she was weighing up her claims. If Edith really was gone, then catching Cess proved nothing. Far from taking Cess to Drax, it might be better to keep her away so that Amelia might prolong the intrigue surrounding her cousin and keep herself in the forefront of Drax's mind.

"I am not a fool. You will promise to make the philter but will not do so and will never return here to bring it to me," said Amelia.

Cess paused and pretended to think hard. "If I give into your keeping the most precious thing I own, to be returned to me if I fulfill my side of the bargain, will you agree?"

Amelia laughed, the sweet sound so at odds with the spiteful, determined face. "Cess, you have nothing precious. You are a bastard!" she squeaked.

But Cess knew without doubt that her singularly vain cousin would not be able to resist the jewel, once she had seen it.

"Let me see what you have and then I will decide," said Amelia imperiously.

Cess feigned reluctance as she opened her purse. The unhappier she appeared giving up the jewel, the more delighted Amelia would be with it.

"You are wearing a purse!" gasped Amelia. No peasant girl should do so. Even a yeoman like Amelia would be reaching above her station to wear one outside her skirt.

"It is only for ease of carrying now I have no home." Cess shrugged, taking out the pendant, being careful not to show the knife. She could grab the athame and fight her cousin, but she knew that was not the answer. This way, there was a possibility Amelia would keep quiet about meeting her so as to keep the pendant and the potions. She handed the pendant to Amelia as if it were a favorite kitten. Amelia tucked her knife into her girdle and took the jewel. Her eyes opened wide in awe as she ran her fingers over the valuable gems in their gold setting.

"You stole this," she breathed.

"I did not," replied Cess indignantly.

"How did you get it, then?"

"You wouldn't believe me if I told you."

Amelia looked sharply at her cousin but did not bother to argue. Nor did she ask whom the portrait depicted, and Cess decided not to enlighten her.

"Very well. I will strike this bargain with you. Leave the philter by the stile tomorrow night, and I will return the jewel. If you do not, this jewel is forfeit."

Cess nodded and disappeared into the forest as fast as she could. She had a feeling the pendant would not bring Amelia any more luck than it had brought her.

CHAPTER 18

Jasper followed closely behind Edith. She moved as quickly as a fox, slinking along hidden paths, stopping frequently as if to sniff the air and listen. Edith had warned Jasper that it would be a long walk, for they would circle the house at a distance and only approach it from the south, where trees gave cover. On every other side there were bowling greens, lawns, ponds, or formal gardens, and they risked being seen. His only weapon was a curious white-handled knife she had given him. Jasper's fear was kept at bay by the elation of being outside and, at last, doing something positive to hasten the end of this nightmare.

The moon gave good light and they made fast progress. Edith kept far enough from dwellings to prevent dogs barking. He knew Cess was out there too, not far away. When he thought about her, he noticed that he no longer felt the urge to slap her. She was stubborn and headstrong and had got herself involved in matters way above their heads, but he grudgingly admitted that she was, at least, interesting.

They crossed a little brook and skirted several long strips of cultivated land. Eventually they came to an avenue of elm trees, which they crossed, and continued through a loosely cropped meadow to the orchards on the south side. They saw a lantern near the house. The night watchman was making his rounds. Edith opened a wicket gate that let them into the orchard, closing it carefully behind her. The densely packed trees and low branches made the way dark and difficult.

Suddenly Jasper spotted a pale shape partly hidden by a tree. It was moving. He ran to warn Edith, but fell over a body in the grass. Guards! They must have been waiting for them. He lay winded, hearing grunting as the guard placed the heavy butt of his pike on his back. Edith was approaching, but how could she fight the guard?

"Are you hurt?" whispered Edith, pushing the great weight off Jasper's back. He turned and saw that the pike butt was the trotter of a huge sow, who was nuzzling him with interest. All around he saw other pale shapes sprawled on the ground or coming to see what was happening.

"We must go, in case they make a noise," whispered Edith, pulling Jasper to his feet. He was pleased that the darkness hid his blushes. He hoped Edith would not mention to Cess that he had been floored by a pig.

At the corner of the orchard they looked over the fence to survey the stables beyond, a long building of two stories. The lower floor contained the stalls for the horses and rooms for tack, bedding, and feed. Above was a low-gabled dormitory for stable boys and grooms. Cess had warned them that the grooms often stayed awake late, playing cards, and were sometimes still at it when she began work. On this night, no candlelight shone through the shutters, nor was there a guard or dog stationed outside. The night watchman's lantern was nowhere to be seen, and so Jasper let himself out through the wicket gate and ran to the stable door. Edith remained in the orchard, keeping watch.

Close to, Jasper could hear snoring coming from inside. It was a human, not a dog. He lifted the latch using both thumbs so as to make no sound, and poked his head around the door. It took a few moments for his eyes to grow accustomed to the darkness. The only light came from the moon through a single open shutter. Jasper saw that this part of the stables was separated from the rest by a wooden partition that ran from floor to ceiling. From the left-hand wall jutted a mezzanine floor supported by two wooden columns, which would surely creak when he walked on it. He could see the top of a number of barrels and sacks—the fireworks, he presumed. Sprawled on a heap of straw at the bottom of the ladder leading up to it was a sleeping man.

Jasper ran back to Edith and reported what he had seen.

"I shall send him into a deeper sleep," said Edith, pulling a tiny clay jar from her purse.

"What is it?"

"A sleeping draught. It is not much used these days, for if it is wrongly brewed the sleep is permanent."

"It kills? What's in it?"

"It is a concoction of bile, opium, henbane, lettuce, bryony, hemlock, and vinegar diluted in wine. If I have the proportions right, he will sleep very deeply and wake feeling dizzy but remembering nothing, for it affects the memory and can give very strange dreams. Have you the ropes?" Jasper nodded.

Edith crossed to the stable as quietly as a shadow, and Jasper followed, waiting by the door. She knelt beside the snoring man, opened the pot, and tipped the contents slowly into the man's gaping mouth. He swallowed, cleared his throat, and grunted. Edith put the jar away and beckoned Jasper, but before he could reach the stairs, the man sat bolt upright. Jasper's heart flew into his mouth and he grabbed his knife, but Edith shook her head. The man glared at Jasper and then at Edith. His eyes were huge and bright, the pupils much larger and blacker than normal. Then, without a sound or hint of recognition, he collapsed back on the straw, eyes closed.

"Go!" whispered Edith.

Jasper raced up the ladder and began passing sacks and barrels down to Edith. He found a box of hemp fuses and three tinderboxes with large pieces of char cloth in them to set the fuses alight. There was also a strange wooden block drilled with holes, which Jasper guessed was to set the fireworks in to light. When he judged that they had all they could carry, he clambered back down the ladder. Edith roped as many barrels and sacks to Jasper as his legs could stand. She then tied several more sacks together and bent down to put the rope over her shoulders. With difficulty, she managed to stand up.

The man began murmuring and singing to himself as Jasper and Edith staggered out of the stable and into the orchard. The night watchman was on the other side of the house, the yard obviously not part of his beat but the responsibility of the poor dolt now moaning into the straw.

"Poor man," puffed Edith once they were a safe distance from the house. "He is going to wake with the most awful pain in his head."

"And on his arse," panted Jasper, "if he's whipped for allowing a thief to walk right over him."

Sir Edward was sitting watching the small flames of the summer fire in the vast fireplace. The morning was raining again and chilly, despite being May.

He was preoccupied by the information he had received about his son's betrothal. If the information was correct, Drax was playing a very dangerous game indeed. His duty was to inform on Drax to the Queen, but he would do that only if he believed his son was truly a lost cause.

His reverie was disturbed by the sound of the outer door opening and a knock on the inner. His steward walked in.

"My apologies for disturbing Your Lordship."

"Come where I can see you."

Sir Nathaniel Davies moved around the high-backed chair to stand before the fire. "I am afraid there has been a burglary." Nathaniel looked worried. "It must be someone who knows the place well."

"What is missing?" asked Sir Edward, glancing at the fireplace.

"Fireworks," said Sir Nathaniel. "The stable in which they were stored was raided last night, right under the nose of the guardsman who was posted in the room. A very large quantity is missing; it must have been the work of more than one thief."

"Fireworks? What on earth could anyone want with those? It would be rather obvious if they tried to use them."

"Indeed, sir, it is very puzzling. My first fear was that they could somehow harm the Queen, but on further consideration it seems improbable. It takes several minutes to light them and there is no way to direct them across the ground to hit Her Majesty. . . . I do not understand it."

"Could the guard have been bribed?" asked Sir Edward.

"It seems more likely he was drugged," replied his steward.

"Drugged? That would require skillful knowledge. He was not drunk?"

"It is hard to say, sir," said Sir Nathaniel, shrugging his shoulders. "The man swears not, but he has a bad head on him this morning."

Lord Montacute thought a moment. "Nathaniel, put a watch on my son. But discreetly—Drax must not know."

The steward bowed and left the room quickly. Sir Edward pulled himself to his feet and looked around the great chamber. Had the thief come into the house too? It occurred to him that things were a little disarranged. A candlestick was missing, and his writing box was not quite how he had left it. He opened the precious object and noticed immediately that several pieces of parchment were gone, and his favorite goose quill was blunt. The small square of vellum had not been taken, however. Hurriedly he walked to the fireplace and pushed on the secret panel. With relief he saw that the scroll was in place. He plunged his hand to the back of the cubbyhole until it closed on the heavy leather purse. He opened the drawstring with shaking fingers, grunting with relief as he saw the gold sovereigns glinting undisturbed. The bag contained the bulk of the cash he had raised to cover the enormous costs of hosting the Queen and her huge retinue.

He replaced the gold and shut the panel, deeply relieved that the intruders had not found his hiding places. He pulled out one of his hairs and stretched it across the closed cubbyhole, fixing it in place with tiny dabs of candlewax. The gold he pushed into his doublet to put in the armory later. He opened the locked compartment of his writing box and took out a sturdy key. Leaving his chambers, he walked down the main stairs to the great hall and then down a narrow spiral stone staircase to the storerooms under the house. He had only been down here once, with the achitect, and it took a few tries to find the right door for the key. Eventually he found himself in the tiny room he remembered, with a narrow staircase. He noticed a large hole in the floor where the stone flags had collapsed into what looked like an ancient cellar or cesspit.

It had seemed fitting to build the secret passages, given his position as spymaster. He thought to use them during the Queen's visit to ensure her safety and keep abreast of what her privy counselors were up to, but had not expected to enter them before that. However, it occurred to him that someone else was finding them very useful indeed.

"Is he expecting you?" said Sir Nathaniel, doubtfully.

"No, but he will see me," said Amelia, lowering her head but looking up at the steward with her clear blue eyes.

"Wait here."

Amelia did not. She was not a peddler to be kept in the vestibule. She strolled through the arched entrance of the ornately carved wooden screen into the great hall. Light filled the room even though it was a gloomy morning. Although her own home was one of the grandest in the village, it would nearly have fitted into this one room alone. The fireplace was so large she could have stood in it without bending her head. The surroundings were grand, but she felt equal to them.

She was shivering, not with cold but excitement. She had felt like this since receiving the pendant a few hours before. She was sure it would be her key to catching Drax. She was wearing it around her neck, but had tucked the portrait into the top of her bodice to keep it a surprise. She knew Drax would not object to watching her draw it out of her bodice, slowly.

"Maid Perryn?" Amelia turned to see Bartram Paget, Drax's page, enter the hall alone.

"I have information about Cecily that will deliver her to you," said Amelia, with a triumphant smile.

The page suppressed a huff; the girl irritated him. "Pray tell me and I shall impart it to His Lordship."

"Oh no," said Amelia. "I must speak to His Lordship only."

The two stared at each other, aware of their rivalry for Drax's attentions and the strengths and weaknesses of their separate positions. Amelia tossed her golden curls, and Bartram Paget stroked the golden embroidery of his livery. With a curt nod, he indicated that Amelia should follow him. Amelia was surprised. Surely they would meet here in the hall or walk in the grounds? It was not seemly to meet a man unchaperoned in his chambers. However, she had little choice but to follow the steward as he mounted the stairs. It was not the grand staircase she had seen at the opposite end of the hall. The page knocked and Amelia's heart lurched as she heard Drax Mortain's gruff "Enter."

"Maid Perryn, with information," said the page through slightly gritted teeth. "I took the liberty of bringing her up, as her message is of a private nature."

Amelia's eyes narrowed. The page was implying that she was a strumpet of low enough class to visit Drax's private chambers without worrying about her reputation. He was also making it clear that he did not deem it appropriate for Drax to be seen in Amelia's company in the public rooms and gardens of the house. It occurred to her that Drax had only ever spent time with her in the maze, where they were hidden from public view, even from the upper floors of the house. She suddenly felt so uncomfortable that she was ready to turn and flee when the viscount walked toward her, smiling.

"It is always a delight to see you, Maid Perryn. How kind of you to take the trouble to bring me information." He cupped her elbow, glared over her head at his page, and led her to the casement, where there was a high-backed chair and a stool beside Mexica's perch. With a flourish he helped her into the grander seat and perched on the stool beside her. Appeased, Amelia gave him a coy smile and tried to look admiringly at the hawk, for she knew the nobleman admired it, although she thought herself a more worthy object of admiration.

"A fine hawk, is she not? She was given to me by the captain of a ship returned from the Americas," he said, stroking the bird's ghostly plumage. "Normally they have a black stripe on their tail and the tips of their wings. This beauty is pure white." Amelia had no real idea of where "the Americas" were; she had not even seen the sea just a few hours north of Montacute, but it was where her father threatened to send them when he was annoyed. Like "heaven," she had always assumed it was a great distance away and not somewhere you came back from. The bird was exotic and inscrutable; Amelia hoped Drax did not seek in his women what he admired in Mexica, for she knew her charms were more local.

"Of course, where Mexica comes from, white is a feared color. It is the color of death and spirits. She is a little unsettled at present, but do not be alarmed if she suddenly takes flight. May I offer you some small beer or wine?" Amelia did not want anything, but she did want the page to have to do something for her, so she accepted. With a scowl, Paget left the room to find a servant.

"Now, what have you to tell me?" said Drax, leaning close to her. Amelia blushed. She had rehearsed the drawing out of the pendant from her bodice many times, to look both seductive and pure, but with Drax so close she lost her composure and pulled it out in a rush. The look of astonishment on Drax's face was not one of the many responses she had envisaged. Excitement, desire, interest perhaps—she had thought he would bend forward and peer closely at the portrait, but he did none of those things. In fact, he paled and moved slightly away.

"Where did you get that?" he asked in a flat tone.

"From my cousin Cecily Perryn."

Drax's eyebrows shot up before he composed himself again. "Indeed? So you met with the little witch. Did she tell you how she came by this jewel?"

"No, my lord, but I have laid a trap that you might catch her and ask her for yourself. She will even bring evidence of her use of philters to bewitch men."

"Good, good, you are a clever maid as well as beautiful." Drax spoke with his usual languor. He seemed to be avoiding looking at the pendant.

Paget entered, followed by a servant carrying a pewter tray on which stood two silver goblets. He offered one to Amelia, which she accepted with what she hoped was haughty indifference.

"Tell us of your trap, Maid Perryn."

"Did anyone see her?" asked Drax a few moments later, when Bartram Paget returned from showing Amelia out.

"Sir Nathaniel," Paget replied.

"His opinion of me is so low he will assume I am trifling with her, though it is not ideal that my father find out at this moment. I must uncover that list of his contacts," he spat angrily, banging his fist against the wall. "I feel them moving in on me. Without it, all our work could fail. With it, my father will be finished. Don't you realize the importance of it, Paget? Why did your prophecy fire fail?"

"With all due respect, sir, the fire was extremely accurate in revealing the whereabouts of your father's hiding places. Why and to where the documents you seek had been removed I do not know, for I cannot always predict the vagaries of human nature. I fear your father's suspicions are aroused."

Drax grunted. "I will find them if I have to rip the house apart. I will look again tonight. Or perhaps a rapier to the old man's heart might be quicker. Send a messenger to prepare both assassins. Once that list is in my hands we will have to work quickly. Inform the Lady Arbella of my intention to come to London, and have a priest made ready for our marriage."

"A Catholic priest?" Paget asked.

"What? I don't give a damn, man. No, not a Catholic, for the union must be lawful in the eyes of the courts and the people. She won't care either. She's just desperate to get out of her grandmother's clutches and has had enough of being the Queen's pawn."

"And the poultry girl?" asked the steward.

"The dogs have her scent?"

"Yes. I took a smock from her mother. I told her we were trying to help."

"She does not know where her daughter is?"

"I believe not."

"And the dogs found nothing yesterday?"

"They seemed confused and out of sorts. They sneezed a great deal. Perhaps it is a bad time of year, fungus spores . . . It is not normal hunting season."

"Have you conjured another prophecy fire?" asked Drax.

Paget frowned. "I have. The results were most unsatisfactory, for it seems she has learned to close her mind to unwanted intrusion."

"Really?" said Drax, raising his eyebrows. "Is that usual for a peasant girl?"

Paget smiled without mirth. "It is one of the reasons I consider her a notable threat."

"Seize her tonight when she meets with Amelia," said Drax decisively. "She is not to be killed yet. I have questions for her."

"There is one more matter to be settled," said Paget.

"What is it?" said Drax.

Mexica was shifting about on her perch. Bartram Paget could see that the bird would happily rip his face to shreds if Drax allowed her. "The boy who does not die is becoming a nuisance, shouting out and goading the monks. They are weary and frightened of him."

"He has been scraped again?"

"Several times, but each time seems to have less effect. Father Garret demands he be dispatched."

Drax nodded. "I will do it," he said, pulling on a thick leather glove and letting Mexica stand on his hand. "Take him to the chapel when you have the girl. As they are such close friends, it will be interesting to see how they face each other's deaths. Take your instruments, Paget. We will need to know who else she has told. Their bodies will be easily disposed of up there, and if they are ever dug up, the deaths can be blamed on the witch."

"I will have to be caught," said Cecily, holding a piece of wood for Jasper and too preoccupied to notice him glance at her approvingly.

Sometimes she was beautiful. It all depended on her expression. When grumpy she looked jowly and dim-witted. When she laughed, her huge hazel eyes flashed and her giggle was so infectious he could not help but join in, even if it was him she was teasing.

"That is too great a risk," said Edith firmly, dipping two lengths of hemp cord in the saltpeter Joliffe had given them.

"She's right," said Jasper to Cess as he tapped some nails into the wood in her hand to make the petard case. "I heard Drax tell his page to take three men-at-arms with him and that he himself will arrive when you and William are in the chapel. That damn bird nearly gave me away. How can Edith and I overcome that many people?"

Cess noticed that Jasper looked exhausted. He had slept for just a few hours before going to the House early to discover the reaction to their night's forays.

"We will have surprise on our side," she said. "Edith, can you prepare a sleeping potion for the guards?"

Edith carefully hung the cords to dry on a rung of the ladder. "Sleeping potion must be drunk, and I doubt we can make them do that. But I can prepare arrows and sharp sticks dipped in deadly nightshade. How is your bowmanship, Jasper?"

"I've only ever shot standing targets," he said, chewing hard on a sage twig stuck between his lips as he concentrated on getting the petard case right.

"We should get one shot each. After that, of course, our presence will be noted. If I can tip the arrowheads correctly, the men-at-arms will become delirious and fall down. But we will have to be very careful that we are not overpowered and the weapons used against us, for I shall make nightshade port strong enough to fell a grown man. That amount would kill any of us."

"You and Edith can use the tunnel to reach the chapel," said Cess.

"But that might not be safe now," said Jasper, looking up. "I told you, when I was leaving there today I heard someone opening the door in the cellar room that leads to the secret passageways."

Cess thought hard. "But you thought that was Sir Edward. Now we know that the man we saw in the cellars with Father Garret was

Drax's page, and that Drax and his father are largely estranged. Do you not think it safe to trust His Lordship?"

"Not sure I trust any of them," said Jasper.

"If you attack from outside, Paget will hear and will kill us before you get in. You will have to use the tunnel and take the risk. Can you block it behind you so that you can't be followed?" asked Cess.

"I suppose so," said Jasper, already thinking how to do it as he started on the second petard casing. "Hold this, please."

Cecily took the wood and looked at Edith, whose head was bowed. When she eventually looked up, Cecily saw such a deep sadness in her friend's eyes that her stomach turned over with fear. What awful news or future event was her friend protecting her from?

"What is it, Edith?" Cecily whispered. "Will William die?" she asked, unsure she wanted to know the answer.

"Death is foreseen," Edith replied.

CHAPTER 19

"The sun is setting," Cess said. "It's time to go." William had endured five days of hell in the cellars. She prayed he would understand why it had been impossible to get him out any sooner. She moved close to Edith, who took out her pentacle and made the sign of the five-pointed star over Cess, whispering three times:

> *With our power, I do lay*
> *Protection on you, night and day.*
> *Gracious Goddess, day and night*
> *Watch o'er this child with all your might.*

Edith and Cess hugged so tightly that Cess wondered if Edith would ever let her go. As they dragged themselves apart, Cess felt waves of nerves flooding through her.

Edith handed her a clay flask.

"This is the so-called philter. If anyone drinks it, they will get a bad case of flux," said Edith, grinning.

Cess put it in her purse and turned to Jasper, unsure whether to shake his hand or kiss his cheek.

As she agonized, Jasper stepped forward and pulled her into his arms. "You are the bravest wench I have ever met," he said. "William is lucky to have you to love him." He held her at arm's length and looked at her intently. Cess blushed. "Don't worry. Whatever happens we will not leave you in the hands of that man," said Jasper, watching Cess as she climbed the ladder.

The hardest thing was going to be looking surprised when they jumped her, they were so poorly hidden. Drax's page and three armed men were crouching behind a hedge close to Amelia.

"Hello, cousin," said Cess coolly as she approached.

"Where's the philter?" replied Amelia.

Cess pulled it from her purse and held it up. They stood either side of the stile.

"And my pendant?" asked Cess, wondering how the guards would overpower her when they were on the wrong side of the fence. She smiled to herself, for it was clear from Amelia's frown that she was worrying about the same thing.

"I have it," said Amelia, patting her bodice, "but you must cross the stile and give me the potion, or you might make a run for it."

Normally Cess would have refused to obey Amelia's orders, but she had to be caught.

She handed Amelia the small clay jar and climbed the stile, carefully turning her back to the guards to save her pretending not to see them. The weight of three men falling on her crushed the air out of her lungs, and she thought she might vomit. She was thrown on to her stomach and her arms pulled roughly behind and bound.

"Well played, Maid Perryn," said Bartram Paget to Amelia,

unpleasantly, as he detached himself from the hedgerow, carefully brushing away stray leaves and twigs.

Cess looked up at her cousin, who seemed uncomfortable rather than victorious at seeing her trussed up at her feet.

"Where are you taking her?" Amelia asked. Cess noticed that the girl tucked the little flask safely into her purse.

"Good night," said Paget, staring rudely at Amelia to indicate she was no longer needed. Amelia looked petulant, and for a moment Cess thought she might refuse to go home, but eventually she turned and walked back toward the village.

Cess watched her go with a sinking heart. Although Amelia had betrayed her, her presence forced Paget to behave. With her gone, the four men could do anything.

"Get her on her feet," Paget ordered, and the men heaved her upright, nearly pulling her arms from her shoulders. Cess cried out in pain and Paget whipped his hand across her face and spat in fury. "Silence! Any sound and you will have your tongue cut out." He began walking across the field to the start of the cart track up the mountain.

Cess could have shown them a much quicker way but kept her mouth shut. The page set a fast pace, despite not lighting the torch he carried, and she stumbled along as best she could with her arms tied behind her. She received regular shoves from one or other of the armed men, all of whom were also carrying unlit torches. Cess noticed that Paget had what looked like a rolled-up piece of leather tucked under one arm. She felt sick as she remembered where she had seen something like it. The barber-surgeons who visited the village every few months used a similar roll to store the nightmarish instruments they used for incisions, lancing boils, pulling infected teeth and toenails, or amputating limbs.

No one spoke until they had climbed the hill.

In the patchy moonlight that seeped through scudding clouds

she could see the building was even more dilapidated than she remembered. The roof was gone and only bare beams stuck into the sky, like the ribs of a dead sheep. The chapel stood in a clearing and the nearest trees were at least ten long strides away.

Bartram Paget opened the door and waved the guards and Cess through. Inside it was dark and bare save for a few broken sticks that might once have been stools. Most of the stone columns that once held up the roof were still standing, although the one nearest them had broken off low down and was lying in pieces on the floor. William was not there.

"Tie her feet," Paget ordered a guard as he dropped his leather roll on a fallen piece of masonry and lit his torch and those the guards held. He placed them in the rusty wall brackets, taking the last with him as he climbed the crumbling stone steps that would once have led to a gallery. There he waved the torch six times across a gap in the wall, as if signaling someone, and descended.

"Stand guard," said Paget, pointing the men toward the door. "Two outside, one in." He pushed Cess sharply so that she toppled over backward onto the floor. Fear spread through her body. Her legs were numb with it, so was her head. However rough, the men-at-arms were less to be feared than Bartram Paget.

Paget shoved his torch into a bracket on the nearest column and opened the leather roll, which contained a number of metal instruments in pockets. One by one he took them out, making sure Cess had a good view of their sharp, twisted, spoonlike, or pinching forms.

"We know about you, Cecily Perryn," said Paget in his nasal, almost hissing voice. "If you had not made such a spectacle of yourself outside the church, then maybe you would have escaped us. A malapert girl like you gets what she deserves, eh?"

Cess felt panic rising in her throat. She tried to think of Jasper and Edith to calm herself.

We are here, Cecily, do not fear. Edith's voice came clear and strong, and the corner of Cess's mouth flickered.

"Amused by my knives?" said Paget viciously, as he stabbed one at Cess, missing her eye by a fraction. Cess cowered back. Paget proceeded to use the blade to clean under his nails, flicking the dirt he scraped away in her direction.

Cess was worried that William had not yet been brought to the chapel. Her intuition told her he was alive, but maybe it was wrong. Perhaps he was already dead and she had made a terrible mistake allowing herself to be caught. Was Paget summoning William or Drax when he waved the torch? If Drax arrived first, there would be one more to overpower. Their plan was beginning to look very flawed.

"You will tell us who else you have told about the priory cellars," said Paget, pulling out a long, sharp skewer. He grabbed her hand and shoved the instrument under her middle fingernail. She cried out in agony as the sharp point drilled into the tender flesh. Before she could speak, a voice called from outside the chapel and the door was opened by a guard. Paget pulled out the skewer.

"The boy's here," said the guard. Cess's heart leaped in her chest, despite feeling faint with the pain in her throbbing finger. She was happy to see William, whatever the circumstances. Through the door came the blond man she knew to be Father Garret, with William over his shoulder. He dropped him onto the chapel floor, and Cess saw that her friend was still very poorly. His skin was blistered and weeping, although perhaps less bloated. He was so painfully thin she wondered how they would ever get him out of the chapel in such a weakened state.

"Tie him to her," ordered Paget to the monk, who looked surprised to be ordered about but did as he was told. He did not look at Cess, but was careful to step on her, butt her with his large feet, and chafe her with the ropes as he tied William to her.

"You may leave us," said Paget. The monk, annoyed at being

spoken to so curtly, bowed and left without a word. However, once outside, he stood by the door and took a small clay pipe from his jerkin. To Cess's alarm, he leaned against the doorway smoking, talking occasionally to the guard. Until he was gone, Jasper and Edith could not start their rescue plan. The monk looked immensely strong and would make the odds against them too great.

Cess craned her neck around to look at William, willing him to look back at her. His head was slumped on his chest. He did not move. Being manhandled up the hill had exhausted him.

"William," she whispered. She glanced at Paget, but he sat still, observing them.

William stirred. His head lolled around as if he were drunk.

"William," she said, louder this time.

"If you shout, I shall run you through," Paget said calmly, indicating his sword. "But feel free to rouse him—we need him awake if he is to watch you die."

Cess tried to keep her panic at bay. She hoped Jasper and Edith could see that Father Garret had not gone.

"Edith, the blond man is still here. Do not attack," she thought as hard as she could, hoping Edith would sense her fear at least.

"William," she said again, as loud as she dared. William lifted his head. It took a long while for him to focus. A flicker of recognition crossed his face.

"Cess . . . why are you here? They've got you too?" he rasped.

Paget sighed with irritation and strode to the door. "This is not time to indulge in smoking and idle chatter," he said coldly. The monk towered over Paget's birdlike frame, and for a moment Cess thought he might pick the page up and shake him. Reluctantly, Father Garret knocked the ash from the bowl of the pipe so that it fell on to Paget's fine boots, and walked off.

Now, thought Cess. Paget moved inside and shut the chapel door, perching back on the broken column. Cess heard a noise.

A quiet thud, ten or fifteen paces behind her. At last, she thought. Two black shapes, like bats, darted in opposite directions across the ruined chapel. Paget looked up and, taking up the torch, peered first in the direction of the noise and then at Cess. Holding William in her arms, she pushed herself sideways onto the floor.

"What are you doing?" he demanded, his eyes narrowing. Suddenly a thin whistling noise filled the air, and Paget leaped back, clawing at his throat. A tiny arrow had pierced the skin below his ear. There was almost no blood, but the page's eyes were already rolling up so that the whites showed. He slumped to his knees and toppled sideways.

"Hey!" shouted the guard. As he ran toward Paget, Cess saw that the arrow intended to fell him had failed to fully pierce his jerkin and was hanging limply, stuck in the leather.

"What did you do to him?" the guard yelled at Cess, pulling her and William to their feet. Out of the corner of her eye she saw a black-cloaked shape close in behind the guard. The outside door opened and one of the guards looked in.

"Watch out!" the man-at-arms shouted from the door. Jasper scraped a poisoned arrow across the back of the guard's neck but could not leap back in time. The guard swiped at him and Jasper flew through the air and landed heavily on his back. The guard grabbed Cess and William again, squeezing so hard they could hardly breathe. Cess kicked out at him, but he appeared not to notice. He was staring oddly, his eyes rolling. He began screaming and pushed them away as if they had turned into evil spirits. The hallucinatory effect of the deadly nightshade was working.

An athame flashed in the torchlight, and Cess and William were freed by Edith.

"Go!" she said. Her cloaked form was racing toward Jasper's prone body. The second guard was edging forward, pike lowered to run him through. The third was racing straight at Cess. She grabbed

William and ran with him toward the back of the dark church. The guard followed them until he came to the trapdoor through which Edith and Jasper had come. He looked puzzled for a moment, then grunted in understanding. He slammed it shut and heaved a huge piece of fallen masonry over it. Cess watched in horror as their escape route was blocked.

Jasper had got to his feet and was watching the second guard, who was waiting for the right moment to strike, wary of the sharpened sticks Jasper was clutching. Suddenly he jabbed forward with his pike. However, it was not Jasper he aimed at but Edith, as she arrived at his side. She jumped back gracefully, grabbing the pike as it came toward her chest and falling to her knees with a grunt, still clasping the weapon as tight as she could so that the guard could not retreat. In that split second, Jasper darted forward and slammed his sharpened stick into the man's upper arm. The guard cried out and dropped to his knees seconds later. The third guard, who had left Cess and William and was running to help his friend, stopped in his tracks. Jasper pulled out another stick and waved it about to keep the guard at bay. He dropped his pike with a tremendous clatter and drew a heavy sword from his scabbard.

Cess left William at the back of the church and ran closer to Edith, who was lying between her and the guard. She was frightened by how still Edith was. She edged closer, watching the guard who was intent on Jasper and his poisoned stick. The guard moved to his left, around a column, creating more distance between himself and Edith so that Cess was able to run to her friend.

"I am hurt," groaned Edith, white as starched linen. "Leave me, I cannot move."

"No," said Cess, shaken.

"Get out of here now!" shouted Jasper to her. But Cess did not go. Instead, catching sight of Edith's quiver of arrows, she carefully pulled one out. She could not see the third guard; he was behind the column, slowly forcing Jasper farther back. Cess ran silently to the column and waited. She would edge around it and come upon the guard from behind. Just then, however, the man let out a great yell and charged Jasper, raising his sword. Cess threw herself at his back and stabbed the arrow into it. The guard cried out in surprise and pain. He swung round to cut Cess down, but Jasper leaped forward and stabbed him again with a stick, this time into his right arm. The guard dropped his sword, staggered a few paces, and then fell, twitching and shouting.

Cess rushed back to Edith and, with Jasper's help, pulled the witch to her feet. They opened her cloak and saw a bloodstain seeping slowly from a hole in the middle of her chest.

"It's not bleeding much," Cess said to Edith as reassuringly as she could. "You will be all right." All color had drained from Edith's face. Her head hung limply, and her breathing was shallow and noisy. The pike may not have pierced deeply, for it had hit Edith's breastbone, but the force of the blow had done much damage.

"We need to get into the tunnel," said Jasper.

"The trapdoor is covered; it will take too long for us to shift the weight on it," said Cess. "We'll have to go into the forest." She ran to fetch William, who leaned heavily on her.

They struggled to the door, but suddenly Cess's heart was gripped with fear. A great white bird landed on the wall above her head.

"Drax . . ." she whispered. Jasper looked up and saw the hawk. William was uncomprehending, and Cess realized that of course he had not seen Drax since the humiliating episode outside the church. "The man responsible for all this," she gabbled, staring around wildly. Edith suddenly gripped Cess's arm, unable to speak but saying all she needed through her bony, firm fingers. Cess took a deep breath and forced herself to calm down. Standing still, she closed her eyes and looked steadily and deeply inward, withdrawing from everything around her: the blood, the exhaustion, her fear. Her breathing became deep and steady. In the silence she saw clearly that Drax was in the forest and that there was a key around her neck that she had forgotten in her panic.

"He's nearby but not on the summit," she whispered, feeling goose pimples on her skin. "We must head to Joliffe's and hide there, now."

"Not the hideout?" questioned Jasper, bowing under Edith's weight.

"No," said Cess shortly. Joliffe was unlikely to welcome her cramming his priest hole with fugitives and witches, but she did not think he would refuse her. With luck, he would be out, drinking.

Cess pulled William through the chapel door; Jasper followed with Edith's arm over his shoulder. Cess headed northwest, sensing that Drax would arrive up the cart track from the south. She heard a whistle and saw the bird fly down behind the chapel wall. He was between them and the hideout, and so her intuition to go to Joliffe's had been correct.

A slight breeze, heralding dawn, moved the trees and made her even more nervous, for she could not hear if anyone was approaching. It felt like the longest walk of her life. Edith's breathing was becoming more labored, and blood was beginning to seep through the cloak. William, too, was painfully slow, but unlike Edith, who was silent, he was whispering without stop.

"I came to find you after the fireworks . . . The man hit me so hard, and when I woke, there were other boys who were dying and I don't know why I didn't, but maybe something Edith did with the pox and . . ."

"William, we will talk of everything later," said Cess, unsettled by the usually quiet boy's need to talk, and concentrating hard on the noises in the woods. Drax Mortain would be able to move much faster than they could. It was with intense relief that she saw the stile that led to the lane and Joliffe's track. It took so long to get Edith over that Cess was sure they would be caught. She hurried them along the lane to the farm, unlocked the door, and let them in. Before shutting the door, she scattered some of the decoy herbs to throw any dogs that might be sent after them off their trail. Then she locked the door and felt her way in the darkness to the far chamber, where she lifted the planks to the priest hole.

"No!" gasped William, shying away when he realized what Cess wanted him to do. "Not in there. No more cellars."

"William, we have no choice. Get in quickly!" she ordered. He scowled but allowed himself to be helped down.

Cess knelt beside Edith. "Edith." Her friend's eyes fluttered. With a great effort, she managed to open them.

"Cecily," Edith whispered, "my pentacle . . ." She could not finish the sentence. Cess found the five-pointed star in Edith's purse and pressed it into her hand. Edith smiled weakly and tried to speak some more. Cess sensed that her friend was fading and might soon pass into spirit.

"Once we are hidden I can help you. . . ." But she could see there was nothing she could do for Edith. Her lips and fingertips were turning blue with the difficulty of breathing. She was mumbling, and Cess bent forward to hear.

"I must tell you something"—Edith coughed, and Cess heard a terrible rattling in her chest—"about your father. . . ."

CHAPTER 20

Drax kicked the men-at-arms and shook his page. One guard was already dead, one was coming round, and the third looked as if he might also survive. Paget was lucky the arrow had struck him only a glancing blow, or he, a slight man, would be dead too. The page's pulse was irregular, and his pupils hugely dilated, when Drax pulled up his lids. He would be no use for several hours. Drax swore and stood up. He walked over to the guard who was slowly coming round, holding his head and groaning loudly. Drax manhandled him into a sitting position and slapped him a few times on the cheeks. The guard slowly opened his eyes.

"Can you hear me?" asked Drax loudly. Slowly the man managed to nod.

"My horse is tethered halfway down the track. Take her back to the great house, do you understand?" Again the man slowly nodded. He tried getting to his feet but kept falling over. Drax eventually hauled him up and held him against a wall until he was steady.

"What do you have to do?" he shouted.

"Horse . . . house."

"Good." Drax pulled the man out of the chapel door and set him going on the track down the hill. The man-at-arms looked as if he were sleepwalking or exceedingly drunk.

Drax stood silently on the summit of the mountain and closed his eyes. He let his mind wander in the way his mother had taught him, although he did not know where she had learned it. He pictured the girl, Cecily Perryn, as he had last seen her, standing outside the church looking up at him defiantly. He concentrated on the image until it was very clear, down to the strand of brown hair escaping from her cap. Drax opened his eyes and began to walk. At first he turned toward the track, but stopped. He turned around completely and walked northwestward into the forest. The going was rough, but he felt sure she and the crippled boy, and whoever had helped them escape, had come this way. They had to be stopped before things got out of hand.

The hill sloped steeply downward. It was slippery and overgrown, but after a while he found the trees thinning and could see where he was. Below him, in darkness, was Joliffe's farm. Drax smiled grimly, unsurprised.

"Joliffe!" he shouted. He walked around the outside of the house but could see nothing through the shutters. The doors were sturdy and locked, but next to the kitchen entrance was a narrow window. He plucked a stick from the wood pile and bashed at the wooden shutters until the catch that held them broke and he could pull himself through.

From the cramped entrance he walked into the dark hall. As he opened the window shutters, a damp, gusty breeze blew into the stale-smelling room. In the glimmer of moonlight, he spied a tinderbox on the shelf over the buffet, and he lit a stub of tallow candle, which was all he could find. Other than the spitting and smoking of the wick, the house was still. The ashes in the grate were cold. The hall was so sparsely furnished he could see at a glance that no one could be hiding there. On the far side of the entrance was the kitchen, which smelled strongly of sour milk. Some stale bread and rancid butter lay half eaten on the table, and a rat scuttled away as Drax entered. The buttery smelled so strongly Drax could do no more than poke his head inside it, and the scullery was piled high with unwashed bowls. The brewery was the only room that showed some order and was clearly in regular use. The embers in the brewing fire had been carefully raked and covered and were still alight. He dipped a finger into the large ceramic bowl over the fire. Strong beer.

"Drunken sot," Drax said aloud. He walked back into the main house, noticing the spare key hanging from some twine on a hook beside the door that would enable him to let himself out. He walked slowly through the hall, where Joliffe's bread trencher lay on the ancient table with a jug and tankard beside it. The chamber beyond had a battered oak table without a carpet covering, a three-legged chair by the fire, a couple of floor cushions, and a chest. Drax poked around but found nothing of interest. He looked carefully into the fireplace in case anyone was hiding in the nook. The ashes here were also cold, and the rush matting particularly dirty and foul-smelling. He had a distinct sense of not being alone, even though the room appeared empty.

Drax walked slowly back into the hall and climbed the narrow staircase, which creaked loudly at each step. Upstairs were three chambers, only one with a bed, in which lay Joliffe. Drax could tell his sleep was genuine. He checked the other two rooms carefully, but one was empty and largely devoid even of furniture, and the other was a storeroom smelling strongly of apples and the previous year's bean crop.

On the way downstairs the candle sputtered out, the wick burned through. He banged into the table and knocked over a tankard as he walked back into the far chamber. Something about this room bothered him. He stood before the fireplace, listening. He heard Joliffe stir in his bed, rise, and cross the floor above, heard the farmer creeping down the stairs and picking up a stool with which to arm himself. It was not he but Joliffe who jumped when he entered the chamber.

Joliffe swore mightily at the nobleman.

"As foul-mouthed as ever, I see," said Drax

"What in hell are you doing breaking into my house?" said Joliffe, red-faced and furious.

"How do you know it was I who broke in?" asked Drax.

"Because you are standing in my chamber! Get out!"

"I would not have dreamed of entering had I not suspected that three runaways are sheltering here."

"Runaways? Rot!" shouted Joliffe. "Intimidation, I call it!" And before Drax could draw his rapier, he felt the farmer's hefty fist slam into his cheek, knocking him sideways so that he fell heavily onto the table. For a moment his vision went black and he remained still.

"If you don't go, by God, I will kill you," snarled Joliffe.

Drax rose suddenly, his rapier at Joliffe's throat. "Unless I kill you first."

The two men stared at each other with pure loathing.

"If I had not to ride to London, I would take your house apart brick by crumbling brick," spat Drax, lowering his weapon and sweeping out without a backward glance.

CHAPTER 21

Cess wept silently as she held Edith's body in her arms. The dark priest hole had become a coffin, as she had foreseen. She wished it was her own and not her friend's.

Heavy footsteps overhead made them hold their breath, but it was Joliffe's face looking down at her when the planks were lifted. He looked gravely at Cess's tear-streaked face above Edith's still form. Without speaking he reached down and helped Jasper and William out of the confined space, then got into the priest hole and knelt beside Cess.

"Drax'll be back before long," he said, softly. Cess nodded mutely, blinded by tears too copious to blink away. Joliffe gently took Edith's body from Cess's arms and lifted her to the floor of the chamber. He helped Cess out, closed the priest hole, and replaced the mats.

"What's that smell?" he asked.

"A herb mixture that Edith made to put off the dogs," replied Cess, trying to get control over herself.

"Drax noticed it, I'm sure. Let's hope he doesn't work out what it is or he'll be back here immediately." He stared down at the once vibrant woman.

"She tried to tell me about my father," Cess whispered, her throat thick with tears. Joliffe stiffened and did not look at Cess.

"What did she say?" Had Cess been less upset she would have heard the apprehension in his voice.

"She died before she could," said Cess. Joliffe grunted slightly but said nothing more as he bent to lift Edith's body. He led the sorry group outside, where he placed Edith's body on a handcart he had wheeled out of the barn and covered it with a heavy woolen blanket. He looked at Cess, who stood motionless, stunned.

"Lass," he said gently, "only you know the way we must go."

"What is happening? Nathaniel! Nathaniel!"

The steward stumbled into Sir Edward's bedchamber, disheveled from sleep and dressed only in his nightshirt.

"Drax and his mounted guard are riding out, my lord."

"I can hear that myself, but it's not yet dawn. Has he not a care that he wakes the entire household?" grumbled Sir Edward. Sir Nathaniel shrugged, but both men looked worried rather than annoyed.

"Something is up, Nathaniel."

"Yes, sir. My man has been shadowing Drax as you requested. He went to the chapel on Saint Michael's Hill during the night and is now riding for London."

"London? The chapel? What in the Devil's name is going on?! Where's his page?" asked Sir Edward, his face growing redder as his temper flared.

"Not in his chamber. No one saw him leave."

"Come with me."

Sir Edward grabbed Sir Nathaniel's candle and strode barefoot from his bedroom to the great chamber. He went straight to the fireplace. The hair across the secret panel had been disturbed. He knew what to expect when he opened it.

"He has the scroll," said Sir Edward quietly, seeing the empty cubbyhole. He went quickly to his writing desk. As the light from the candle fell on the beautiful object, he saw that it was smashed and splintered, the vellum cipher gone.

"My God," breathed Sir Nathaniel, horrified. "Surely Drax would not . . ."

"Until we ask him we cannot know," Sir Edward said in a calm, steel-edged voice. "We must see how many of our informants' addresses we can remember, for there is no copy of that scroll, and now their lives are in jeopardy. Have the fastest rider made ready."

The sun was high; it was after midday, and Drax and his men had been riding since dawn. He was tired. For the last few hours a voice had been nagging at him, telling him to go back, something was wrong. He had been trying to ignore it. His business in London was vital to his plans, but still the voice needled him with questions. What drug or bewitchment had felled his men? How had the girl evaded all his efforts to find her? Why had the dogs not sniffed her out? Drax had been so angry when he had discovered the chaos in the chapel, it had taken all his willpower not to run the unconscious Paget through.

Now, however, it was the seemingly trivial details that were bothering him. Joliffe's house was not clean, but why were the rushes in his chamber dirtier than elsewhere, and what was the strange smell in there? Was this girl, as Paget believed, his most invincible foe? He had noticed something about her from the moment he first saw her. He felt drawn to her, but it was not sexual desire. It was puzzling.

The beat of hooves was hypnotic against the buzzing and whirring of his brain. He tried to shut out his thoughts and concentrate on the rhythm of the galloping animal beneath him. After some time, answers came fluttering down to him like leaves. If he tried to catch them too eagerly they escaped, but by half shutting his mind, they fell into place. He pulled his horse up sharply and swore under his breath. His men stopped too and looked at him questioningly.

Drax knew that the success or failure of his plans depended on the decision that he was to make in the next few moments. Should he continue to London to destroy his father's spy network and seal his marriage, or return to deal with the poultry girl? He sat still in the saddle for a long while, allowing the breeze to cool his overheated brain. Eventually he took a deep breath and held it for so long that his skull felt fit to burst with shooting stars. Only once he was sure of his decision did he breathe again.

He took a leather scroll case from his saddlebag and handed it to his chief guard. "Carry on without me. You know where to deliver this. Take six men."

The guard pointed to the men who were to accompany him, and they rode away at a gallop.

"We return," said Drax to the remaining four guards. They nodded without hesitation.

Stroking Bess's neck, he turned her westward. They were both weary, but would have to ride fast to reach Montacute by nightfall.

When he arrived he would send Paget and a handful of his men to Joliffe's farm. He had finally understood why the smell and dirty rushes in the chamber had been bothering him when the stench and filth in the kitchen and buttery had not. The scent in the chamber was some sort of herbal mix designed to confuse hunting dogs. The girl had been right under his nose all the time. Still, with a little persuasion from Paget and his tools, Joliffe would tell them where she was hiding. The farmer's death, and those of the girl and her companions, would have to look like accidents; he did not want the Queen's visit delayed. He had received news that the sweetmeats that would bring about the demise of the Queen and her heir were ready. Her first outriders would arrive at Montacute at the end of the week. Nothing must be allowed to disrupt plans that had been in the making for a decade.

Cess woke in the tunnel hideout. She did not move but lay still, watching Alathea as she covered Edith's body with flowers and moss. She was not surprised that Alathea had come. The pain that had torn her body as Edith died could surely be felt by the coven leader too. Cess's stomach lurched painfully at the thought that her dear friend and protector was dead.

Cess did not move for a while. She thought about Edith, reliving the moment that she had died in her arms. Her sacrifice must not be wasted. Although tired and bruised, Cess felt a fire inside. She must make Edith's death mean something.

Alathea came over and kissed her. There was no need for words between them about Edith's passing, but other matters were urgent.

"The storm is about to break over our heads, and we must be ready. I have called the coven to us," said Alathea.

"Drax said to Joliffe that he was going to London today. But I am convinced that the danger looms close and we will have to face him very soon." Cess tried to sound strong as she spoke, but Edith's death had shaken her and made her realize how fragile life was.

She slowly raised herself on her pallet and looked about. Jasper was beside the small fire, and William was sitting a little way away, staring at Jasper's sleeping form.

"How are you feeling?" she asked, moving to sit beside him. He shrugged. She could tell he was angry.

"We came for you as soon as we could, William. We did everything possible."

William did not reply. He sat winding the ribbon he had given Cess around and around his fingers. The beautiful colors had become gray with dirt, so obsessively was he twisting it.

"What is it, William? What is the matter?"

Slowly he turned his hostile gaze upon her. "Why did we come here and not to our homes?" he asked.

"We are not safe in the village. The man who seeks to kill us is at Montacute House and can find us easily in the village."

"Who is that woman?" he asked in a hoarse monotone.

"A friend of Edith's who has come to mourn her."

"She was mumbling over me. I stopped her," said William, looking suspicious.

"She sought only to help you, to heal you."

"She is a witch," he spat, beginning to rock his body, his eyes so wide he looked almost possessed. Cess noticed that he was shivering, and she pulled a blanket from the pile and placed it tenderly round his shoulders. William ignored the gesture completely.

"Who is that?" he asked in a harsh voice that she barely recognized, jerking his head toward Jasper.

"Jasper. He comes from Yeovil and has been helping us."

"Why?"

"He did not have much choice." Cess smiled. William did not smile back but glared without blinking. "He is helping us defeat Drax and stop the awful things that are happening in the priory cellars."

"Do you have feelings for him?"

Cess was taken aback by the directness of William's enquiry, and was about to snort and tell him not to be silly, when she realized she could not. With a strong and unexpected surge of warmth in her body, she recognized that she did feel something for Jasper that she had not felt for any other boy, even William. She looked over at him, sleeping beside Edith's body, and her chest tightened. When she looked back at William, his eyes were brimming with tears.

"When I was down there, when I thought my life was being taken from me, I came to love life so much that even my clubfoot was beautiful to me. It also became clear that in life only love matters.

Other things, like having glass in the windows or a sheet on the bed, being a physician or a blacksmith, being plain or handsome, are nothing. I tried to tell you on your birthday that I loved you."

Cess, uncomfortable with this proclamation, bowed her head and fiddled with her hands. William carried on, ignoring the embarrassment he was causing.

"When I saw the ribbon, I nearly gave up. I know you did it so I would remember that you had been there, but I would never have parted with something you gave me; I would have found some other way. I would not have left you. I would have died with you. It made me realize something had changed. When I saw you with that boy, the pain was as bad as anything the monks did." William stopped, the tears constricting his throat. Cess tried to hold his hand, but he snatched it away.

"William," said Cess gently, "we risked everything, even Jasper, who had never even met you. Edith has died to save you. Does all that mean nothing?"

William showed not a flicker of appreciation but turned and lay down as if to sleep. Cess wondered at his understanding of her feelings for Jasper before she was aware of them herself and considered what she could do to ease his disappointment. A bang on the hatch above their heads made her jump. Jasper, who had been deeply asleep, leaped to his feet and stared wildly around him, a hand to his white dagger. Alathea alone looked calm.

"They are coming," she said simply, and climbed the ladder to open the hatch. A man and a woman climbed down into the cramped space and knelt for a long time beside Edith before sitting on the floor. Alathea welcomed them, speaking quietly and offering what little beer and food they had.

"I cannot introduce you formally," she explained, "for we use witch names that I cannot reveal to the uninitiated. Nine more will arrive, as covens have thirteen members. They will be coming from three or four miles distance, but as it is daylight they must take extra care not to be seen."

By mid-afternoon, the little hideout was crammed with people. When the last appeared, a quiet goodwife from the village, whom Cess was amazed was a witch, Alathea stood to address them.

They listened silently as she told them all Cess and Jasper had discovered. They shook their heads or mouthed incantations against evil, but none interrupted.

"Dear friends," Alathea concluded, "there are sufficient number of us gathered that we must act. I am not alone in prophesying the events now unfolding and the involvement of this young woman," she said, indicating Cess. "The scriers in this and other covens have all seen her these past months, alongside such visions of evil and danger, not just to ourselves but to many others, that we cannot sit idly by. If Drax Mortain's plan to become King succeeds, a great evil will spread over the entire land and destroy what peace and prosperity we now enjoy."

Cess sat silently for a while, but the sense of tension was so great, she found it hard to concentrate. A tall figure stood. He pushed back his hood to reveal a long, pale face, weathered by many summers.

"Permission to speak, my queen."

Alathea nodded.

"What of our oath to harm none? Are we not here to safeguard our covens until such time as we can once again raise our heads and live in peace with non-witches?"

Cess gaped at the man, aghast. It had never occurred to her that the coven members might refuse to help. Without them there was no hope of defeating Drax. Trying to control a rising sense of panic, Cess heard another sound, faintly. For a moment she could not identify it. As it got louder and more insistent, she realized it was the sound of galloping hooves riding fast. It was accompanied by an increasing sense of dread. Suddenly she stood.

"I know you have seen me in your scrying and that I am meant to have some power that will help us. I have not yet discovered what this is, I will be honest, but even so, I am willing to risk my life to overcome the evil we have witnessed. If we fail, then the lives of every person, everywhere, will be at risk. With this pestilence at his fingertips, Drax Mortain will be able to control us all through fear and destruction. If we do not act, we will fail in the sacred task performed by witches for thousands of years, that of preserving the dignity and preciousness of all life."

The witches sat silently for a while, then turned to each to confer.

Cess remained apart. She knew the meaning of the galloping horse. Drax Mortain had finally understood what was crucial to the success of his plans.

"I can feel something, Alathea," said Cess quietly to the witch queen. "Drax Mortain is coming back. I can sense his approach. Have you felt nothing?"

"No," said Alathea, "but I believed him to be London-bound so have not thought about him. Do you often dream of him?"

Cess was startled. "No."

Alathea waited.

"Well, I have disturbed sleep, and sometimes he is in my mind when I wake. . . . Why?"

"Sometimes people have feelings for those who threaten them— not the feelings you might expect of anger, hatred, and revenge, but more of desire and longing. It is a strange thing, but I have seen it before."

"Desire! I don't feel any desire for him!" exclaimed Cess. "He makes my flesh crawl. He is a cold-hearted snake."

"Come, Cecily, do not close your mind to uncomfortable things. You have a connection with him that none of us shares—no one else has seen him returning, and many amongst us are experienced scriers."

"Then maybe I am wrong. Maybe it is just my fears."

"What do you feel?"

"He is coming to kill me."

"How much time do we have?"

"Very little," said Cess.

The old man who had started the debate stood, and Cess's heart flew into her mouth. Their fate rested on the coven's resolve: to hide or to fight?

"We have come to a unanimous decision." He spoke gravely, looking at Cess. "We will fight."

CHAPTER 22

William waited. It was late afternoon when the chance came. Alathea called the coven, Cess, and Jasper to enter the woods for a ceremony before the fight. He was left alone, in feigned sleep, with Edith's body. He looked dubiously at the mouth of the tunnel that led downhill. It went near the priory cellars, and William decided that he could not face that. The tunnel sloping upward, he guessed, went to the chapel, and that was blocked. He had no choice but to go up the ladder.

Gingerly opening the hatch, he listened and looked around but could hear and see no one. He climbed out, shut the hatch, and set off downhill. He felt dizzy and unsure on his feet, but he stumbled along, choosing a route that took him due south. Through the canopy of trees he could see that the sun was already dipping to the west and that he had very little time.

No one would miss him; he was just a hindrance to them, even to Cess. He knew he was considered too weak to play an active role, for they had not asked him to take part. He was to be left out, this time by the person he loved and who he had thought loved him. It was not entirely her fault. That ringlet-headed ass was to blame. Without Jasper, she would have loved him; she was beginning to, before all this happened.

If she did not love him, then there had been no point enduring the torture in the cellars. He could not bear seeing her with someone else. Her plans were too risky, and that knave Jasper was allowing her to put herself in terrible danger. She had to be stopped.

He muttered to himself, wondering whom he could persuade to believe him and his account of all he had heard in the hideout. His father might be so grateful to Cess and Jasper that he would join their fight. Anne Perryn could do nothing. The parson would not believe a word he said and would never act against Drax Mortain.

The shadows were lengthening, and Amelia was anxiously twisting the gold chain of the pendant around her thin fingers, pacing up and down the chamber she shared with her siblings. There had been no message from the House. She did not understand it. She had delivered Cess to Drax, but now she had no idea what was happening. Amelia felt angry that she was being excluded from something that she had, after all, initiated. But she was also nervous. She had wanted Drax's attention but had not expected the hunt for Cess to become so hostile. She was realizing that Drax was a powerful man but not a kind one, attractive but not lovable.

She was fed up sitting around indoors, so she threw on her cloak and left the house. Not feeling like talking, Amelia avoided the main street and headed for the stile where Cess had been caught. Perhaps she could find something out.

As William came to the bend in the hedge just above the stile, he collided with someone coming the other way.

"William!" cried Amelia. She seemed astounded by his reappearance. William cursed his bad luck to bump into someone so soon. He had not yet formulated a plan. "Where have you been? You look awful!" said Amelia.

"I was kidnapped. I have only just escaped."

"You were really kidnapped?" said Amelia, her mouth slack with surprise. "People said you were taken by witches."

"Not witches. Torturers and murderers. They tried to kill me."

"Who are they? Are they close by?" asked Amelia, looking around anxiously.

It was beginning to dawn on William that Amelia might just be the person to stop Cess's dangerous plan to blow up the cellars. Amelia was the daughter of Richard Perryn, the most important yeoman in Montacute, with influence among the villagers. Amelia was so vain that she would love to be the one who persuaded her father to take some villagers up to the hideout to stop Cess. He had to think swiftly, though. If the Perryns knew that Drax Mortain was involved, they would be much less willing to act.

"Amelia, I need your help. To save Cess."

"She needs saving?" said Amelia—rather calmly, in view of her previous anxiety, William thought. "Where is she?"

"She's with some idiot called Jasper, and she has a stupid plan to blow up the cellars of the priory. They stole fireworks from the great house to do it with."

"What?!" William was confused by Amelia's reactions. "But . . . she was with . . . I mean . . ."

"Will you help?" said William, frustrated by Amelia's bewilderment.

"Why does she want to blow up the cellars?" asked Amelia, mystified.

"There are men living in the cellars. They are doing evil things and she wants to stop them," said William, being careful not to mention Drax or his page, "but she never will; it is too dangerous. She must be stopped and then a proper plan worked out, perhaps with your father in command? It will bring great rewards to your family to expose what is happening down there. It is a plot to kill the Queen!"

"No!" cried Amelia, her eyes glistening. "Is that true?"

"I promise it is all true, and if you don't help, Cess might get there first and get killed . . . or get all the glory."

"Of course," said Amelia, hanging on William's every word in a way she had never done before. "Tell me everything. How can I help?"

"I shall go and say good-bye to William," said Cess, opening the hatch and descending the ladder. She returned almost immediately.

"Alathea, have you sent him somewhere for his safety?"

"No."

Cess felt her stomach flip over. "He's gone. Alathea, I am a fool!" she cried. "William was angry with me. I never dreamed he would do something like this, but now I can see it was obvious. He will betray us. We must catch up with him."

Alathea rapidly called out four names, and the witches quickly gathered.

"You must find a boy called William Barlow. He was here when you arrived, lying on the pallet. You will recognize him by his clubfoot."

The witches stood quietly in a tight group, eyes shut. One by one they opened their eyes, and each spent a few moments looking intently at the other, as if testing that they could hear each other without speaking. Then they were gone.

"If they don't catch him, perhaps he will tell only those who will be favorable to us," said Alathea doubtfully.

"No, Alathea," said Cess quietly. "His time in the cellars has changed him; he is not at all the boy I knew." She sighed. "Since Edith was killed, I feel like I am standing on the edge of a deep hole, able to fall in at any minute."

"You are. So are most of us, once we have experienced deep loss or humiliation, as you have both. Your spirit is strong, but you must train it. Do not give in to fear, self-doubt, or loathing, but seek the path forward. You will become a person of strength and wisdom such that obstacles will be an opportunity to demonstrate your growth. Edith had complete faith in you. Show me that she was right."

Amelia left William at his cottage and scurried along the lane to Montacute House. She could hear hooves approaching fast, and turned to see Drax Mortain riding around the bend at full tilt. She raised her hand to wave, but he galloped so close that she was nearly knocked to the ground. She looked down at her patched cloak and muddy hems.

He must have mistaken me for a peasant, she thought crossly, but hurried on regardless. She had information that would be worth a great deal to him. Of course it should not be Cess or even her father who led the charge against those evil people in the cellars, but Drax Mortain. If it really was a plot to kill the Queen, then he was the most worthy to foil it. Perhaps he did not even know that Cess had escaped. She had much news for him. He would be very pleased with her.

As she approached the impressive edifice of Montacute House, she wished she had stopped at home to change and to order a servant to accompany her and knock on the door. It was not seemly for a gentleman's daughter to knock on doors herself, like a common hawker. As William had told it, however, there was no time for such niceties.

"Maid Perryn," said Sir Nathaniel smoothly when the servant showed her into the great hall, "how may I be of service?" He looked pink-faced and disheveled, as if he had dressed hurriedly after a bath. Amelia had to suppress a smile at the thought of this dour man splashing about in a tub.

"I have an urgent message for His Lordship."

"Of course. Come this way," he said immediately. Amelia was surprised not to be questioned but allowed herself to be led up the grand staircase. The steward ignored the manservant standing by an elaborately carved and beautifully polished door and knocked on it himself. It was an older voice that answered. In a flutter, Amelia grabbed Sir Nathaniel's arm.

"No, not him, the young Lord Montacute."

"Ah, you mean Viscount Drax Mortain?"

Amelia nodded vigorously. "I have always called to see the younger, sir. I assumed you knew who I meant," she stammered desperately, blushing at this show of her ignorance of courtesy. Sir Nathaniel studied her coolly. For a moment, Amelia believed herself to be safe, but even as he smiled, he swept the outer door open.

"I am sure the Earl of Montacute will be delighted to talk with you. The viscount has just returned from a long ride." The lesson was lost on the terrified Amelia, who was stuck fast and only moved when Sir Nathaniel opened the inner door and propelled her inside.

"Nathaniel?" questioned Sir Edward.

"Maid Amelia Perryn, my lord, cousin to the missing poultry girl, Cecily. She is here to visit Sir Drax, who is changing after a fast ride back to Montacute. It seems he changed his mind about going to London."

Lord Montacute's eyebrows came so low in a frown that they completely obscured his eyes. "Come," he ordered Amelia. "Stand where I can see you." Amelia, quaking, felt as if she were being measured for her coffin, but managed an unsteady curtsy.

"What is that?" asked Sir Edward, seeing the heavy gold chain around Amelia's neck. It took her shaking fingers a while to locate

Drax's necklace and pull the ruby pendant out of her bodice.

"A gift, my lord, from your son," she said, wanting Sir Edward to know that Drax Mortain had encouraged her in her attentions.

He seemed unimpressed. "Not that one, the other."

Amelia thought she would faint. Without touching it, she bowed her head meekly. "A pendant, my lord, recently entrusted to me by a relation."

"Let me see."

Amelia noticed that the steward also edged into the room. Amelia wished that she had not charged into the house with so little thought. Reluctantly, she walked closer to Sir Edward so that he could inspect the jeweled portrait.

"A relation gave you this portrait of my late wife?"

Amelia's eyes nearly jumped out of her skull in surprise. She had not thought who the woman was, but certainly never dreamed it was Lady Mortain. It was a few moments before she collected herself sufficiently to reply. "My cousin, my lord. I know not how she came by it, but she swore to me it was not stolen." She noticed Sir Nathaniel looking rapidly between the pendant, his master, and her.

"You have seen her recently?" asked Sir Edward.

"Yes." Amelia hesitated. How much of William's tale was it safe to tell? She wanted to be the one to inform Drax, but surely Sir Edward would want to protect the Queen too?

"She was kidnapped and so was William, but they've escaped and . . ." Before she could say more, there was a knock at the inner door.

"Come," said Sir Edward.

A manservant entered the room. "Viscount Drax's page requests an audience, sir," he said.

"Tell him to wait," Sir Edward replied decisively, standing. Once the manservant had closed the door behind him, he walked to the corner of his room and opened a hidden door in the wood paneling.

"Nathaniel, I want you to witness what occurs without being seen yourself. Should you need it, this is the key for the door into the cellars, where you can get out," he said, pulling a key from his doublet. "Be careful—the floor in that room has collapsed into the foundations of the old house or some ancient cesspit, I am not sure. It is not yet mended."

Sir Nathaniel bent down and entered the secret passage, and Sir Edward shut the panel behind him. He then turned and stood so close to Amelia that he towered over her.

"If you say one word about what you just saw, you will regret it bitterly, do you understand?" Amelia nodded mutely, too scared and surprised by the events unfolding to know what to think.

Sir Edward was walking to open the door to Bartram Paget, when Drax Mortain swept into the room, still lacing his doublet, followed by his page, who Amelia noticed looked very unwell, pallid and sweaty. Both bowed to Sir Edward.

"What is the meaning of this intrusion?" said Lord Montacute coldly. To enter a room without being invited was the height of rudeness.

"Father, there was some urgency," said Drax, ignoring Amelia.

"Indeed? There seems to be a great deal that is urgent just now. This highly adorned young woman is known to you, I understand?"

Amelia saw Drax's eyes flicker to the pendants she wore, but his expression did not alter. "Father, Maid Perryn has been most diligent in her service toward us and has been rewarded."

Amelia felt as if she had been struck. Drax saw her as a mere servant?

"She has a message for you." Sir Edward turned to Amelia. "Please deliver it." Amelia noticed Drax's eyes narrow to slits. Bartram Paget looked worried too. Amelia felt like a cornered deer about to be shot with arrows from all directions.

"My message is unimportant," she said in her meekest voice, her head lowered. All she wanted to do was go home. Drax had been using her, she knew that now. "Please excuse me, I should not have come." She curtsied and turned to leave.

"Wait," said Sir Edward, glowering at her. He raised his eyebrows, and it took Amelia a few seconds to understand what he wanted. With trembling fingers she took the pendant from around her neck and handed it to him. Strangely, she felt relieved.

"It surprises me that you have received visits from this girl under my roof without informing me," said Lord Montacute to his son, a resonant note of anger in his voice. "I hear also that you are betrothed but do not speak of it with me nor seek my permission. These are acts of great defiance, Drax, and need some explanation, as does the fact that my writing box is smashed."

The silence that followed Sir Edward's speech was so thick, Amelia felt her body grow heavy with it. Father and son were locking horns like stags in the forest. There would be blood between them. Amelia could not believe how stupid she had been to get involved in a family battle, as well as everything else. She inched toward the door. But Drax was aware of every movement in the room. He indicated to Paget to stop Amelia.

"Ah, good Paget," said Sir Edward with mock friendliness, looking away from Drax. "I am so glad that you are encouraging our young friend to stay—her stories of kidnap and escape promise to be most diverting."

Drax spun round to look at Amelia. "What has been said?" he asked her sharply.

"Her tales were just getting interesting when you arrived," interjected Sir Edward. "Pray continue, Maid Perryn."

"Take her away," said Drax to Paget.

"What!" exploded Sir Edward. "You would contradict my orders in my own house?! You insolent . . . Guar—" A hand clamped over his mouth before he could finish the word, and he was pushed back into the chair by Drax, who unsheathed his dagger and held it to his father's throat.

"If you cry out again, you will die," said Drax, slowly taking his hand from his father's mouth. "Get something to tie him up with," barked Drax to Paget, who looked at the table and tapestries doubtfully. Spying Amelia's tattered cloak, he took it from her and ripped long pieces off the hem. Adeptly he tied Sir Edward to the heavy oak fire chair.

"What on God's earth are you doing?" said Sir Edward. "You will never get away with this."

"On the contrary, Father."

"Preposterous! If you kill me, the Queen herself will have you hung, drawn, and quartered. Don't be a fool, man!"

"I have no intention of killing you."

"If you ever let me loose, I will kill you!"

"No, Father, you will not," said Drax calmly, looking at his father as the old man struggled against his bonds, with a coolness as if he barely knew him. "You will need me. I have deciphered your list of spies, who will soon be, shall we say, out of service. For a long while I had to live in your shadow. After that, I chose your shadow, for it gave me freedom to plan greater things. Now it is your turn to know darkness. Accept it gracefully and we can carry on as before. You will meet the Queen. No one will be any the wiser, but you will answer to me. Resist and I shall have to kill you. I will make your death appear to be from natural causes; you will not be long mourned. Either way, I win. Consider your choice overnight." Drax turned to Paget. "Gag him. Lock the door. I will tell the servants His Lordship wishes to work undisturbed. The fire should last for a few hours at least," Drax said, turning back to his father. "I am sorry not to leave a piss pot, but then, you would struggle to use it."

Amelia began to inch to the door, but Drax took hold of her hand. She stiffened at his touch. Once she had found it exciting to be near him, now it was terrifying. Having witnessed this scene, she doubted whether he would let her walk out as if nothing had happened.

"My lord, my parents will be anxious about me. I must return."

Drax laughed contemptuously. "Even if they knew you were with me? I thought they were positively throwing you at my feet." Amelia blushed, for it was true. She glanced toward Sir Edward, who was staring at her. She knew he was warning her not to give away Sir Nathaniel's position. Even with that advantage, it seemed to Amelia that Drax was the most likely victor in the battle between father and son.

Gripping her arm so tightly she cried out in pain, Drax whispered into Amelia's ear, "Now, what did you come to tell me, my sweet?"

CHAPTER 23

Cess could hardly breathe for fear and excitement as the witches left the tunnel and formed into their coven above ground. They were armed with staves and knives, and from their girdles hung bags and vials of hallucinatory and sleep-inducing concoctions. Linen masks soaked in linseed oil were tied over their faces, which made a strange and frightening sight. They moved in silence and with ease, as if the clearing were illuminated by brilliant sunshine rather than the pale evening glow. With no perceptible signal being given, they moved off as one, out of the clearing and down the mountain toward the ruined priory.

Once they were out of sight, Cess climbed down the ladder and saw Jasper staring up at her.

"Let's go," she said, more confident in her role as leader than she could have believed possible. She had never before been in charge of more than a few hens. How many thousands would perish if she and Jasper failed?

Shouldering a heavy sack each, they entered the tunnel by the light of a single lantern. They quickly made their way to the bottom of the hill, turned right at the fork, and hurried to the end of the tunnel. In front of them was the smooth stone panel of a large sarcophagus. Beyond it was the priory crypt. There was just enough space between the tomb and the crypt wall for them to squeeze through.

Once in the crypt, Cess stood quietly while Jasper pulled the sturdy wooden block from one of the sacks. Into each of the drilled holes he pushed a long wooden dowel, to which were attached the paper tubes of fireworks. From the bottom of each tube hung a fuse.

"The coven is ready," whispered Cess to Jasper, sensing that the witches were now gathered outside the dovecote. With Cess carrying the sacks and Jasper the firework block, they moved quickly out of the crypt and into the passageway. As they expected, to their right was a dead end. They walked left until they came to a junction. Ahead was the exit to the dovecote. To the right were the cells and workroom. The door was open as before, and they could hear voices. They crept as close as they could without being seen. Jasper knelt down and angled the block carefully so that all the fireworks were pointing into the room. He lit the fuses with the lantern candle, and he and Cess flitted past the door to hide behind it.

The fuses made quite a noise as they burned, and Cess and Jasper looked at each other, worried the monks would come out to investigate before the fireworks ignited. After a few moments, they did hear someone shushing the others and the sound of a bench being pushed back. Through the crack they could see a figure come to the door. The fuses were almost gone. Cess and Jasper covered their ears, which muffled the sound of the monk's surprised yell.

Even covered by her hands, Cess felt her eardrums would burst with the force of the fireworks exploding in the confined space. The screaming noise of the rockets shooting upward was terrifying, and within seconds the workroom was filled with burning shards of paper and wood and thick, sulphurous smoke. Some of the men's robes caught fire, and they ran from the room, screaming. Coughing, blinded by smoke and fumes, the rest fumbled their way out of the room and up the passage toward the exit. Cess smiled at Jasper through the thick darkness. The plan was working perfectly.

Before the last monk had stumbled from view, Cess and Jasper covered their mouths and noses and ran into the workroom with the second sack. Eyes streaming, they pulled out the two petards and nailed them to the underside of the trestles.

"I've made short fuses—we will just have to run fast once they're lit," said Jasper.

"I'll check the cells," said Cess, leaving the room. The first was empty, the second contained two bodies. As she checked the third cell she heard distant yells and the noise of fighting echoing down the passages. She felt a stab of intense fear. Alathea was talking to her. "Get out of there, Cecily. Get out, quickly."

Amelia stumbled into the hall and blinked in surprise at the number of faces turned to her.

"Amelia, what has happened?" cried her mother. Amelia's hair was disheveled, her clothes dirty, and her cloak gone. She collapsed into a chair by the fire, too exhausted to make sense of why Peter and Margaret Barlow, William, Joliffe and Anne Perryn seemed also to have just arrived at her home.

"Who did this?" said her father.

"Drax Mortain, Father," she mumbled, terrified to admit to all what she had been doing these past days. She shot an angry look at William. "Why didn't you tell me he was involved?" she spat.

Attention turned to William. He scowled defiantly. "How was I to know that you would head straight off to the great house? I asked you to get help from your father. What did you tell Drax?"

"Plenty," said Amelia, her chin lifted. "He had a dagger at my throat. He is heading to the priory already. He left me tied up with Sir Edward."

"So how are you here?" asked her father.

"Sir Edward's steward released us. They are going to fight Drax, but they will be too late and too few." Amelia seemed defeated.

"We must go," said William, struggling to his feet.

"No!" said Goodwife Perryn, with sudden force. "No good will come of charging off in the night and interfering where we have no business. Richard," she said sharply to her husband, "we must wait to see the outcome."

"Are you mad, woman?" shouted Peter Barlow, red with fury. "There are foreigners in our midst murdering our children and working to kill our Queen, and you want to see if Drax defeats his father before you act?" He turned from her in disgust. "All those who will fight, let's be gone."

Cess's throat dried up. Drax Mortain was close. As she peered out of the cell door she saw a tall figure stride through the smoke and enter the workroom, rapier in hand. She ran closer, noticing that the sound of fighting was growing louder.

"Drax Mortain!" yelled Jasper in warning. Through the gap between the door and the jamb, Cess saw Drax pointing his rapier at Jasper's heart.

"You have an accomplice?" said Drax, sounding icy calm. "Ah." His face lit up with understanding. "Where is she?"

"Who?" said Jasper.

"Don't play with me," Drax snarled. "The girl, Cecily Perryn."

"Maybe dead," Jasper said, indicating the battle sounds overhead.

"Then you have outlived your use," said Drax calmly, hanging his rapier back on his belt and retrieving a long dagger. He forced Jasper's head back to cut his throat.

"No!" yelled Cess, running into the room. Drax twisted around, shoved Jasper away, and grabbed Cess. She did not flinch. Drax stared at her, then slowly lowered his dagger.

"Maid Perryn," he said, forcing her to kneel next to Jasper, his dagger poised. "We meet, at last." Cess scowled but Drax appeared intrigued by her. "Not as pretty as your cousin, but interesting none the less. So, you planned to blow up all our hard work?" drawled Drax, never taking his eyes from her.

Fury rose in Cess's chest that William had betrayed their plans. Many lives would be lost because of it.

"A prophecy told me that I had met my greatest foe," said Drax, walking around Cess to look at her from all angles. She squirmed inwardly. Jasper was staring too, from Cess to Drax and back again. "It took a while for me to realize that it was a wench from the lowest orders. Why are you my enemy?" He had finished his examination and looked at her expectantly.

"You took my friend," replied Cess vehemently. "That was enough. Then I heard your plans for our Queen. How could I not fight you?"

Drax acknowledged the courage of her answer with a nod. "I thought you an unworthy opponent, witch or not. Now I see yours will be a noble death," he said, only slightly mocking. "One last question: how came you to wear my mother's picture?"

"I found it. I heard she could have been a very great woman but was ruined by her pride and ambition. Perhaps you will be ruined in the same way," said Cess boldly, not sure what instinct was driving her to goad this man.

Drax's eyes narrowed to slits, but still he stared at her intently. "Thank you for your insights, Maid Perryn. Now remove your cloak and lean forward," he said. Cess slowly did as she was ordered and looked up at Drax with her clear, hazel eyes. "Stay still or it will be more painful," he said.

Cess had never really thought she and Jasper would die. Jasper moved to throw himself between them, but Drax drew his rapier with his left hand, spun it in the air so that it came to rest the right way, and pressed its lethal tip into Jasper's chest. "Do not test my skills," he warned. "I can kill with either hand."

Drax put his dagger to Cess's throat, but then he paused. She could see that a thought or question had been nagging at him since she entered the room, and that he could not bear to kill her until he had the answer. Suddenly his eyes widened, and he pulled back, the color draining from his face.

"You are thirteen?" he asked abruptly. Cess nodded, nonplussed by the question. "Jesu in heaven!" mumbled Drax, rubbing the edge of the dagger against his chin and staring at Cess like she was the Angel of the Annunciation.

"What?" asked Cess, encouraging his strange change in mood but looking all the time for a way to escape.

"Do you not know? Really?" he said, seeming to will her to see what he could.

Cess was bewildered and shook her head.

Drax looked at her, clearly weighing up what to tell her. He let out a short bark of joyless laughter that made Cess and Jasper jump. "Can you not see it ... ? I am your father."

For a moment, Cess could hear nothing. Her world was silent. She stared at Drax Mortain as if he had breathed fire rather than spoken. Then a wave of nausea engulfed her, threatening to knock her over.

"No," she whispered in horror, looking desperately at Jasper to tell her it wasn't true.

But Jasper was nodding. "It's true, he is your father. You look like him. That is your power."

Cess pulled herself to her feet, but was trembling so violently she had to hold the edge of the workbench. She stared at Drax and knew that Jasper was right. That was the power she possessed that had been foreseen by the witches. It was the power of her blood, the same that ran in her enemy's veins. That was her way into his seemingly impenetrable heart. That was his vulnerability. His tremendous belief in himself would extend to any that came from him, to his children. Images and snippets of words from the whole of her life fell into place. This was her father.

Before anything more could be said, footsteps clattered down the passage and Bartram Paget burst in.

"My lord," he said breathlessly, "your father's men-at-arms have arrived, led by Sir Nathaniel. Sir Edward is here too."

Drax turned to stare at Cess. "What witchcraft have you done to make this so?"

Cess was shaking so hard she could barely reply. "It is not my doing, Father." She used the word deliberately, for she knew it was the key that would open his head and heart to her. Everything she had learned from Edith and Alathea flowed into her at that moment, every surviving witch was willing her on, the power of Nature and the strength of Mother Earth were at her call. She could see him recognize in her all the features he had possessed as a young man. Her innocence and bravery, her faith in justice. Here was a product of his own seed, a girl of outstanding courage who had caused him so much trouble.

"So much for your prophesying, Paget. Meet my daughter," drawled Drax. Paget's goggle-eyes bulged so alarmingly, it looked as if they would pop out of their sockets. "Get back up there. I hope to God you're a better soldier than you are a sorcerer."

Paget ran out and Drax moved closer to Cess but did not touch her. She could feel his emotions as clearly as if they were her own. Even his dreams flowed through her. She would be his heir and ally,

225

the most powerful woman at court, daughter of the King. What a life it would be! Indeed, her own heart was wrenching at its bonds. A part of her was thrilled to know her father at last. She wanted to embrace him and be embraced in return. Cess looked into her father's eyes and saw feelings he had denied for two decades fighting to emerge once more—feelings of belonging and protection.

Jasper, seeing his chance, darted as quick as a ferret to a torch on the wall. He dived under a trestle and lit the petard's fuse, then rolled to the second and lit that. The salty tang of burning saltpeter filled his nostrils immediately.

Drax jolted himself out of his reverie, but Jasper had already seized Cess, and they were pelting out of the room. Cess's heart was pounding so loudly she could not tell if her father was behind her or not, and she dared not stop to look back. They were just beneath the hatch to the dovecote when the blast threw her against the wall, and her ears were filled with a tremendous roaring. She crumpled to the ground, and as the noise faded, she could see and feel nothing.

CHAPTER 24

Alathea fell to her knees as the ground shook beneath her, and witches and soldiers alike paused in the fighting. For a brief moment, they all feared the ground would open up and swallow them. Sir Edward was the first to recover.

"Attack!" he yelled at his men, who raised their swords and advanced.

Alathea looked around. Despite the gathering darkness it was clear that the battle was going against them. Drax's men-at-arms outnumbered Sir Edward's, and the coven members were not equipped to battle trained fighters. Alathea silently commanded the witches to fall back to the woods. Three had been killed by Drax's men, who had arrived sooner than Alathea had hoped. She had wanted to flee but sensed that Cess and Jasper needed more time to execute their part of the plan.

"Cecily needs help," said Alathea urgently. "Now that Lord Montacute's men are here, we can go to her. Who is uninjured?"

Only three lifted their hands. "Two of you, come with me." Pulling their hoods over their faces, the three witches ran swiftly across the field to the dovecote. The small building was filled with smoke, and Alathea had to crawl her way to the hatch. Peering down, she saw Jasper struggling to climb out with Cess's limp form. The three witches helped him out as quickly as they could, for the tunnels looked close to collapse, and there was a risk of infection from the shattered experiments. Between them, they carried Cess away from the dovecote, skirting the fighting men.

"They're losing," said Jasper, looking anxiously at Alathea. Drax's men-at-arms were inflicting heavy casualties on Sir Edward's men. Through the gloom, Jasper recognized Bartram Paget on his horse, a poor fighter but seemingly a good tactician. Beyond the clashing men he saw Sir Nathaniel and Lord Montacute, mounted, surveying the scene and occasionally shouting orders. As he watched, Sir Nathaniel spotted Drax's page. He spoke to Sir Edward, who nodded. Then the steward plowed valiantly through a group of Drax's men toward Paget. Sir Edward also seemed unable to remain a bystander. He swung his sword arm a couple of times, then spurred his horse into the morass.

Jasper helped lay Cess, still unconscious, on the floor of the wood.

"Stay and tend to those hurt," Alathea ordered an unwounded witch. "You, come," she said to the other two.

"I shall come too," said Jasper, grabbing a stave from one of the wounded witches.

"You are injured from the blast," said Alathea, looking concerned by the blood running from a head wound.

"No matter," said Jasper. "It does not hurt."

"That's what worries me," she said, smiling at his bravado. She picked up her stave and several poisoned sticks, and ran back to the fight. It was a near suicide mission, Jasper knew, but he could not sit idly by while Alathea and her witches were slaughtered.

As they neared the battle, another sound could be heard above their panting. Shouting and banging.

"What now?" groaned Jasper. But as he drew closer, he saw a crowd of villagers running from Abbey Farm toward them. "It's Joliffe!" he shouted wildly.

Armed with smithy tools, farm implements, and the occasional old sword, the villagers crashed headlong into the fray, attacking the guards in Drax's livery with tremendous force if not great skill. The women encircled the battleground and used pitchforks to push back any of the enemy who tried to escape.

Jasper laughed. He could see defeat on the faces of Drax's men, pulled from the jaws of victory by a crowd of untrained villagers. Bartram Paget faltered. Sir Nathaniel was closing in and Drax had not emerged from the cellars. With the villagers attacking from every side, Paget looked suddenly isolated and fearful, his own life at risk.

"Desist!" he shouted from his horse, pointing his sword downward. "Desist!" The soldiers around him stopped fighting, and those in Drax's livery pointed their swords down warily, alert for any last-minute parries. Across the battlefield came the sound of swords being dropped in surrender. A cheer rose up from the victors.

Paget, glancing left and right, suddenly raised his sword and slammed it down into the back of the soldier who had grabbed his mare's reins. As the man collapsed screaming to the ground, Paget dug his heels into his horse and cantered away into the darkness.

She was on a ship, rolling on a gentle swell. She had dreamed such things, and now it was happening for real. She could see the mast against the light. Edith was beside her. Cess knew Edith had been keeping her company for a while. The rolling was getting worse, but there was no breeze. The smell was strange. There was no salt or tangy weed, just lavender and woodsmoke. It was not a mast but a bedpost. Edith was backing away, smiling. Cess moved her head. It was not Edith but her mother.

"Cecily." Anne smiled. "You are waking," she said with relief. Cess could see her mother's lips moving, but heard only a mumble. Her head hurt as if had been split in two with an axe, and the bed was still moving.

Anne Perryn leaned forward and adjusted the fine linen bandages around Cess's head and removed large pads of soft wool from her ears. Cess saw brown stains and cried out.

"Shh, child, the blood is old," said her mother. "Your ears are healing. Can you hear?"

Cess tried to nod, but her head hurt too much. Her mother's voice was still muffled, although she could understand what she said. Trying not to move, she looked around the room. She was propped up in a large, canopied bed, with posts and curtains pulled round. Her mother, who had been sitting on the bed watching her, slid down and opened the curtains on one side. Windows, several paces away, were shuttered.

"Where am I?" whispered Cess, and coughed. Her mother gave her a sip of watered wine from a glass.

"We are in Montacute House," said Anne, a little uncomfortable in her grand surroundings. She spooned some bitter liquid into Cess's mouth. "This is willow water."

Cess grimaced but would have swallowed anything to ease the drumming in her skull. "How is Jasper?" she asked, dreading the answer.

"He is well and asks after you constantly."

Cess smiled. "And the others? I heard fighting."

"None of the villagers were badly hurt, although poor Joliffe lost a finger. Quite a few of the men-at-arms on both sides are dead. And three of Alathea's friends died."

"Drax," said Cess suddenly, pulling herself up in bed, nearly vomiting with the pain. "Drax Mortain," she whispered, remembering again what the explosion had temporarily knocked out of her. A flare of anger bit into her heart and she stared at her mother.

Anne looked down at her hands, took a deep breath, and began to talk. "It seems the time has come to tell you the truth. The night you were conceived, Joliffe and his friend were drunk and started a fight with Drax Mortain. Mortain was a big drinker too in those days. He often came into the village with rowdy friends to pick fights. I saw what happened. Drax killed Joliffe's friend. I was the only witness because Joliffe was too drunk to remember. Drax . . . caught me . . ." Anne stumbled on, her throat thick with grief and shame. It was hard for Cess to hear her. "He forced himself upon me. Afterward he threatened to have Joliffe hanged for murder and violation if I told anyone what happened. It was my word against his, and I would never win; his father was chief magistrate." There was a long silence, broken by Cess.

"Did you tell anyone?"

"Only my father. I wanted him to know that I had not sinned with Joliffe. I made him promise not to tell, but he did. He marched over to Montacute House and demanded an audience with Sir Edward. His Lordship refused to acknowledge what had happened, although he did send Drax packing to a tutor in Windsor. He was a much harder man in those days. His ambition was so great that he did not want a whisper of scandal to disrupt his rise at court. He dismissed your grandfather and refused to deal with him thereafter. That is why your grandparents struggled for money in the last few years. Sir Edward must have felt some guilt later, as he gave you the position of poultry girl. Every time you told me he had visited the yards, I wanted to scream. I had to hold so much in." Anne took a deep breath and continued. "Drax Mortain passed me on his horse the day he left Montacute for Windsor. He seemed not to recognize me at all. I think he managed to block his memory of the whole event."

"Why did you tell me nothing of this?"

"Would it have helped? Could you have borne our shame any better, knowing that your father was a noble gentleman who was not even aware of your existence? I wanted to protect you from the bitterness I felt."

Tears were running down her cheeks. Cess hesitated, then reached out and hugged her mother. "That is why Joliffe was so angry?" she asked into her mother's hair.

"If I had told him the truth he would have insisted on vengeance," said Anne, helping Cess back onto the pillows. "Drax would have killed him. He broke off our engagement." Anne wiped her tears and managed a smile. "We are betrothed again now, though, Cess," she said gently. "As soon as I told Joliffe the truth, he proposed. He also said he could think of no finer girl than you to have as a step-daughter." Anne's smile broadened. "I am very happy." It was true. Cess had never seen her mother's smile so warm.

"But what about Drax Mortain. Where is he?"

"No one knows. He was not seen to come out of the cellars, but his body has not been found. His bird was discovered dead in the woods this morning. She appears to have died of a broken heart."

The following evening, with Cess still feeling sore but much recovered, she and Alathea made their way up to the clearing on Saint Michael's Hill. The surviving coven members had already brought Edith's body from the hideout and were kneeling beside her and her three fallen comrades.

"Shall we bury Edith close to where her hut was?" Cess asked Alathea. "She was happy there."

"It is best that they remain in the center of the clearing, and we will form a sacred circle around them."

"With the ten of us?"

"More will come," said Alathea, sweeping the clearing with Cess's help and forming a circle with salt and purified water. As night deepened, the forest came alive with silent hooded figures. They walked out from the trees and stood around the dead witches, holding hands and creating unbroken circles, tightly packed liked a closed bud, keeping safe the precious souls at the heart of the circles. Cess counted seven complete covens, over ninety witches, men and women, heads bowed, keeping vigil.

The circle closest to Edith and her three dead friends were those who knew them best in life: Alathea, Cess, the surviving coven members, and several men and women Cess had not met before.

Most of the witches faced inward, focusing their thoughts upon the bodies. Only at the edge of the circle did the sentinel witches, thirteen of them, look outward, creating an invisible but impenetrable barrier against evil spirits and earthly intruders. Hooded and still as rocks, they made an awe-inspiring sight. There were no candles or torches. The waxing moon lent her light.

The hairs on Cess's arms were standing upright, not with cold but with the strength of the power moving within the space, from hand to hand, jumping across the circles of witches, holding the deceased in its gentle power and allowing their spirits to move joyfully and with speed into the next existence.

Although not a single word passed between the witches, they moved as one. Everyone except the sentinels pushed back their hoods, and each circle began moving, one clockwise, the next widdershins. Like the grinding of millstones, their movement generated tremendous heat and power. Faster and faster they went, suddenly changing direction and then back again, without collision or noise. Soon they were running, as fast as they could but as if they had wings, without becoming breathless. Cess felt the grief and heaviness of her heart start to change, to move outward instead of crushing inward.

An energy, a blissful feeling, poured out of her into Edith's body and spun through the circles around her. She could sense by the intense tingling throughout her body and in the air that everyone was experiencing the same.

Gradually, the witches slowed and stopped. Again without speaking, each member sank to their knees and placed their hands over their heart. Cess broke from the circle and knelt at Edith's feet, holding them gently in her warm hands. Three coven members held the feet of the other dead witches. Alathea knelt by Edith's head, cupping one hand over her beloved friend's lifeless cheek. She held her other hand up to the moon. For the first time that night, she spoke aloud:

> *Witch, sister, friend, Goddess,*
> *Wizard, friend, hero, brother*
> *Soul, moving to another*
> *Place.*
> *Love, walking you over*
> *Threshold, found at the end of*
> *Life.*
> *Never dying in our hearts,*
> *The gift of knowing you,*
> *Eternal.*

Silently, each witch came forward and kissed the fallen witches on their lips. Then four male and four female witches removed the flowers from the bodies, folded their hands over their chests, and tucked a few blooms into them. Cess saw that Edith was lying on a shroud. The witches wrapped it over Edith's body, tying knots at her head and feet so that she lay in a cocoon, and repeated these actions for the other three. Then they lifted the bodies onto their shoulders, three each side, and all the other witches formed two lines. Slowly, the bodies were carried down the lines of witches, each one reaching out as they passed to touch them and say farewell. At the end of the lines the witches paused while the sentinels broke the ring of protection and turned in unison to watch and honor their fellows as they passed out of the sacred circle and into the forest. Within moments the pale shrouds disappeared into the deep gloom under the trees and were was gone.

After a few minutes' silence, the sacred circle was re-sanctified with water and salt, and the witches formed into two concentric circles. The thirteen sentinels looked outward again, and the witches of the inner ring turned to Alathea and Cess, lowering their hoods. Cess felt light-headed and a little sick with nerves. This was to be her initiation. Although her novitiate had been short, Alathea agreed that she had already proved her loyalty and courage.

"We gather this night to welcome a new witch into our coven," said Alathea in her clear, musical voice. Cess felt a moment of intense sadness that Edith was not with her.

"Our sister Edith, recently passed into spirit, is joyful you take her place," said Alathea with conviction.

Two witches moved to stand on either side of Cess. They removed her cloak and revealed her to be wearing her undersmock. It reached only to her knees, but far from being embarrassed, Cess was filled with a sense of power and freedom. Without outer clothes she was neither peasant nor princess—she was a creature belonging to Nature, as the otter or the owl.

The witches took a length of twine, which they held from her head to her feet and then around her chest and head in order to make her "measure" or shroud.

"Anyone who has a witch's measure can do them great harm," explained Alathea, "so the coven leader keeps the shrouds to ensure the initiate does not betray them." Once the measurements were complete, Alathea leaned forward and whispered a name into Cess's ear. This was to be her witch name, known only within the coven. Then she began the ceremony of giving Cess her eight magical tools. The first was a small sword, simply but beautifully made and light to hold. It symbolized a trained and focused will, without which her power would be weak and ineffectual. Second was a black dagger, her own athame, and third was a ritual white-handled athame, to be used inside a consecrated circle. Alathea then placed a wand carefully on Cess's upturned palms.

"This wand has been harvested and fashioned for you alone. I made it many months ago, after I first dreamed of you. I have chosen hazel, a wood that lends the wand special power for protecting its owner and increasing her magical powers. It was harvested under a blue moon, which will lend your wand potency. It has been treated with the finest beeswax, harvested at full moon. Use it to focus your own magical abilities, and ask of it only that which harms none." Cess could feel the wand's smooth warmth. It was so light it would take some practice not to grip it too firmly.

Alathea then stepped forward with a five-pointed-star pendant enclosed in a circle within an up-pointing triangle on a leather lace, which she passed over Cess's head and positioned over her heart. "For protection."

At her feet were placed a small copper pan, in which powerful herbs could be burned to create sacred smoke during rituals; a whip, to remind her of the punishment she would receive from the gods if she broke the trust being shown in her; and some rope, symbol of all that held her back, her fears, her wants.

The moon reached her zenith in the night sky. She blazed above their heads, still for one precious instant. An inward breath completed before an outward commenced. Across the world the tides waited, pausing before their turn. At that moment of pure peace, pure power, Alathea spoke.

"A witch's strength comes only from within. There is no part of us that is not divine. If it harms none, do what you will."

As one, the gathered witches spoke to Cess. "We salute you in the name of the Goddess and the God, newly made witch." Their voices echoed richly around the clearing and into the trees, as if telling the whole of Nature that a new witch was born.

EPILOGUE

Montacute House had never looked more magnificent. Each diamond pane of glass in every window had been polished with vinegar and paper until it shone like a jewel. The statues of saints and knights had been scrubbed, the woodwork oiled, the drive raked, and the lawns and bowling green cleared of every leaf and fallen blossom. The knot garden, herbarium, rose arbor, maze, formal lawns, meadow lawns, love seats, tree swings, and ponds had been cleaned, pruned, replanted, or restocked. The poultry yards and pigsties were spotless, the orchards scythed and tidied. The kitchens and pantries were groaning with food and drink, every delicacy and speciality of the region, and others shipped in from the trade routes of the world.

Inside the house, the oak floors had been scrubbed, oiled, and perfumed, fresh rushes laid, and herbs spread. The fireplaces had been cleared and relaid, the mantelpieces washed, the tapestries and carpets beaten, the plate was polished, the sheets whitened in lime, dried in the sun, and ironed. The portraits in the long gallery were dusted, and the family crests around the house were given new paint.

Although the house was buzzing with servants, hundreds more lined the drive, including Sir Edward's surviving men-at-arms. The Queen's forerunner had arrived that morning, announcing her arrival around noon. Her outriders had then appeared and been stabled. The Ladies of the Household had followed, to prepare her rooms and personal belongings such as cutlery and serving dishes, her bed, hip bath, chairs and cushions, clothes, books, and musical instruments. The armorer had arrived next with the strong boxes containing gold and silver coins, silver and gold plates and drinking vessels, the Queen's jewelry, and seals of office.

It was past noon when Cess, watching from the long gallery at the top of the house, saw the Queen's gilded carriage. It was pulled by eight white horses, their tails and manes dyed orange, surrounded by exquisitely dressed mounted knights carrying pennants. In front were about twenty men and boys on horseback, wearing the green and white Tudor livery, blowing trumpets and beating drums. A little way behind rode her ladies-in-waiting, ladies and gentlemen of the court, pages, and attendants. Stretching into the distance, farther than Cess's eye could see, was the baggage train of nearly three hundred carts pulled by oxen or heavy horses, carrying the personal effects of the entire retinue and the tents and cooking and washing facilities for the men-at-arms and all those who would be camping.

As she looked down, she saw a growing crowd milling about by the main entrance to the House. She could hear Lord Montacute, her grandfather, calling her. He had named her his heir as soon as she had recovered from the explosion. Sir Edward had disinherited his son and had brought Cess into his great chamber to tell her his decision to make her heiress of Montacute House. Cess had felt as overawed as she was pleased.

"You have the wit, child, that is sure enough. You needn't be afraid to go to court—you've proven yourself a survivor amongst scoundrels and murderers," Sir Edward had said with a sad smile.

Down below she could see her mother, arm-in-arm with Nicholas Joliffe. William was also nearby. He would soon be going away, as Sir Edward had offered to send him to a tutor for schooling. If he studied hard, he could pursue his dream of becoming a physician. He seemed happy to be leaving. Cess wished things between them could go back to how they were before, but William had admitted to loving her, and she had not been able to love him back the same way, so they were changed forever.

The Queen's retinue was at the end of the long drive to the house. Amelia and her parents were jostling to secure a good position at the front. Amelia, chastened for a few days by her treatment at the hands of Drax Mortain, was back to her old self. She was dressed in her best, and hoping to secure the affections of one of the Queen's knights, at the very least. The parson was hovering about, talking to no one in particular. He had refused to marry Cess's mother to Joliffe, his disgust at Anne having had a child out of wedlock making it quite impossible, but after Sir Edward had suggested he seek a parish elsewhere, he had found it more acceptable.

Sir Edward had now come into the sunshine and was looking around, for her, probably. They had spoken frankly about all that had happened, and he had admitted to putting the pendant in the coop. He had not felt ready to accept her as his granddaughter, but wanted to mark her thirteenth birthday and give her a hint of where she came from. Drax had been a guest for several weeks by that time, and Sir Edward was realizing that his son might not make a reliable heir. It was time, he had thought, to discover whether Cecily might. He had watched her leaving the house the day she found the jewel, and had felt guilty when he saw her uncomfortable clogs and ill-fitting clothes. His own grandchild, a poultry girl. He had decided he would tell her the truth after the Queen's visit.

"I'm sorry, Cecily," Sir Edward had said. "I only wanted you to have something precious for your birthday. I thought you might guess at its meaning, as you look very like your grandmother. It never occurred to me that you had no mirror, nor any idea of how you were conceived."

"Is it safe to wear?" Cess had asked Alathea.

"It is always the wearer that gives power to a contagious object, Cecily," she had said. "I would advise you to wait until matters are more settled." Cess had locked the pendant back in the armory without regret.

She knew she must go down to join Sir Edward, but she did not yet feel ready. The idea of being presented to the Queen frightened her almost as much as blowing up the cellars. Her grandfather had spent many hours over the past days preparing her. She had been given instruction in the geography and politics of the land, the greatest classical authors, and the main characters at court. She was told the Queen's likes and dislikes, and taught the dances she would be expected to perform. Sir Edward had conceded, regretfully but to Cess's intense relief, that there was insufficient time to master a musical instrument or a foreign language. When first she had eaten with him, he had grimaced and lectured her severely.

"Those at the top table use pewter trenchers on which to put their food, not a piece of bread. The little dip in the corner is for your salt—it is impolite to dip your meats into the main salt dish." Cess had carefully speared a small pullet with her knife. "No, child, that dish is for four. You must let those of higher degree serve themselves before you. Do not load up your trencher, for it is impolite, and use the spoon, knife, or your fingers to put small pieces of food in your mouth." Cess had withdrawn her knife and instead spooned a little sauce onto her trencher, believing her grandfather could not object to that. "Never leave your spoon in the communal dish—that is the height of bad manners, as is putting your leftovers back into the dish that others are eating from." Cess hurriedly picked up her spoon, splashing a tiny bit of sauce on her bodice in doing so. She wiped at it with the tablecloth and heard Sir Edward tutting loudly. "Try not to dirty your clothes—they are very expensive—and watch the ruffs at your wrists. Everything you do must appear effortless and graceful, to reflect the gentility of your station. Take that napkin beside you and fold it over your left arm or shoulder. Have you ever used one before?"

"Not quite like this," said Cess, remembering the square of dirty old linen she used to cover her lap as she sat round the fire pit, bread trencher in hand.

"It is to keep your face clean and to wipe your mouth before you drink. You will share your cup with the person sitting next to you and possibly with one or two others. When the Queen dines with us, of course, we shall have no cups upon the table, but you may call a servant to you whenever you wish for a drink, and he will bring you one from the cupboard. Hold it with both hands and do not put your elbows on the table for fear of rocking it." Cess dabbed at her lips in what she hoped was an effortless manner, even though she had not yet eaten anything.

"Do not spit or pick your nose at table, of course," continued Sir Edward, "although if you must blow it, be careful to wipe your fingers before putting them in any of the food dishes. And do not throw bones on the floor; there is a bowl for that."

Cess had, understandably, eaten very little in Sir Edward's company.

Her only sadness was that she had known Drax Mortain to be her father for just a few minutes before he was taken from her. She had seen into his heart and believed he could have been turned to good if the circumstances had been different. If only for a few heartbeats, he had been proud of her.

Suddenly, she saw Jasper run around the corner and up the steps, looking about, something dangling from his hands. She could not see what it was; it looked like a piece of knotty string. He seemed to be looking for her. Sir Edward had agreed to take him into the household, even when it traveled to court, to his mother's immense delight. A few moments later, the sound of pounding feet on the stairs announced his arrival in the long gallery. He came to her side, and they smiled at one other. In his hands was a daisy chain, and he put it over her head with great ceremony. To Cess, it was much more valuable than the pearls she now wore.

With a sigh, she got up from her sunny vantage point and headed a little unsteadily to the staircase. She was not accustomed to the weight of the clothes she was expected to wear, now that she was heir to the Montacute estate. Her kirtle was of thick silk, embroidered with so many flowers and seed pearls that it stood up on its own. It stuck out almost an arm's length away from her hips on a farthingale, a great cage of wood and linen tied round her waist. She felt like an ox with a wooden yoke. She had a bodice as before, but this one had whalebones sewn into it to keep her posture straight and push up what little bosom she had. Her sleeves, so tight she could not bend her arms, were tied to the bodice with silk cords, and the gown dragged on the ground behind her. Two heavy strings of pearls constantly caught the little hairs on the back of her neck. Her headdress was the most uncomfortable change, used as she was to a linen coif. It felt like she had a roof on her head, and the pins to attach it were pushed so firmly into her skull that her scalp ached.

"Perhaps the noble life will be terribly dull," she worried out loud to Jasper, quite convinced it would be impossible to have any adventures in such attire. The shoes, however, made up for much. They were cut from the softest leather and dyed a deep rose madder to match her sleeves and skirt panel. They were so light she could barely feel them on her feet, and made her want to dance.

As they came down through the house, the rooms were still and watchful. The hubbub from outside was muffled. The last of the servants had gone outside to wave to the Queen as she progressed up the drive, and they had the place to themselves. The House, grand beyond her imaginings, was now her home.

As Cess walked into the sunshine, Jasper squeezed her hand, which was a little clammy with nerves, and together they went to join Sir Edward as he bowed to the Queen.

ACKNOWLEDGMENTS

The Weald and Downland Open Air Museum in Sussex is a treasure trove of a place with historic buildings rescued from destruction that bring to life homes of the past. Thanks to this place, I learned what Elizabethan England smelled and tasted like, how drafty were its glassless houses, and also what few crops were harvested in May.

Montacute House in Somerset is owned by the National Trust and is a very beautiful place to visit. I grew up knowing it well, as my grandparents lived in the village. I spent many days getting muddy on Saint Michael's Hill. The dovecote and priory gatehouse still exist, as, it is rumored, do the tunnels. Thanks to Brendon Owen for old maps of Montacute, and Joseph Lewis for information about Yeovil market.

Vivianne Crowley's *Wicca: The Old Religion in the New Age* was informative about witchcraft rituals and beliefs, and was a source of inspiration for the witches' chants.

Dr. Susan Doran helped me with modes of address, and Sarah

Dunant, Gilliam Slovo, Preti Taneja, and Gabrielle Séguin gave me help and encouragement just when I needed it. Thank you especially to Sarah Odedina, Isabel Ford, and Talya Baker at Bloomsbury, my patient and clever editors, and my agent, Eugenie Furniss. Lily, Jasmine, and Cecily, I love you.